THE RISING OF ⑧ THE SHIELD HERO

Aneko Yusagi

Naofumi Iwatani

Rishia

Kizuna Kazayama

THE RISING OF 8 THE SHIELD HERO

"Rafu!"

Something came bounding straight at me out of the smoke.

"Wh . . . What the . . . ?"

I caught whatever it was in an instant.
I looked down and saw a small creature that looked like a mix
between a raccoon and a tanuki.

Table of Contents

Prologue: The Never-Ending Labyrinth

"—Fumi-san! Naofumi-san!"

Someone shook me awake. I could hear them shouting my name over the persistent dripping of water.

"Ugh . . ."

I was dizzy and shook my head to try to steady my senses as I slowly sat up to get my bearings.

"Oh thank goodness. Naofumi-san . . ."

Rishia looked at me, her eyes filled with worry. She sat with her legs splayed out like a duck.

"Where are we?"

"I . . . I don't really know."

I looked around the room. It was a small dark room, with walls built of stone—very dank and depressing. Behind me was a pile of damp straw on the ground. A crude bed lay in the other corner and iron grating formed the far wall.

"It looks like . . . a prison."

"Feh . . ."

What the hell was going on?

I climbed to my feet and analyzed the situation further.

The iron grate made it clear that we were in a prison cell of some kind.

But jeez . . . How did we end up here? My memory was still fuzzy with sleep. I better go over everything I can remember and try to clear my head.

My name is Naofumi Iwatani.

I was a normal university student with otaku tendencies back in Japan, but that all changed on the day I went to the library and found a book called *The Records of the Four Holy Weapons*. I started to read it, only to find myself summoned to another world and treated as if I were one of the characters from the book—the Shield Hero.

The people that summoned me said they needed me to save the word from a great calamity called "the waves."

At first I was thrilled to find myself in a new dream-like world, but things didn't end up going so smoothly. Despite the fact that the people in charge of the country—Melromarc—had summoned me to their world of their own accord, they didn't waste any time framing me for a rape I never committed so that they could throw me out into the streets, penniless and alone.

Eventually, after going through all sorts of hardships and trials, I was able to get rid of the people who were behind a conspiracy to destroy me, the Shield Hero. I was finally cleared of all charges, and the people that had framed me were punished.

Finally cleared of the charges against me, it was time to

fight against the waves as a true hero—or so I thought. As it turned out, there was still plenty of trouble waiting for me.

The first problem was the most fundamental. I was summoned to serve as the Shield Hero, but the Shield Hero was specialized for defense and was completely unable to attack enemies on his own.

I was one of four holy heroes, and the other three were heroes of the sword, spear, and bow. All of them had been summoned from Japan, just like I had been. But there were many different Japans in different dimensions, and none of them came from the same one that I had.

What's that? Why do I remember all this stuff about them?

The important thing about the other heroes is that, back in their own worlds, all three of them had played games that were remarkably similar to the new world that we had all been summoned to.

The world we found ourselves in really did have *a lot* in common with video games. People had levels and stats, we earned experience points by defeating monsters, and those points could be used to raise your abilities.

Naturally there was magic, and the world was stalked by creatures I'd never seen in Japan. Because you could grow stronger by battling your way through the world, obviously any information you had ahead of time would be useful.

But the other three heroes liked to keep secrets. They didn't care at all about the conspiracies that had been plotted against me. And they certainly didn't care enough to tell me any of the things they knew about this new world.

After I'd been cleared of all the charges leveled against me, I was able to convince the other heroes to sit down together so we could discuss what we knew about how to power up our weapons. Over the course of our meeting it became increasingly clear that they were having the time of their lives using their own secret knowledge to play the role of the world's heroic saviors. They were so pleased with themselves that none of them had stopped to realize that they each only knew a single part of the full method.

After they had heard of the other power-up methods each of the other heroes were using, each one of them still only understood the method they previously knew about from the games they'd played. So they continued to battle against the waves with underpowered weapons. The stupidity was nearly too much for me to bear. In the end, I tried using all of the methods that we discussed during the meeting, and I quickly became much more powerful than any of them. It was a good thing I did, too. Soon after that we ran into all kinds of dangerous situations that I never would have survived had I not powered up the way I had.

A bunch of things happened, but the most notable was

probably the battle with the Spirit Tortoise, an enormous monster that could save the world but could only do so by sacrificing a large portion of the world's human population.

The Spirit Tortoise was a protective beast that existed to save the world, albeit in a very different way than we heroes were supposed to. The other three heroes all went to attack the beast on their own, were defeated, and then went missing. As usual, their failure became my responsibility. I faced the Spirit Tortoise in battle and was eventually able to stop it in its tracks.

With the immediate danger put to rest, my friends and I searched for the missing heroes, hoping to find and rescue them from whatever dire fate they'd encountered. It wasn't long before we discovered that we weren't out of trouble yet.

At around the same time that the Spirit Tortoise first appeared, a mysterious woman in a robe came to me and insisted that I should kill her. Her name was Ost Horai, and she was a Spirit Tortoise familiar (human type), a soldier of the enemy. Worse, she carried the burden of the Spirit Tortoise's will within her.

I didn't understand what was happening when she first appeared, and she vanished before I could ask anything further. That's why I was a little slow in responding to the threat. The next time I saw her, she appeared to tell me that the Spirit Tortoise was still alive, despite the fact that we had already blasted its head off. When she appeared before me again, she begged me to finish the job.

She told me the Spirit Tortoise was being controlled by someone. This prevented it from carrying out its true purpose: using the souls of living things to form a magic barrier to protect the world from the waves. She said that if the Spirit Tortoise couldn't carry out its true intentions then it would have to be defeated.

After that there was a long series of battles.

My friends and I joined forces with Ost to fight the Spirit Tortoise, and we were able to sneak inside of its body. We tried to defeat it in different ways, like attacking both its heart and head at the same time (a method we'd researched beforehand) and using a sealing spell on its heart.

Nothing worked. But then Ost helped us find the Spirit Tortoise's core, and it seemed like we might be able to defeat the Spirit Tortoise there. That was where we ran into the strange scientist-like madman that had taken over control of the Spirit Tortoise's body: Kyo Ethnina.

He wasn't the only person we found in the core chamber. The three missing heroes were there, too. After their pathetic loss to the Spirit Tortoise, Kyo had taken them prisoner.

Kyo manipulated the core and used it to produce powerful Spirit Tortoise familiars to cause us grief. In the middle of the fight, Glass and her friends appeared and joined forces with us in the battle against Kyo.

Speaking of Glass, she was a human enemy that came out

of the dimensional rifts during the second wave we fought against . . . or at least that's what I'd thought. We found out that Kyo came from the same world that she did, and he possessed something called the book of the vassal weapon. According to Glass he had crossed over to our world to use our protective beasts in order to cause destruction and chaos—and that was something that could not be permitted. We shared a common goal. So we teamed up to defeat Kyo.

But Kyo had the power of the core behind him, and his attacks were extremely powerful. He used the energy the Spirit Tortoise had gathered to make himself even more powerful, and for a while we weren't able to hold our own against the strength of his attacks.

His defenses were formidable too, and just when I thought we didn't have a chance, something snapped in Rishia, and she and let loose a fury of attacks that, luckily enough, broke through his defenses just in time for me to use the special power that Ost had imbued my shield with: The Spirit Tortoise Heart Shield.

It had a special effect called Energy Blast—which was exactly like the killer attack the Spirit Tortoise itself had used against us when we'd fought its head.

I did as Ost asked and directed Energy Blast at the Spirit Tortoise's core and was able to destroy it—breaking Kyo's connection to the Spirit Tortoise in the process. Realizing he'd lost his advantage, Kyo opened a portal back to Glass's world and escaped through it.

And so, finally, the curtain closed on the Spirit Tortoise's rampage affair.

We were victorious, but the victory came at a heavy cost.

Ost asked me to destroy the Spirit Tortoise's core, knowing all the while that if I did she would die. I knew it, too, but I did as she asked.

When the Spirit Tortoise was defeated, the energy it had gathered would awaken the next protective beast, and no waves were supposed to occur until that time. But the energy had been stolen, and Ost had interfered, so the next beast didn't awaken, and the waves threatened the world as they always had.

We joined up with Glass and her friends and followed them back to their world to hunt down Kyo, the man responsible for all the destruction in the first place. The other three heroes were just as useless as ever, so we left them in back Melromarc.

So . . . how did we end up in a jail cell?

"Where are Raphtalia and the others?"

"I do not know. When I woke up, I was lying here with you in this room."

I decided we'd better start by figuring out what was going on.

"Huh?

I decided to start by checking out the shield I was equipped with, because something clearly wasn't right. I'd had the Spirit Tortoise Heart Shield equipped before I lost consciousness, but now I was equipped with something else—a feeble looking thing I'd never seen before. If it reminded me of anything, it was the Small Shield from a long time ago.

Beginner's Small Shield
abilities locked: equip bonus: defense 3

What was this thing? When did I get stuck with this? I decided to change to my strongest shield, but an icon popped into my field of view when I tried.

Change conditions not met.

Um . . . What the hell?

I called up my weapon book and quickly scanned the list of shields. There was a long list there, but it was nearly all greyed out.

"What the hell is going on here?!"

I couldn't use any of my shields!

"Um . . . I . . ." Rishia hesitantly raised her hand. I had a really bad feeling about what she was going to say, so I didn't even want to ask. Then again, avoiding the truth wasn't going to make it go away. Besides, I had a pretty good idea what she was going to tell me.

"I'm afraid to ask, but what is it?"

"I just checked my status, and it says that I'm only level 1 . . ."

That's what I was afraid of. Before we'd gone through the portal, Rishia had been at level 68. How could she be at level 1 all of a sudden?

Maybe the dragon hourglass had somehow returned her to level 1 while we were unconscious. I didn't know what happened, but I knew what I had to do next. I didn't want to do it, but I slowly, hesitantly, opened my own status menu.

Naofumi Iwatani

job class: other world Shield Hero level 1

equipment: beginner's Small Shield (legendary weapon) ○ ▼ ◆x type 2

"Nooooo!!!"

"Fehhhhh?!"

I screamed, and Rishia was so startled she screamed with me.

I was level 1, too? All that work—it had all been for nothing?!

Not good at all! This might have been the worst thing that has ever happened to me!

Shit!

I checked the party functions menu, only to discover that

there weren't any party functions available. Raphtalia and Filo's names were nowhere to be seen. Rishia's was the only name listed. Everyone else was gone.

Even the slave- and monster-controlling spells . . .

The slave spell, by the way, was a special spell that could be applied to someone, and then that person would have to follow orders or they would be punished instantly—and Raphtalia was my slave. Actually, at one point the slave spell was taken off of her, but she knew that I wouldn't be able to trust anyone that wasn't forced to obey me, so she volunteered to become my slave again so she could earn my trust.

I bought her from a slave trader shortly after I was framed and persecuted, back when I had completely lost the ability to trust anyone at all.

She was a young demi-human, which was a race of humans in the new world that had animal-like characteristics—she had ears and a puffy tail that looked like they were from a tanuki, or a raccoon. That made sense, because she'd said she was a "raccoon-type" demi-human.

She looked like she was about eighteen years old. She was actually younger than that, but demi-humans matured physically to match their current *level*, not *age*. She had long chestnut hair, a pretty face, and very fine, clear skin. Even Motoyasu, the Spear Hero, who was the most voracious consumer of female beauty I could think of, counted her high on his list of beauties.

I'd always been an otaku, so it's natural for me to describe her as one of those beautiful young women you see in video games and anime. She was at least as beautiful as they were.

The first weapon I gave her was a sword, and she quickly grew proficient with it. I was useless when it came to offense, so she cut down enemies on my behalf. Personality-wise she was very serious, and she was always quick to correct me whenever I said something improper.

When the first wave of destruction washed over the world, it took her village and family with it, so she had a lot of heavy emotions connected to the waves. Her family was gone, and in the aftermath she was captured by slave traders and sold to the highest bidder. It was a dark time in her life.

In the end, I bought her from another slave trader, and we began to fight together. Now she's my most trusted, dependable companion.

I normally never had to use it, but the slave spell was capable of telling me where she was at any time.

If I was ever going to use it, this was the time.

Out of slave spell observation range.

Well I guess that was that. What about Filo?

I received some funds from the crown after distinguishing myself in the first wave of destruction, and I used some of them to play a monster egg lottery-like game back at the slave trader's shop. Filo hatched out of the egg I got. She was a young monster girl called a filolial—and she loved to pull carriages. Filolials were . . . Okay, it's a little hard to explain. They are large bird monsters and looked like beefed-up ostriches. But Filo wasn't just any old filolial. She was a higher-ranking monster—a queen? A mutant?

She was a filolial queen—a sort of boss filolial. She looked different from the others too. She was much fluffier and built like a mix between an owl and a penguin. Her coloring was mostly white, but streaks of pink ran over her feather tips.

Oh—she could transform into something resembling a human whenever she wanted.

When she was in human form, she looked like a little angel. She had long, wavy blonde hair and innocent blue eyes. She was as innocent and mischievous as she looked. She was a bubbly, bumbling ten-year-old girl with wings on her back.

Her hair was bright and smooth. Her skin was just as taut and clear as Raphtalia's. And her face was pretty, too. She really looked exactly like a typical blonde-haired, blue-eyed, angelic little girl. She mostly wore a white one-piece dress with blue accents.

Her favorite weapons were her iron claws. When she was in human form she equipped them on her hands, and when she was a monster she wore them on her feet. She switched up her fighting style to suit whatever the situation called for. About her fighting abilities—well, she was even stronger than Raphtalia. She'd gotten us out of more tough spots than I could count.

I tried to use the monster spell to figure out where she was, but just like the slave spell, it didn't work. For whatever reason, the spells wouldn't even specify what direction they'd disappeared to.

Rishia was the only party member left.

Rishia used to be a member of the Bow Hero's team, but Itsuki framed her for a petty crime as an excuse to kick her out of his party . . . You see, you couldn't really depend on her for much.

She wore her hair in a French braid, and she came off as a bit of a sheltered, bookish girl. And truthfully, ever since she joined my party, she'd only proved herself useful outside of battle, with her knowledge and research. But that's not how she saw herself—she kept saying that she wanted to be a stronger fighter.

After Itsuki saved her from a perilous situation, she fell head over heels for his commitment to justice and asked to join his party. It all fell apart pretty quickly after that. She went through the same thing that I did. Her teammates framed her for a crime and kicked her out of the party. In the end, it turned out that Itsuki himself had planned it.

My theory was that he didn't like the fact that she had been more useful than he was in the battle with the waves.

She was very pretty, just as pretty as Raphtalia. Motoyasu, the Spear Hero, certainly spent a lot of time appraising the beauty of women—and Rishia was near the top of his list, too.

She, too, looked younger than she really was. I guess most people in my party don't look their age. If you took a glance at Rishia, you'd probably think she was fourteen or so, but she insists that she's actually seventeen. To sum it up, she looked really young, and I never really got the sense that I could depend on her for very much.

That reminds me. Lately she'd taken to dressing in a very strange way. She'd been wearing a kigurumi that looks just like Filo. She says she wears it because no one can tell if she's crying or not when she's in a kigurumi.

She had more surprises in store than just that, though. When we asked the queen for a battle specialist to help us improve our fighting skills, the old lady that showed up (who was a master of the Hengen Muso style) declared that Rishia had the sort of innate talent that only came around once every hundred years. And to be fair, she did pull off a good hit every once and a while. Actually, it was thanks to one of those lucky hits that we managed to make it out of the last battle alive. But most of the time she wasn't so great.

But damn it! What were we doing in jail?! How were we supposed to get out?

It could only mean one thing: we'd been captured by Kyo. But how?

How could this have happened to us?! Damn it!

"Let us out!" I shouted, rattling the door of the cage. I had never been thrown in jail before. I wasn't about to start crying about it, but I certainly didn't want to be there. Since I'd come to the new world, I'd done plenty of things that could have gotten me thrown in jail. But I'd never actually ended up in one!

I was innocent! I'd been proven innocent!

Or . . . Maybe someone had just found me passed out and put me in a jail cell because they didn't know what to do with me. I might be level 1, but I'd still find a way to fight back! A long time ago, an accessory dealer had taught me a lot about working with metals and jewels. Maybe I could fashion a key to get us out of there.

As I shook the door, I wracked my brain for a solution. I was thinking so hard about it that I barely noticed when the door just suddenly swung open.

"What the . . . ?"

"Feh?"

The door wasn't locked. What was the point of jail cell if you didn't lock the door? Whatever—it was better than being locked in.

"Um . . . okay. Well, let's figure out where we are. Raphtalia, Glass, and the others might be somewhere nearby."

"Alright."

We quickly slipped out of the jail cell and looked around

the stone-walled prison. The next room over was furnished pretty nicely. It looked like someone was living there. There was a thick bed, a sofa, and a bag that appeared to be full of food.

One of the jail cells had been renovated into a proper room. Raphtalia and the others were nowhere to be seen.

"Raphtalia! Filo! Where are you!? Answer me!" I shouted. There was no answer, so at the very least they couldn't have been within earshot.

"Alright, I'll lead the way. You follow me and keep an eye out. I'm depending on you."

"Um, okay! I'll do my besties!"

Oh jeez. Now I was even more worried than I had been.

"Hm . . ."

The prison must have been empty, because we didn't run into anyone at all. The further we walked, the more confusing it got. Walking around an unfamiliar building made me feel like I was in a labyrinth.

Something wasn't right. If we were in a labyrinth, I'd expect to run into monsters or something. Luckily enough, we hadn't come across anything dangerous . . . yet.

We went along lazily following the path until we came to a dead end. There was a mysterious door set in the wall, and it was glowing with colorful, rainbow-like light. It was built under a strange arch, and the colors all swirled in strange patterns over its surface—like the surface of a bubble in the sun.

"What . . . What is this?"

"I don't know."

If I'd learned anything from my years of playing video games, it was that strange objects like this normally teleported the player to a new location. But I'd never seen anything like it since I came to this new world.

"Nothing's going to happen if we stand here being scared of it. Let's go through."

"Feh . . ."

"What are you so scared of? Let's go."

Rishia stood there hesitating, so I grabbed her hand and pulled through the doorway with me. But what I saw on the other side left me speechless.

"What the . . . ?"

We were standing on a white sand beach. The sun blazed overhead in a clear blue sky, while waves rolled on in the distance. I turned back to where we came from and saw the doorway standing behind us in the sand.

"Feh! What's going on here?!"

"How should I know?"

I didn't know what was happening, but I knew that whatever this doorway was, it was capable of teleporting us through space.

"Get it together. We need to figure this out."

I turned away from the ocean and looked the opposite way.

There was a grassy field that was bordered by the beach and a close thicket. We didn't have any other leads at the moment, so I decided to head for the field.

I hadn't heard from Raphtalia or the others yet, so there was no time to waste standing around. We were running out of time. We had to find Kyo and make him pay for what he'd done.

"I know all this seems a little crazy, but we have to keep going. Would you rather wait here for help? Who knows if anyone will come?"

"Feh . . ."

I didn't want to wait. I didn't want to sit around hoping for something that might never happen. When I was framed and thrown out into the streets, there wasn't anyone who could help me. Even if I found someone who believed me, they didn't give me any way to prove my innocence. That's when I learned not to depend on others. It's true what they say—if you want something done, you had to do it yourself.

"I'm coming with you. I'm coming, so please don't leave me behind."

We headed for the field.

It wasn't long before a creature I'd never seen before approached us, looking pretty angry the closer it got. I still didn't know where we were, but the world seemed to function the same way the last one did—which is to say there was status magic that you could use in battle.

Maybe it was because I was down to level 1, but now that I couldn't use any of my other shields, I was stuck with the one I had, and I wasn't sure if it could actually protect us from anything.

Luckily all the status boosts and special functions I'd earned by unlocking all my previous shields were still in effect, which meant that I was more powerful than my lowly level 1 would imply. Furthermore, the power-up method that I learned from Itsuki, the one where you use the materials from defeated monsters to raise your stats, tied those boosts to all my shields at the same time. So all those boosts and abilities were still accessible.

Taken all together, I figured I could probably hold my own against a mid-level monster if I had to.

There was a monster in the bushes, something kind of white and angular. I looked at it closely, and its name appeared in my field of view.

White Box

I'd never seen the monster before.

It turned in my direction and came flying straight at me.

I immediately shoved my hand forward and snatched it out of the air

The monster was about the same size as my head. It was

white and . . . square and . . . Wait . . . Was it a cardboard box?

It must not have appreciated being grabbed, because it opened its mouth—or whatever it was—and bit me.

It wasn't strong enough to deal any damage. I'd never seen one of them before, but I had memories of something similar.

"This thing is like a balloon. Rishia, have you ever seen one of these things?"

"Feh? No, this is the first time I've seen one. I've never even seen one referenced in a book."

Hm. If Rishia—by far the most bookish person I knew—had never heard of these things, then we must have been in a very strange place indeed. If you could depend on her for one thing, it was her knowledge.

"It's just a weakling. Here, I'll hold it. You stab it."

"Okay!" she said, and then stabbed the white box with her sword.

The box let out a crushed sound, folded up flat, and X's appeared where its eyes had been. It stopped moving.

What a weird little monster.

It acted just like the weak little monsters you'd find in a field of any online RPG. Oh well. I guess the balloons back in Melromarc were sort of the same thing.

Received 15 EXP

The monster was really weak, but it gave quite a bit more experience than the balloons had.

"It was pretty tough."

"You're just not very strong."

Even if she leveled up, she didn't have any abilities. I checked her stats, though, and they were actually pretty high, considering her low level. So maybe these boxes actually were a bit tougher than the balloons.

I absorbed the fallen white box into my shield.

Just as I suspected, the monster was like the balloons in another way. It unlocked some status-boosting shields when I absorbed it.

Beginner's Small White Shield conditions met!

Beginner's Small White Shield
abilities locked: equip bonus: defense 2

Well, that settled it. It unlocked a shield with the exact same stat boost that the first balloon I killed had. It was basically just a small boost on top of what my shield was already giving me. I'd seen it all before.

"Here's the plan. I'll hold the monsters down while you kill them."

"Alright! Tee-hee!"

Oh jeez. More giggling.

Rishia was such a klutz. Now we were out leveling together, just the two of us. It reminded me of when Raphtalia and I had started leveling up. I wondered if I had been safer back then. Oh well, no point in dwelling on it. We kept on walking over the field. As we wandered around leveling and searching for our friends, I also found a lot of plants that looked like they were medicinal herbs. I figured they must have been, because they looked a lot like the plants we used to make medicine back in the last world.

And just like in the last world, the plants unlocked a shield like my Leaf Shield.

This time it was called a Tree Leaf Shield, which was weird because the leaf that unlocked it didn't come from a tree—though the plant did seem to have the same status effects as the medicinal herbs I was used to.

As we came across a variety of monsters, I noticed another strange thing. Almost none of the monster's names were written in katakana. Creatures resembling the rabbit-like usapils I'd come across in the last world were replaced with similar monsters, but this time they were indicated with the kanji for "rabbit."

And like I'd noticed when we defeated the white box, the monsters seemed to give more experience points than I was accustomed to. In the few hours we spent wandering the field,

I had already reached level 9, and Rishia had reached level 16!

I was careful to thoroughly break down any monsters we defeated for materials and drop items. We spent a few hours leveling up.

After I'd gained a few levels, a few of my shields became available again. I couldn't help but notice that certain shields were still unavailable. I didn't have any idea what the problem could be. What if I could never use the Soul Eater Shield, or the Chimera Viper Shield, again?

"Huff . . . Huff . . . I'm getting tired," Rishia sighed as she followed close behind me. She was clearly out of breath.

"Let's take a break."

I was a bit surprised that there were so many monsters in such a place. Maybe it was because of the strange way we got here. Where were we?

I sat down to rest for a bit. I was starting to get really thirsty.

We didn't bring a bottle or canteen or anything like that, so we were going to have to find some way to access fresh water. I habitually picked medicinal herbs when I walked, so my bag was starting to get full of them. Of course I hadn't brought my pestle and mortar, or any of my other compounding or crafting materials, so I'd have to use my shield to make things. I put some materials into the shield and had it start compounding from a recipe I'd memorized. It seems the recipe was flexible enough to work with these new plants, so it appeared to be working.

Maybe if I were a chemist by trade I'd have been more excited about experimenting with a whole new array of plants—but I wasn't, and it kind of annoyed me that I'd have to study all these new things.

"We're doing pretty well for ourselves, don't you think Naofumi?"

I was deep in thought for a little while, and Rishia wasn't able to tolerate the silence any longer.

"Yeah, I guess you're right. Good thing the monsters aren't too strong around here."

"I've gotten a little stronger, haven't I?"

" . . . "

Should I have told her that even though she'd gained fifteen levels her stats had hardly changed at all? Any change was so minimal it could have been attributed to a margin of error. I sat there worrying about how to best respond to her, when I noticed the sound of bubbling water nearby. There must have been a river.

I should have known! We were by the ocean, so of course there'd be a good chance of a river being nearby. I was thirsty, too, so I decided to go check it out. I pointed in the direction of the sound, and Rishia nodded, understanding exactly what I meant. She must have been thirsty, too.

We followed the sound and came across a riverbank.

There was a bridge made of fallen trees a little further down the bank from where we stood.

I had no idea where we were. I had no idea if the water was safe to drink. I took a long hard look at the water—it seemed clear and fine.

I scooped some up and drank it.

"Whew . . ." Rishia sighed. She relaxed after taking a deep drink.

We had come quite a long way from the shoreline.

Sitting there, drinking at the river, I was reminded of the day that we all camped out by the riverside in Melromarc.

At the very least, we were still capable of surviving here. We might have not been very strong yet, but we could survive. When I saw that I was at level 1, and that I couldn't use any of my shields, I'd been really worried. But we still didn't know where we were or what was going to happen next. It was no time to let our guard down. Whatever was going on, I knew one thing: I had to unlock more shields and get them powered up.

Maybe it was because of our low levels, or maybe there was something else going on, but I wasn't sure when I should start thinking about powering up the shields. If I found a better shield right after I powered one up, it would be a waste. On the other hand, if I didn't power up what I had, I might run into a monster that I'd be unable to overpower.

I was running the various options through my mind when

I noticed a strange monster splashing through the river nearby.

"Is that a kappa?"

Sure enough, it was. The monster was green and frog-like, its back was covered with a tortoise shell, and it had a little water-filled saucer balanced on its head. It looked almost human, and it walked upright on two legs, just like how my childhood yokai picture books had depicted them.

"Gwah," the kappa barked at me. It seemed angry.

Looking at the strange monster, I wondered what it would be called in the world I'd been summoned to. Was it a monster? A demi-human? A beast-man?

My shield was capable of translating the speech of people, so I wondered if it could translate what the kappa was saying. Unfortunately there was no time to find out. The kappa's throat puffed up wide, and it was clearly about to attack us.

"Air Strike Shield!"

The kappa barked and sent a high-pressure stream of water shooting at us, so I quickly used Air Strike Shield to block it. The shield appeared in mid-air between the kappa and us, just in time to intercept the beam of water. But the attack was too powerful, and the shield shattered in an instant.

It must have been because my level was still so low. I hadn't powered up my shield, either, and . . . this kappa monster was surprisingly powerful. If it thought we were enemies, then it didn't really matter if it was a monster or a human.

It opened its mouth and started to charge up for another water beam attack, but we sprinted over to it before it got a chance to use it.

"Gwah!" it barked, swiping at me with its claws. I blocked with my shield, and it swiped at me with its other arm.

"Second Shield!"

Another shield appeared in the air and stopped the monster's claws. That was my chance! I slipped behind him and grabbed his shoulders so he couldn't move.

"Rishia!"

"Feh?!"

Jeez . . . Rishia! Did she have to be confused about everything?

"Hurry up!"

"O . . . Okay!"

"Gwah!" the kappa croaked, preparing to shoot a beam of water straight at Rishia. Like I'd let that happen!

I tightened my grip on its shoulders and forced the monster to the right, causing the water beam to miss. The kappa was kicking and writhing in my arms, but it couldn't slip out of my grip.

"What are you waiting for?! Hurry up, Rishia!"

"Fehhh!" she shouted and stabbed at the kappa's stomach, but the little thing was tougher than I'd expected, and it didn't show any signs of going down yet.

"I am the Shield Hero, the source of all power. Hear my words and heed them. Give her everything!"

"Zweite Aura!"

I cast support magic on Rishia, and a big chunk of my magic power vanished. I would have preferred to end the fight without resorting to magic, but Rishia looked like she was at her limit.

A piercing pain shot through my back.

"Ugh . . ."

Was there another kappa? I turned to look, and sure enough, another kappa had snuck up behind us and plunged its claws into my back.

It really hurt. These things were pretty damn tough!

"Rishia, hurry it up already!"

"I . . . I know! But it's too tough! I can't get the sword through!" she shouted. She was stabbing at the kappa with all of her might, but the blade kept ricocheting off of the monster's belly. I had already cast support magic on her. Had we already run into a monster we couldn't defeat?

Damn! The second kappa sliced at my back again, and I felt a trickle of blood dribble down my back.

Things weren't looking good. I wasn't sure how much longer I could keep my grip on it.

"Hurry up! I can't hold on! If you can't kill it, then we'll have to make a run for it!"

If they were as strong as they seemed, we didn't stand a chance. Our levels clearly weren't high enough to take on these monsters. But I also wasn't sure that we'd be able to escape.

The water beams looked like they packed a serious punch, and we'd be wide open for attack from behind if we tried to run.

We were really stuck in a tough spot now, and things looked like they were getting worse by the second. Was I really going to die in a place like this? I wasn't going to give up, but I was also fresh out of ideas.

A third kappa appeared a little ways down the river and started running toward us. We were about to be surrounded.

"Fe . . . Feh!"

Damn it. Was this the end? Now I didn't see how we'd be able to escape.

But then . . .

The kappa that had been running at Rishia suddenly stopped in place. Then its head went flying from its neck.

"What the . . . ?"

"Blood Flower Strike!"

There was a flash of light along with an unfamiliar voice, and then the kappa that was attacking me from behind, and the kappa I was restraining in my arms, collapsed in a bloody pile.

What was going on?

I felt like I'd just witnessed a new, mysterious art form. Was it a skill?

Skills were special powers and techniques that only heroes like myself could use, like Air Strike Shield. But Glass and her friends could use them, too, and they weren't heroes. Sometimes we call magic "spells" and techniques "skills," which made it a little confusing. I wasn't sure if what I'd just seen was actually a skill or not.

"Are you okay?"

I noticed her ferocious eyes first. They were deep brown eyes. Her skin was . . . the same color as my skin. I don't mean that she had masculine skin, only that she was clearly human. It looked very healthy, a bright white tinged with pink here and there. It was tight and clean.

She was about as tall as a sixth grader, or maybe a seventh grader, but she carried herself with a confidence and dignity that made me think she might have been older than she looked.

Her hair was long, and pulled up into two pigtails on either side of her head, and she wore very feminine clothes that seemed to contradict her powerful and confident carriage. She wore a gothic dress and covered it with a threadbare haori. As for her chest . . . Even accounting for the extra frills and folds of her dress, there didn't seem to be anything there.

For a moment, I wondered if she might be a he . . . but I decided against it. It would be creepy for a man to wear his hair in pigtails. Besides, her face sure looked like a girl's. She had a soft aura about her as well, and I couldn't picture her as a man.

A pole—or no, a fishing rod—hung at her waist.

Her face was really pretty. She seemed strong, but still feminine. I might even go so far as to call her a tomboy. It was hard to tell how old she was.

And there was something . . . undeniably Japanese about her. Was I just imagining it?

"I only looked away for a second. I'm surprised they made it this far. If I hadn't shown up, that would have been it for you."

She clearly wasn't our enemy, but that didn't mean she was our ally, either. It was easy to imagine someone pretending to be our ally just so they could stab us in the back later.

I didn't have enough magic power left, so I used the medicine I had to heal my wounds. I spread the ointment on the surface of the kappa's ragged claw marks, and they healed before my eyes. I had to admit, that was one of the things I liked about being summoned to a new world. Back in Japan, wounds took a lot longer to heal.

"I've been watching out for you since you two fell out of the sky."

"Who are you?"

Of course I was grateful that she'd saved us from the monsters, but I still had to figure out whom we were dealing with. You could never be too careful. It was good to have people owe you a favor, and who knew what she was really after?

"You don't trust me?"

"Of course not. We get out of a prison, only to end up in a fight we can't win just in time for you to show up and save the day like a hero. It's hard to attribute it all to coincidence."

"Oh, right. I guess that makes sense. I guess," she sighed, annoyed, and scratched her head.

What was with this girl? Was she the one who'd returned us to level 1?

I decided to err on the side of caution and slowly slipped into a defensive position.

"We might as well get acquainted, considering we were lucky enough to meet out here. Let's chat."

"Maybe you should offer your name before you ask for someone else's."

"I guess you're right. Okay, I'll go first. I'm Kizuna Kazayama, and I'm one of the four holy heroes—the Hunting Hero, to be exact."

" . . . What?"

What the hell was she talking about? She was a holy hero? The Hunting Hero?

As far as I knew, the four holy heroes were the Sword, Spear, Bow, and Shield Heroes.

"I gave you my name. Now give me yours," she said, irritated to see me standing there speechless. I decided it was best to tell the truth and see how she reacted.

"My name is Naofumi Iwatani. I'm also one of the four holy heroes—I'm the Shield Hero."

" . . . What?"

Kizuna looked just as confused as I was. She even said the same thing I had.

"Is there a problem?"

"No. I've just never heard of a 'Shield Hero.' Are you sure you're one of the four holy heroes?"

"Oh yeah, well, I've never heard of a 'Hunting Hero.'"

Kizuna crossed her arms and pondered. "Hm . . ." If she was curious, she didn't show it for long. She immediately looked at Rishia and clipped, "You're next."

"Feh?!"

"Rishia, introduce yourself. I don't think she's our enemy." At least not for the moment.

"Oh, um . . . Okay. My name is Rishia Ivyred."

"Oh, so you're not calling yourself a hero?"

"No, she's just my friend."

Kizuna looked Rishia up and down and then nodded to herself.

"Okay, so, Naofumi—Can I call you Naofumi?"

"Sure. I'll call you Kizuna. What is it?"

I could tell from the way she spoke. Her name had been a dead giveaway. The holy heroes were all summoned from somewhere else, so . . .

"I guess it's safe to assume that you were summoned from Japan, right?"

" . . . Yeah, whatever that's worth."

"I don't know what you mean by that, but I've never heard of a 'Shield Hero,' which makes me think you must have been summoned to a different world to serve in a different set of holy heroes."

" . . . It does sound that way, doesn't it?"

We had followed Glass and her friends, so we must be in their world. Which meant that this girl Kizuna must have been one of the four holy heroes in this world.

"I don't know how a hero from another world ended up here . . . but things don't look so good for you."

"Why do you say that?"

"You're right that there's a prison here, but it's not a good one—it's one of the worst."

"Elaborate."

"This place is a never-ending labyrinth. To make it simple, there aren't any guards, but it's impossible to get out. It's a special kind of space."

An inescapable, special kind of space? Ha!

"What's so funny?" Kizuna seemed irritated again.

But how was I supposed to keep from laughing?

"It's nothing. They summoned me to the previous world, and I'd been looking for a way out ever since. I'm pretty accustomed to these 'inescapable spaces' by now. I've been in one for months!"

Isn't that basically what Melromarc had been the whole time? They summoned me to serve as the Shield Hero, but they wouldn't let me leave. The way I saw things, the whole world was a prison. Now Kizuna says I'm in a special space. It was all the same to me. Another trap I could only escape by breaking through a dimensional wall.

Anyway, the first thing I had to do was confirm that we were in the right place—Glass's world. If Glass was from another world, then there was no guarantee that that we'd come to the right one. Maybe there were more.

"That sounds like a very broad interpretation."

"I guess you're one of those people that just can't get enough of life in these crazy worlds. Is that it?"

If she was a holy hero, she might have been just like the other three heroes from my world. But she didn't confirm or deny it.

"I . . . I wouldn't say that, exactly." She turned her eyes away, which only made me more curious—the heroes I knew wouldn't act that way. No way. All three of them were over the moon to be where they were. Kizuna's ambiguous reaction made me suspect that there was more going on. But it wasn't the time to dig into all of that. I had to find Raphtalia and the others and make sure that they were okay. That was my highest priority.

The next priority was Kyo. I had to make him pay for what he'd done.

A long, thin blade hung from Kizuna's waist. It looked like a tuna knife. I'd never used one, but I'd seen them before.

The Hunting Hero must have used hunting tools for weapons, but was that sort of knife considered a hunting tool? What was a Hunting Hero, anyway? Could she use anything related to hunting?

That seemed like a very broad category. Compared to the Shield Hero, who was stuck with shields and shields alone, it seemed like a much better title to have.

"What is it?"

"Nothing."

Kizuna inspected the kappa corpses. She seemed confused.

"That's odd. I killed the monsters, but I didn't get any experience points for it."

"Probably because there's another hero nearby, don't you think?"

"Is that how it works?"

Didn't she know about the interference phenomenon that kept the heroes from fighting together? Whenever a hero fought a battle near another hero, neither of them received experience points. That was why the heroes always had to split up and go on adventures on their own.

When the waves came we had more important things to

do—and hordes of monsters to defeat—so there was no reason to worry about experience. I explained what I knew about it to Kizuna.

"Interesting . . . I'd never heard of it."

"You haven't met any of the other heroes in this world?"

"No, I haven't."

I was so jealous! I couldn't stand it!

But weren't all four heroes summoned together at the same time? I was thinking it over when I noticed that Kizuna was giggling to herself.

"What is it now?"

"It's nothing. I just haven't talked to anyone in years—it's so much fun!"

"What?"

What did she just say? She hadn't spoken to anyone in years? Was she some kind of antisocial maniac—someone that could never figure out how to enter conversation, so they just didn't ever say anything? She didn't seem like the soft-spoken type to me, though . . .

"Of course I haven't. I don't even know how long it's been since I was thrown in here—at least a few years, though, I'm sure. When I tried to count the time, it just made me sad, so I stopped."

"What about when the waves come? Don't they teleport you out of here?"

That's right, I forgot to mention it: whenever the waves came, the dragon hourglasses automatically teleported the heroes to the site of the wave's occurrence. I hated it. It meant that you had to fight even if you didn't want to.

"Waves? You mean the legends about the stuff that happens in the outside world? Are they real?"

"You've never fought in the waves?"

"I already told you, this space is separated from the outside world. I don't know what's going on out there," Kizuna said. She looked depressed.

I slowly opened a menu and called up the hourglass counter that had been moving, back before I came through the portal, and . . .

—:—

It was blank. It wasn't counting down to anything.

Huh? Did that mean that I wasn't going to be summoned to fight in the waves as long as I was in this place? The space was so inescapable that the hourglasses couldn't even summon me to fight in the waves? Just how isolated was this place?

"Anyway, what do you want to do with these things?" Kizuna asked, pointing to the dead kappas.

"Turn them into materials? Break them down?"

Kizuna nodded.

"I got all the materials I needed from these things ages ago. The drops are boring now, too."

"Then I'll take it."

I absorbed the kappa body into my shield.

A sound indicated that I'd unlocked a shield, but my level wasn't high enough to access it yet. The drop item wasn't very good, either, but it was better than nothing.

"Um . . ."

I turned to look at Rishia, who looked ashamed. She wasn't a hero, so she should have gotten some experience from the battle—that is, as long as this world functioned the same as the last one.

"Can you still form parties here? Some stuff seems to be different from the world I came from, so I wonder . . ."

"As far as I know, heroes won't be able to get experience when they fight together. But Rishia isn't a hero, so can you try giving her your points?"

"Huh? Oh, sure. Even if it doesn't work, I don't mind. Which one of you is the leader? Send me an invite."

I raised my hand. Kizuna clearly understood what I meant, so I went ahead and sent her an invite. At least party formation appeared to function the same way in this world.

She joined my party, and the experience from the battle naturally went to Rishia.

"This isn't the best place to sit and talk. Let's go somewhere safe."

"Sure."

Kizuna led us back down the path we'd come by, all the way back to where we'd first appeared on the beach.

"This is one of the safest spots around. If you put on equipment that lets you breathe underwater, then you can go into the ocean and walk on the ocean floor, but you'll soon discover that it's a maze down there, too. This is an island, so if you walk inland it'll soon turn into thick forest, and that's a maze, too. Once you get to the other side of that field, you'll be in the woods."

She explained the situation like it was the most obvious thing in the world. I guess it was safe to assume that we'd been dropped into a place that functioned similar to a roguelike game.

"It's pretty weird, isn't it?"

"Yeah."

"It's a tough place. I hear it's made so that you can't get out."

"And how do you know that?"

"I heard about it before I ended up here. They say that once you enter, you can never leave. The labyrinth is basically a world in and of itself. I've spent a long time exploring it, and I've gotten pretty far." She sighed and then spat. She looked stressed out. "As far as I can tell, they were right. There's no way out."

So even though we were supposed to have followed Glass back to her world, I ended up with Rishia, stuck in some mysterious labyrinth instead.

"It's best to go back to the jail cell if you want to sleep. But it's safe enough to talk here." Kizuna pointed to a house built near the beach and started walking in its direction.

"Ah . . ."

She was right. It was probably best to take a break. I had no idea how long I'd been unconscious, but I was definitely approaching exhaustion after all those battles in the field. We could all use a rest.

"Feh!" Rishia gasped, still surprised by every little thing. When was she going to come to terms with what was going on?

"I have to say . . . You both certainly have an interesting way of dressing." Kizuna took a seat in a sooty chair at the beach house and looked us over.

I couldn't disagree with that, either. The Barbarian Armor +1? was really beat up after the fighting with the Spirit Tortoise. I tried to look into the state of the armor using the status magic system, but all the letters were garbled and illegible.

It was so banged up that it probably didn't even count as armor anymore. I slowly slipped it off and . . . Yup, my stats didn't change at all. The armor had become completely ineffective. The old guy at the weapon shop had made it especially for me, but there was no point it wearing it if it wasn't doing anything.

"Rishia, how's your kigurumi holding up?"

"Feh?!"

She looked through her equipment menu and squealed in surprised.

"Feh?! It says something strange!"

I suppose that meant that at the very least her equipment wasn't so beat up that it was ineffective.

Something odd must happen to equipment when it crosses the barrier between worlds. That would explain why Glass and her friends were dressed so strangely when we ran into them inside of the Spirit Tortoise.

"Take it off. There's no point in wearing it if it isn't helping."

"O . . . Okay."

Rishia obeyed my order and slipped out of the kigurumi. Finally, she was wearing normal clothes for once.

"So? Kizuna, how did you end up in this place?"

"I'll tell you, but I'd rather you explained how you got here first. It wouldn't be fair if I was the only one answering questions around here."

She had a point. Besides, she was probably only answering my questions because she wanted to find out more about us.

"Where should I start?"

"Tell me how you got here. I'm curious what brought you to a place like this."

She was one of the four holy heroes, so there was probably

nothing to lose by cooperating with her . . . right? Then again, I didn't really want to cooperate with the other three heroes I knew. They didn't listen to anything I said. But my level was so low here that I didn't see what choice I had. I needed her help. If she decided to turn on us, we wouldn't stand a chance.

I decided to carefully watch to see how she reacted to my story.

"First things first . . ."

I started with how I was summoned to the world, how I was framed, and how I was exonerated, and I went on to tell her the main points about the other three heroes.

"Uh-huh. And then? What brings you to this place? To my world? I thought the four heroes weren't allowed to cross between the worlds."

"Ah, so you know about that?"

When Kyo escaped after our battle, I tried to follow him through the portal—only to discover that I couldn't get through it. A warning appeared, saying that the four holy heroes were not permitted to cross over to other worlds.

Ost, just on the verge of death, intervened on our behalf, which is how we were able to get through the portal. Kizuna seemed to know all about the difficulties that crossing over entailed.

"There was this giant monster called the Spirit Tortoise that collected the souls of people killed in the waves and used them to make a barrier to protect the world from the waves. Anyway, someone took control of the monster and used it to go on a rampage."

"Heh . . . A protective beast? We've got something like that over here, too. We've got the Black Turtle and the White Tiger, but I don't know much about those legends. You say someone took control of this thing?"

"That's right. He was crazy. His name was Kyo Ethnina. We chased him through the portal he made back to this world."

"Hm . . . Maybe you played right into his hands. Maybe this was a trap."

" . . . I'm starting to think the same thing."

Kizuna rocked in her chair and nodded. "I see. Sounds like a real disaster."

"It was terrible. Still, Kyo was obviously violating all sorts of rules, so a few people, who were our enemies, ended up helping us out."

"I don't really understand it all yet, but you say they were your enemies?"

"Yeah. Glass and L'Arc Berg."

I remembered everything about Glass and her friends and what had happened before we woke up in this place.

As things stood, we had put aside our differences to focus on fighting our common enemy, Kyo. Still, I wouldn't call them allies.

I'll start with Glass.

She was a beautiful woman with long black hair, and she wore a kimono, which made her look very Japanese. When we fought with her, she used folding fans for weapons, and her fighting style looked like dancing. Even after implementing all of the other heroes' power-up methods, she was still so powerful that I wasn't able to defeat her.

I don't think she was human, because she seemed to turn a little transparent from time to time. I still didn't know very much about her—she was a mystery.

L'Arc is next. His real name was L'Arc Berg. When I first met him, he seemed like a dependable, nice older-brother kind of character. He was laid back and easy to talk to.

After I was exonerated of my crimes, I met him on a boat we took to the Cal Mira Islands. There was a special event happening on the islands that would give us more experience points than usual for our battles with monsters.

I didn't know we were enemies at the time. I just thought that he was a tough fighter and a nice guy. In fact, we even fought together for a little while. But then a wave occurred close to the islands. We were in the middle of fighting against it when he turned on us. According to him, he had to kill me for the sake of his world. Glass said the same thing.

He had spiked red hair, and he was very muscular. He clearly knew his way around the battlefield. He was handsome, too, but unlike Motoyasu (the other handsome guy around here), nothing about him was irritating or obnoxious. I actually liked him. If we weren't enemies, I would have wanted him to join my party.

He fought with a giant scythe. Just like Glass, it was a special sort of weapon.

It was as powerful as you'd expect, but apparently he only had as much power as he had during our fight because we happened to be fighting at the same time as a wave. Still, he held his own just fine in the battle with Kyo, so it's safe to say that he was a pretty powerful fighter.

At the very least, he was certainly stronger than the other three heroes in the previous world.

He had another person with him: a woman named Therese.

I hadn't spoken with her very much, but she was clearly his partner.

She wore her glossy, blueish hair pulled back in a French braid. The color of her hair seemed to change a little depending on the angle you viewed it from. And when she used a magic spell, her hair turned red, which is something I'd never seen happen to a human—at least not humans in the world I was from.

She was calm, and warm, the sort of woman you'd go to for help. Both her and L'Arc seemed to be kind and dependable people.

She was a magic user in battle, and she normally used magic to cast support effects on L'Arc and Glass. The magic she used was strange, though. It seemed to depend on the accessories she wore in battle. When she cast spells, her accessories would flash and create a magic effect. I assumed it was a special form of magic from their world.

I can't speak authoritatively on her personality, but from what I'd seen, she was very emotive and sensitive. I made her a bangle once, and she was very appreciative.

I think she was probably L'Arc's . . . girlfriend. Maybe.

Anyway, those three were helping us chase down Kyo.

We had to find a way to punish him for what he'd done in Raphtalia's world—for all the chaos he'd sown. That was why we followed him through the portal. We had to make him pay.

After we jumped into the portal, I found myself in some kind of fast, ferocious current, bathed in light. I thought that if we let the current carry us along, it would take us to Glass's world.

That's it—I remember now.

The direction the current carried us started to change, darkness swallowed the light, and suddenly we were being carried along by the current in dark space.

And that was when I heard it, the voice of the enemy. I heard Kyo speaking to us.

"Heh heh . . . You didn't think there would be a trap? How stupid are you?!" He laughed, and lightning crackled in the space around us.

I held up my shield and prepared to blast through whatever trap he'd prepared for us.

But it didn't work. A crashing sound filled my ears and pale lightning crackled in the darkness.

"Ahhhh!"

"Ugh, damn it!"

"Mr . . . Mr. Naofumi!"

"Ugh . . ."

The current that carried us along suddenly split, branching off in different directions and carrying us away from each other. It was like one of those tubular waterslides that split into different paths.

"Raphtalia!"

I reached out to her, desperate to keep us together, but it was too late. I couldn't reach her, and she slipped away.

Damn it. I wondered . . . Could I save her with a skill?

"Air Strike . . ."

Before I could finish calling for the skill, Raphtalia and the others had already slipped far, far away.

"Mr. Naofuuuuumiiiiiiiii!"

"Raphtaliaaaa!"

I lost consciousness.

And according to Kizuna, I woke up in the middle of an inescapable labyrinth.

When I finished telling my story, Kizuna stopped rocking her chair and jumped to her feet.

"Glass! Where did you meet Glass?!"

"Do you know her?"

"She's a close friend. She's the person who gave me this haori."

I'd wondered about her outfit, a haori paired with a western, gothic dress. It made sense if it had been a present. Still, she wore it naturally enough that I'd assumed it was some kind of fashion I didn't know about.

So she knew Glass well enough to have received a present from her—what did it mean?

"If Glass has teamed up with you to take that guy down, he must really be a bad guy. No doubt about it," Kizuna nodded, more energetic than she had been.

If she knew Glass, then that settled it: Kizuna must have been one of the four holy heroes from Glass's world.

"And L'Arc nii-chan was with her, too? How's he doing with Therese?"

"How should I know?" Seriously. I had barely even held a conversation with Therese. How should I know about their private lives?

"Is Glass here, too?"

"I don't know. We fell into a trap of some kind while we were moving between worlds, and I ended up here."

"Right . . . right. I probably would have known if she was here, anyway . . ." Kizuna muttered, nodding. I guess it's my turn now."

"Yeah. Start with how you ended up being summoned to another world in the first place."

"You want me to start way back then? Well, I guess you told me your story . . ." she said, and began to speak.

Chapter One: The Hunting Hero

"I had the chance to participate in a special game with my two sisters . . ."

"A game?"

"At first I thought that I was in that game world, but no matter how long I waited, I never met my sisters. A bunch of stuff happened, and eventually I realized I was in another world altogether. I'll spare you the details."

How was she supposed to enter a game world with her sisters?

Her story reminded me of the other three heroes, except that they had all mentioned something about dying. But hey, she was skipping over some important stuff—what was all this about "entering a game world?"

"Are you talking about VRMMOs? Did this game happen to be called Brave Star Online?"

"I've never heard of that."

"One of the heroes in my world said that the world was just like that game."

"Oh yeah? My game was galled Second Life Project. There was another one was called Dimension Wave, too."

"Second Life Project?"

I'd heard of Dimension Wave before. It was the console game that Itsuki talked about. I couldn't help but be intrigued by Second Life Project, though.

"It's just how it sounds. It was one of those simulator games where you get to have a second life online. The game prepared these special pods that you go inside to enter the game world. They liked to say that a day on the outside is equivalent to a few years on the inside."

It sounded a lot like what Ren talked about, but the technology seemed older. Ren had made it sound like VRMMOs were commonplace, the sort of thing that a normal family might have in their living room. At least, that's how I'd pictured it.

"It's a great system for working people that don't have a lot of time to spend on games. It's a quick way to feel refreshed. I think they call them VRHMMOs? It's short for Virtual Reality Healing MMO."

"Sounds like a real time-saver."

Time is a seriously limited resource, and playing games takes a lot of time, even more so if you play online games. Back when I was in college, I knew someone that had to stop playing games altogether when they got a job. On the other hand, I knew someone that quit their job so they'd have more time to spend on their online games.

"Game 1 let in anyone that wanted to play, but you had to

be admitted by lottery to enter Game 2. Of course my sister was admitted, so the three of us were able to join."

"Hm . . ."

"Everyone starts the game together and ends it together. The game has a schedule that everyone has to commit to."

That sounded like a bit much from what I was used to. It's not that I couldn't understand it; it just sounded like the plot of a futuristic movie or something. But if everyone started and ended at the same time, and if everyone was online at the same time, then that sounded like a very fair system.

And if it only took one day in the real world, that would save a lot of time.

"So I thought I was joining that game. After they summoned me, they started explaining a bunch of stuff. I just thought it was the tutorial."

Oh man, now she really sounded just like the other three heroes in the previous world.

She thought she was playing a game but was actually summoned to another world. At least that was better than the other heroes, who knew they were being summoned.

And I had just read a book. How boring!

"Huh . . ."

"There weren't any waves when I was summoned."

"Then why did they summon you?"

"Because the ruler of the monsters, the Dragon Emperor, was causing havoc."

"Sounds like a retro game to me." It sounded like an old RPG to me.

"I know. That's what I thought. It didn't sound like the kind of game that was on the website. Even the instructions made it sound like something else."

"So then what happened?"

"I went on a few adventures. I took a journey by boat. One day an ominous wind was blowing, and a ghost ship appeared. Glass and her friends helped me solve the mystery of the ship, and it disappeared. We ended up crashing, and I found myself alone in unfriendly lands. I was captured and thrown into this labyrinth. I already knew what sort of place it was, so you can imagine how angry I was to end up in here. I couldn't stop thinking that I'd be here until I die."

"Yeah . . ."

Just how unlucky was this girl? I felt like we'd been through similar things, so I was starting to sympathize with her.

"From then on, I've been struggling through every day, here in the labyrinth. I decided to stop counting the days—the years—a long time ago."

So that's why she didn't know anything about the waves— or about the world.

Whatever the specifics were, we'd both been through similar hardships, and now we were both stuck in the same prison.

"How old are you, anyway?"

She looked like she was about middle-school age.

So if she was as old as she looked, then she must have been summoned to the world when she was still in elementary school. I guess I could picture that. I'd seen plenty of anime that involved young kids being teleported to other worlds. Maybe that was what had happened to Kizuna.

"Me? I'm eighteen."

"Ha! You're kind of an old loli-ba . . ." I stopped short of saying what I was thinking. Raphtalia would have been disappointed in me if I'd let that slip.

Speaking of Raphtalia, she looked like she was about the same age I was, but in truth she was only about ten years old. If I made fun of Kizuna for the opposite thing, it would hurt Raphtalia's feelings.

"What's the matter? Weren't you going to call me a loli-baba?"

"It's nothing. But hey, you know what that is?"

"I know I look young for my age, okay?! So I'm an otaku, so what?"

Heh, it was starting to make sense. All the summoned heroes shared certain otaku-leaning traits. But wait a second— what if people with legendary weapons stopped aging? In some ways that would be a great thing, but what would people think if you came back after being gone for thirty years and you hadn't aged at all? I don't think that would go over very well.

But there was no point thinking about it until I found a way home.

"Anyway, what're you going to do now?"

"Do I have a choice? I can't exactly stand around killing time here."

"That's what I thought. But you know, I've been looking for a way out of here for a long time."

"You can tell me to give up, but I'm not going to."

On the one hand, it would be nice to avoid the waves for the rest of my life, but on the other, I didn't want to spend eternity wandering around the labyrinth.

"Feh . . . Naofumi, I haven't understood anything that you two are talking about."

"You're supposed to be smart, but you can't keep up with a simple conversation like this?"

"Hey, you're making fun of me, aren't you?!" Rishia cried.

I sighed. I was starting to miss Raphtalia.

Why did I have to get stuck with Rishia? Raphtalia was so much easier to talk to.

"Feh . . ." she whimpered, backing away from me.

God, she was annoying.

"I'm not telling you to give up. I haven't given up, either."

A grumbling sound roared from Rishia's stomach. It had been a long time since we'd had a meal, and we'd done a lot of fighting since then. I asked her about it, and she started to giggle.

"Perhaps we should eat?"

"What do you have to eat around here? I'm guessing monster meat."

"There's fish, too. We're right by the ocean, so you can fish all you want." Kizuna went back toward the labyrinth for a minute and came back with food. It was mostly dried meat and fish and a few pieces of fruit.

"If you want sashimi or something, I could go catch a fish or two."

"Do you have any medicinal herbs? I have some things, too, and if we combined our resources we could come up with some seasonings."

"Yeah, I might have just the thing. Want to go get some?"

"Fine by me. But you should know that our equipment doesn't seem to have any effect here, so we won't be any help at all if we run into a strong monster on the way."

Kizuna thought for a minute and then produced a drop item from her weapon. It looked like some kind of equipment. "I have some basic stuff I was going to use for crafting later on, but you can use it now."

"Sounds good to me."

She passed me a wooden piece of armor, some light clothing, a short sword, and a set of double swords.

"I don't need any weapons."

"Ah, I guess the heroes in your world are just like the ones here. We can't use weapons aside from the ones we've been assigned."

"That's right. That's a real problem for me, because I don't have a way to deal damage directly to enemies. I'm stuck with a shield."

Rishia took the weapons from Kizuna and equipped them. She was the only one who could level up, anyway, not that her levels were helping her stats much. Her stats changes so little that it made me wonder if leveling up was good for anything at all.

I guess she made up for it with—surprisingly—decent base stats.

"Can't do direct damage, eh? So I guess you have to use counters and stuff?"

"Correct. Unlike you, I don't have a wide range of weapons to pick from."

What did a "Hunting Hero" actually use, anyway?

If it was anything like how it sounded, she must have had access to a wide variety of weapons.

"Yeah, I guess I can transform my weapons into all sorts of things. This is a tuna knife, for breaking down dead monsters. I can also use bows, and slings, and spears and stuff."

"Quite a range."

I'd figured she could use different tools, but I was surprised at just how many categories she had access to. I supposed I should have expected it, considering the vague title "Hunting Hero."

"You think? Well, I guess it would be inconvenient to be like Glass, with the fan of the vassal weapons, limiting her to just fans. Is that how you feel, Naofumi? Limited?"

"Yeah, I've only ever been able to use shields."

It wasn't that none of my shields had good abilities—that's not what I was saying. It's just that I was always on defense, and there was no getting around that. The only shields I had that could do some damage were the Shield of Wrath and the Spirit Tortoise Heart Shield.

But the cursed Shield of Wrath was impure, and it cursed me whenever I used its skills.

The Spirit Tortoise Heart Shield was capable of a devastating attack called Energy Blast, but I couldn't use that shield in this world. I couldn't use any of my shields.

"I don't have as many options as you. I'm the Shield Hero, and I just focus on protecting people.

"I'm not as all-powerful as you seem to think. My weapons have limitations."

"Like what? I told you about my limitations, so you can tell me about yours."

"Hm? Well the Hunting Hero is supposed to, well . . . hunt. That means I can't really fight other people. I'm just like you. I can't hurt people. I can't fend for myself if people come attack me or capture me. All I can do is run away."

So Kizuna couldn't fight other people. She was limited to attacking monsters.

"If you don't believe me, I'll prove it," she said, and immediately sliced at us with her tuna knife. I raised my shield to block it, but when she drew the blade back, it struck my cheek.

"Feh?!"

Rishia dodged the first attack, but the blade hit her the second time.

The cold steel felt awful on my face, but . . . it didn't hurt. In fact, I could hardly feel it. I touched my skin, and there was no blood—not even a scratch.

Rishia was so surprised she looked like she was about to faint, but the attack hadn't done any actual damage that I could see.

"See what I mean? I couldn't hurt you if I wanted to, so you can relax."

"You could have warned me." I had done the same thing to the other heroes before. Once I'd even punched one of them with my bare fists, just to prove I couldn't hurt them.

"On the other hand, I'm very effective when it comes to fighting monsters."

So she was a hero that specialized in monster battles? It wasn't quite the same deal I had, but it was similar in a way. The Shield Hero was probably supposed to have taken all of a normal hero's attack power and dedicated it to defense instead. The counter-attack effects of the Shield of Wrath and the Spirit

Tortoise Heart Shields were nothing but by-products.

But if I had a way to go on the offensive, maybe Kizuna had some special abilities that would let her hurt other humans.

I wasn't about to take her word for it.

Still, she didn't seem to think of us as enemies, so it was in our best interest to cooperate for the time being.

"Then let's go look around, shall we? I've been cleaning this place out periodically, so there shouldn't be anything too strong out there. Still, if you go too deep, we might run into something rough. Keep your wits about you."

"Got it."

Monsters were like wild animals, so hunting them wasn't exactly the easiest thing in the world.

Kizuna led the way, and soon we were walking through a thick forest.

I didn't see any monster footprints or anything, but it wasn't long before Kizuna held out her hand and told us to stop.

" . . . Something is close."

I held my breath to listen, and sure enough, I could hear something breathing in the bushes. Maybe it was because of my low level, but I felt like my intuitions were a little duller than usual.

"I don't think it's anything to worry about. Let's hurry up and kill it."

"Okay."

Kizuna slunk over to the bushes, and a group of monsters leapt out when she approached.

They looked like very large green rats.

And that's exactly what they were called: large green rats. It looked like there were four of them . . . at least!

"Hya!" Kizuna shouted. Her attack immediately killed two of them. The remaining two must have figured out that Rishia and I were the weaker opponents, because they came running over to bite us.

"Wait! Damn—Naofumi, don't let them get away!"

"Alright! Don't send any more of them in my direction!"

"I know!"

I blocked the first rat with my shield, but the second one got around me and bit into my arm.

"Ouch!"

I was surprised that a monster like that was able to hurt me. They looked like low-level, early-game monsters, and normally my defense would be too strong for them. The kappa looked pretty strong, so I could understand that. But now I was getting beat up by a rat? My pride could hardly take it.

I really needed to level up. I couldn't help but yearn for my lost stats and power-ups.

"Feh!"

"Quit whining and do something!"

Kizuna was busy dealing with the hordes of rats attacking her. "Rishia, it's up to you now!"

"O . . . Okay!"

Rishia dashed forward and plunged her sword into the rat I was holding down.

"Thrust Attack!" Kizuna shouted, thrusting her weapon at the rats. A shockwave with Kizuna at the center exploded outward, sending the crowd of rats flying. They died when they hit the ground with a soft chirp. They must have been cut by a blade of wind, because many of them were sliced clean in half.

"Flying Sparrow!"

Another blade of light shot through the air at the rat that was still attacking Rishia and me.

Judging by the appearance of the attack, it must have worked similar to Motoyasu's Air Strike Javelin, which worked by hitting an enemy with a weapon formed from energy.

"Those things are a kind of tough."

"Yeah, but they're weaker than the kappa. Most of the adventurers in my world need to be at level 15 before they can kill one."

We were struggling to defeat monsters that a level 15 adventurer could defeat. Rishia wasn't the toughest girl around, so for her, at least I shouldn't have been surprised.

"Let's get back to our search."

"The hero interference effect is making this more difficult than it should be."

"Want to go on without me?"

"We don't have the time to spend leveling up. We're just out here to get food."

"Yeah, right. So let's get going."

We restarted our search, and soon we found some banana-like fruits and some herb-like plants. Luckily my appraisal skills were still working, and Kizuna was able to confirm which plants were poisonous and which ones were useful. So we were able to collect a fair amount of medicinal herbs.

Like Kizuna said, the monsters we ran into along the way weren't very powerful, and she was able to dispatch them without any trouble—as in, with only one hit. How strong was this girl, anyway?

Rishia was starting to get some useful experience.

We were only out hunting for two hours, but Rishia had already reached level 20. She was leveling really quickly.

Unfortunately, the hero interference phenomenon kept Kizuna and I from leveling up at all. As soon as Rishia and I were strong enough to survive on our own, it would be best to part ways with Kizuna.

"We should start cooking soon."

"Good point."

"You could wait for me, you know."

"I don't want to think about what would happen if you fed us something bad."

"You're not very trusting, are you?"

THE RISING OF THE SHIELD HERO 8   73

We went back to the beach house, built a fire, and grilled some mysterious meats and fish with the herbs. I thought about maybe making some barbecued skewers for later.

"Is there any drinking water? I was going to make a soup . . ."

"Yeah, there's an underground spring over there. I normally drink from that."

We were so close to the sea. I should have figured that any water in the immediate vicinity was going to be seawater.

Looking out at the ocean, I felt like I was back in the Cal Mira Islands.

Kizuna pulled out a water bottle and filled a large wok-like pan. Then she built a new fire beneath it. I added the bones and head of a fish and let them simmer.

Kizuna ended up with free time on her hands while I was cooking, so she decided to go fishing in the ocean. She said we could eat anything she caught as sashimi.

A few minutes passed, and . . .

"It's done! Kizuna, it's ready!" I shouted. The food was ready.

"It's done already?"

"Yeah."

"I have a big haul, too," she said, smiling. She carried a line with a heavy fish dangling from it. She must have been pretty good.

"Let's eat."

"Yeah. Dig in!"

"Looks delicious!"

Rishia and Kizuna started to eat the food I'd made. Kizuna swallowed the first bite and nodded to herself. "Yum."

"This is delicious. Naofumi, I didn't realize you were such an accomplished chef."

"I had to learn after being summoned to the last world."

"I had to start cooking for myself after I ended up in this place, but I still can't cook very well. I thought about grilling salted fish, but making salt from the seawater is too much work."

"Don't be so lazy. Fortunately, I found some rice, too, so I went ahead and made a paella. You want some?"

"I'm telling you, it's really good! I never knew what to do with rice. All I could think of was making onigiri."

I couldn't imagine where she got rice for herself, but I found it among her things, so I made a paella. She didn't have a great pan for it, so I had to make it in a clay pot.

"Is that better or what?"

"Feh!"

Kizuna was already done eating, but Rishia was still working on it, and tears streamed down her face. Had she really been that hungry?

"Alright. So what's next?" Kizuna murmured as she

watched the sun sink into the ocean. "You guys still up for some action?"

"I'm not against it, but if you've got a way out of here, you better tell us."

"It's not impossible . . ." she said, pulling something from her pocket. "Remember what I said? About how hard I tried to get out of here?"

"Yeah. You said you'd gone deep into the labyrinth."

"I did. I really put my life on the line. I wasn't sure I'd survive."

"Where are we now as far as the labyrinth is concerned?"

"Pretty much at the very beginning. It isn't such a bad place to live, I figure, out by the ocean like this."

She sat cross-legged and watched the sun set.

She looked . . . sad. An air of loneliness hung about her.

"So anyway, when I was really deep in the maze, I found this flying thing there," she said, passing me a flat disc that looked like a CD.

What was it for? How did you use it?

I was low on magic power, so I tentatively touched the disc, but nothing changed.

"You want to see where I got it?"

"If we can survive the trip."

"I'll go ahead to check the route," she said, climbing to her feet and tossing the disc aside.

But before the disc hit the ground, it paused in the air, hovered, and started spinning and glowing. Kizuna ducked into the light and disappeared . . . Then she stuck her head back out.

"Looks fine to me. You want to come?"

"How amazing!"

"You're full of surprises, aren't you? You know . . ."

That thing looked like it might come in handy.

I did what she said and followed her into the disc of light.

On the other side, I found myself standing in sand . . . which was strange, because I was also in a large, solemn stone-walled room.

"Over here," Kizuna said, pointing.

I looked to where she indicated and saw a stairway that led up out of the room and toward another archway of light. But there was a field surrounding the archway, and it looked just like the barrier I could make with Shooting Star Shield.

"I think we can go to the next space if we can find a way around this thing. Come take a closer look." She climbed the stairs up to the magic barrier and motioned for me to follow her.

"What is it?"

"If we can find a way through here, I think we can get out of the labyrinth."

"Why do you think that?"

It sounded like a major discovery to me. Had she been this

close to getting out but just not had the manpower to break through? Had she been wandering around this whole time? Was that it?

I turned and saw something across the sandy floor. Two paths led out symmetrically from the center, and they each had a button-like object at the end. Maybe we just had to push them at the same time.

"That's not the real problem. It's here," she said as she pointed at the archway again.

"What?"

"We can't get in now because of the barrier, but if you get closer, you'll see. It reacts to our weapons and won't let us through, because it leads to a different world."

Say what?

Kizuna watched my mouth drop open as I stood there, nodding.

"I get a warning that says the weapons are not allowed through. I don't know what's on the other side. I couldn't disable the barrier by myself . . ."

I inched closer to the barrier and a warning flashed before my eyes.

Error.
The four holy heroes are not allowed to cross between the worlds.

This action has been rejected.

Whatever was on the other side of the archway, it must not have been my world.

"I figure that, no matter where it leads, it's got to be better than just hanging around here, right? But if we go in there, we'd be summoned when the waves came, right? So maybe we could use the wave-summoning effect to be sent back to our previous worlds. You know?"

"Maybe. But I can't get through."

Just permit the action already!

What if Rishia opened it? Then maybe Kizuna could get through?

But . . .

"What if it's just more of the labyrinth on the other side?"

"I know . . . That's why I don't know what to do."

"What to do . . ."

It was worrisome, for sure.

"Let's head back for now."

"Okay."

Rishia had been studying some writing on the walls, but now she came trotting over and joined the conversation. "If we solve the puzzle, can we get out of here?"

"Not exactly. It goes to another world."

"Oh . . ."

"Let's head back for now."

"Okay."

Kizuna used that teleportation item of hers and brought us all back to the beach.

The sun had set completely while we were gone, and the beach was drenched in the colors of night.

"The stronger monsters come out at night, so we should get back to the starting point. It's safe there." Kizuna led us back to the prison cells, and we decided to rest up.

"Umm . . ."

Kizuna, Rishia, and I all started to think about what to do next. I crossed my arms and tried to review what I knew.

There was a path through the archway that led to another world, and judging from the way my weapon reacted, it didn't lead back to mine.

Rishia turned to Kizuna. "I've been thinking. Who built this place?"

I'd been wondering the same thing.

"Hmm . . . Well, I only know what I heard from Glass, but they say it's a relic from a long time ago, when an ancient wizard made it with special spatial distortion magic."

"Hmm . . . I wonder why he made it?"

"At first it was supposed to be a fortified castle, but there was a problem with the spatial magic, and it transformed into this inescapable maze . . . or something. There are a lot of old skeletons and books around that tell the story."

"And no one has ever escaped?"

"Right. But I have heard of monsters coming out of the entrance of the labyrinth."

"Hold up—that means the monsters were able to get out!"

"I don't understand it. But from what I've seen, giant dragons and unusual magical monsters were thought to have come from the labyrinth."

Huh?

There was a hint in there somewhere.

Were we really supposed to believe that giant monsters solved the labyrinth's riddles and were able to escape?

"Could exits occasionally appear in random places maybe?"

"I guess they could. But how would you ever find them?"

Good question. You can't wait around expecting an accident. That was just idiocy.

But why would only large monsters find their way out? There had to be a reason.

"So have you ever seen any of these monsters?"

"I've seen something like them."

So how were they getting out?

Just a second—she said the labyrinth was formed when the wizard's magic went wild and stitched together a bunch of different spaces, right?

"Could those monsters . . ."

"You have an idea?"

"Just a hunch. What if a really large monster wandered into a small squeezed space?"

"Uh-huh."

"If the monster had too much mass for the space itself to contain, then . . . maybe they get popped out?"

I'd played a game like that once, a long time ago.

In the game, you collected furniture and used it to furnish a house. But if you put too much heavy furniture on the second floor, the game would warn you and then the furniture would break through the floor.

This place was complicated; there were so many spaces stacked and connected that the exit had disappeared.

So what would happen if a monster living in a small space grew too large for that space to contain it? Would it stretch the limits of the space and eventually get ejected out of the labyrinth?

"It's not a bad idea, but what are you going to do? Raise a giant monster from the egg?"

It was going to take some creative thinking.

It would be easier if I could control a monster, like I could with Filo. But I didn't know if it was even possible to add monsters to your party here.

Kizuna's question was an answer itself.

If we found an egg, it would still take a long time to raise the monster. And I wasn't able to invite an already grown monster into my party, either.

"It won't work."

"Just trying it would be a ton of work."

We could keep the idea as a last resort option.

Damn it . . . I was all out of ideas.

And I didn't want to waste any more time in this damn labyrinth!

Ost sacrificed herself to make this path for us. I had to find Kyo and make him pay for what he'd done!

Maybe it was more realistic to take the path that Kizuna had found. We didn't have any other options, anyway, so I started to fold up the Barbarian Armor, and the Filo kigurumi, so they'd be easier to carry.

Then I saw something. There was something in the pocket of the Barbarian Armor.

I'd forgotten all about it. Actually, I'd put it there just in case I ever needed it.

And now I'd found it.

Then I looked through the drop items I had stored inside my shield.

"Hey, Kizuna."

"What?"

I smiled.

"I think I have an idea."

Chapter Two: Escape

"And this is the smallest space around, right?"

Kizuna led us to a small room in the labyrinthine structure.

We ran into a few monsters on the way, but we followed Kizuna at a distance, so she was able to take care of the monsters before they could pose a threat to Rishia and me.

The room she led us to was small. Its few seats and small altar gave it a church-like atmosphere. Inside, a large suit of armor paced back and forth like it was on patrol, clattering and crashing the whole time.

"As far as I know, this is the smallest room in the labyrinth. I can't think of a smaller one."

"Hm."

The stained glass was broken, and I could see darkness outside. I wasn't sure if I was looking at the night sky or not.

"Can you see outside through that?"

"I think I saw some dark clouds and a forested area. The spaces aren't connected naturally, so you can't actually reach that place. Judging from the look of the walls and floor, I think we are underground."

Every time I had an idea, a new obstacle popped up to stop me.

"Hey, I did what you told me, but do you really think it will work?"

Since I was such a low level, I didn't have enough magic power to do it myself. I had to ask Kizuna, who was a much higher level than I was, to do it instead.

I wasn't sure it would work, but when she added it to her weapon, the same skill unlocked, which struck me as a good sign.

"It's really interesting. Does it work like a shikigami?"

"Don't get too excited. I don't have very much left," I said, making sure she understood before turning it over a few times in my hands and finally giving it to her.

"I don't know if it will work, but there's no harm in trying."

I ducked through the archway that connected the spaces and aimed for the back of the room. Then I tossed the bioplant seed. Luckily it landed on the ground, between two split stones near the altar, and I saw it take root in the dirt there.

The suit of armor noticed us and started clattering in our direction, but we slipped out of the archway before it could catch us. According to Kizuna, the monsters couldn't follow us through the archways.

"Did you do it?"

"Yeah. It took root and started growing really quickly."

Standing on the other side of the archway from the church, I noticed a snapping, crackling sound. It looked like the plant had shot straight through the suit of armor.

It got worse—the plant grew inside of the suit and started to control it.

"Uh-oh. What are those seeds doing?"

"Making monsters."

The suit started to prowl around the room, but the plant must not have had complete control over it yet, because the movement was tilted and strange.

I was watching the suit of armor when I started to hear a loud rumbling. Looking up, I saw that the archway itself was shaking, and sparks were flying out of it.

"You want to go through that? Doesn't it look dangerous?"

"I know how you feel, but have you ever seen an archway do this?"

"No," Kizuna said, smiling. She must have been thrilled at the chance to escape her boring life inside the labyrinth.

"Feh . . ."

"Rishia, stop freaking out and use your head."

"Oh . . . Okay . . ."

Ugh . . . Without Raphtalia around, I had to depend on Rishia to get experience points. It was almost too much to bear. I couldn't get experience by fighting with Kizuna, because she was one of the four holy heroes.

"He who dares wins! Let's go!"

"I'll go first. You two follow me."

"Got it."

"Here I go!" Kizuna shouted as she ran to the arch and swung the lure of her fishing rod at the rampaging suit of armor. A second later, she ran her tuna knife through the monster with ease. It clattered loudly to the floor.

It was amazing . . . or it looked amazing. I didn't actually know how strong the monster was.

We ran through the sparking archway and found the church bursting at the seams with the rapidly growing bioplant. The whole space itself began shaking. The bioplant started to swirl and spin like a vortex, like it was being sucked into another place. Then the whole space started shaking violently, like an earthquake.

The black clouds started to suck in the walls of the room, and everything except for the area around the bioplant began to vanish.

"That hole! Let's go through it!" Kizuna shouted while she sliced through the bioplant vines that whipped and snapped at us.

"Okay!"

"Wah!"

"Be careful!" I grabbed Rishia by the hand and pulled her after me as I ran for the hole, jumping and bounding over writhing bioplant vines along the way. A large one whipped in front of me, but I jumped onto it, used it as a springboard, and jumped through the hole.

It reminded me of what happened when I used Portal Shield. The scenery around us changed in an instant. There was a split second when I could see the church crumbling far off in the distance.

Then my field of view was filled with blue sky . . . and I realized I was falling.

Far below I saw a building that looked like a Shinto shrine set on manicured grounds. I couldn't tell how far down it was, but I knew it was far enough that the impact would kill me.

"Air Strike Shield!"

I had very little SP, but there was just enough to use Air Strike Shield to make a landing pad. The shield wasn't very large, but it was big enough to stop my fall.

"Feh!"

Rishia was hanging off the side of the shield by her fingertips.

Not to be the bearer of bad news, but the shield wasn't going to last very long, anyway—and I didn't have enough SP to use the skill again.

"This shield is about to disappear . . ."

"Naofumi."

Kizuna held her hand out from her little space on the floating shield.

"You have an idea?"

She nodded, so I grabbed Rishia and took Kizuna's hands.

Then Kizuna swung her fishing rod over her head and cast the lure far down to the shrine, where it hooked onto the roof. There was a high-pitched whir as the reel activated, and the whole shield lurched down toward the building.

"The shield is going to disappear. There's no time."

"We're going to make it."

The shield vanished, and I felt my stomach turn as we began falling again. The ground rushed up at us, but then I felt a strong jerk.

We'd stopped in the air, hanging by a thread, a mere two meters off of the ground.

"Looks like we made it."

"Guess so."

We jumped down and took in our new surroundings.

I looked at the building that looked like a Shinto shrine. We seemed to be on its manicured property. Then I saw the bioplant that had fallen with us. It was still growing quickly.

What should we do about that?

I passed some of the weed killer I'd made earlier to Kizuna.

"That thing is dangerous. If we don't kill it now, it'll destroy this whole place."

"Looks that way. You said you increased its mutation and growth abilities? We better get rid of it now."

Kizuna kept her distance from the approaching bioplant while she jumped in circles around it, scattering weed killer over its writhing body the whole time.

When I made the seeds, I gave them very weak immune systems, so the bioplant died quickly. I'd have to be careful. Anything left alive that still touched the dirt could easily spawn another main body.

The bioplant shriveled up and died, shooting a bunch of fresh seeds at us when it did.

I picked them all up, just to be safe.

"So? Think we made it out?"

Kizuna jumped when I spoke. She must have been zoning out. Then, when she realized where she was, a huge grin spread over her face and she started to jump up and down.

"Yes! We're out! We're finally out! This is it! This is a different world for sure!"

"Oh yeah?"

"Thank you! Thank you! Oh! I can't believe it! I don't have to be alone anymore!"

I couldn't blame her for being excited, especially considering how many years she'd been locked in that labyrinth.

I had to start figuring out what to do next. My level hadn't changed—it was just as low as it had been. I checked the hourglass icon in my menu. Once again, it displayed the time left until the next wave, and it was counting down.

There was no doubt about it. We were out of the labyrinth.

"So where are we?"

It looked like a shrine enclosed with a low wall. The entrance to the shrine itself seemed to be locked, and we weren't able to see inside.

As for the wall, it looked like it was made of wood, but for a wooden wall it looked very tough and imposing. The gate was closed tightly. Even though the wall looked pretty tall, I figured I could probably think of a way over it.

Kizuna must have been thinking the same thing. She swung her fishing rod and caught the lure on the top edge of the wall. "You can go first," she said.

"Are there guards or anything?"

"It's the entrance to an inescapable labyrinth. Why would anyone want to get near it?"

"There could be monsters that escaped?"

"That hardly ever happens. I'm pretty sure it's safe. Actually, it's probably more dangerous to keep standing here."

She had a point.

"Rishia, stick with us, okay?"

"Alright, what should we do with our belongings?"

That's right. Between Kizuna's things and our equipment, we had quite a bit of stuff with us. It would be hard to climb a wall with all of it on our backs.

"I'll bring it all. Hurry up and climb," Kizuna said.

"Are you sure?"

"It's fine."

She insisted, so I climbed up the wall first. When I got to the top, I looked back down.

It was a very tall wall. It must have been four meters off of the ground. Still, it wasn't so tall that you couldn't get down if you hung and dropped.

"You're next, Kizuna."

"Okay, I'm coming up—move over and make space."

I did as she said, and she flipped the reel on her fishing rod. The reel whirred as it effortlessly carried her up to the top.

I was starting to like that fishing rod of hers. Then again, I had the Rope Shield, and I was pretty sure that I could do something similar with it.

"Alright! Let's get out of here!"

"Yeah, before anyone comes to check on the place."

"We . . . We're running away?"

"Of course we are! This place is a labyrinth . . . a prison!"

As far as anyone that was associated with the labyrinth was concerned, we were their prisoners—and we'd basically just pulled off a shocking prison break.

We jumped down from the wall and cautiously left the grounds.

Chapter Three: The Unknown World

We ran through the forest, keeping an eye out for any trouble the whole time, and then we came across a road. We started to let our guard down a little bit, figuring that we were far enough away from the shrine.

"So? What's next?"

"What do you mean?"

"We only teamed up because of the circumstances, right? So what do you want to do now? Split up?"

"Why would we do that?" Kizuna asked, apparently confused by the suggestion.

"Feh . . . Naofumi? We should stay with Kizuna. It's dangerous out here."

It was probably the best way to avoid trouble. But we had only known her for a little while, and she herself said that she was friends with Glass. So I had to be sure.

"Well, if I don't make sure you're on our side, you might lead us straight to the altar."

"You really aren't very trusting, are you? Besides, if you're working with Glass then I'd have no reason to challenge you. Besides, I'm not on very good terms with this country, so I'd rather not travel alone. I'd really prefer if we stuck together for now."

"Hm . . ."

I didn't really understand the particulars of her situation, but she said she didn't want to be alone.

"Crossing the border may prove difficult."

"Can't you use a teleportation skill?"

Hey, there's an idea. I decided to check out my Portal Shield skill.

I called up the list of saved locations, but it was empty.

I guess you had to start over when you went to a new world. The skill itself was still available, so maybe . . .

I looked in the help menu but couldn't find any useful information.

I guess the only way back to my world was to wait for the next wave to come.

"There are limits on what I can do. To go anywhere with it, we're going to have to get there first. Our skills might work differently."

"I guess so. Mine is called Return Transcript. But you need a tool to make it work, and I can't use it in this country."

"Mine is called Portal Shield. I can save three places that I've already been to, and then I can teleport to them whenever I want."

"How convenient."

"But right now, it looks like all the places I saved are gone. It must have something to do with the distance to the destination."

"I get it. Sounds like a great skill—but you still can't use it," Kizuna said as she brushed dust off of her haori. "We have a couple of options. One of them is that we could head for the border. That way we can get to a country that is safer than this one."

A border crossing . . . I hadn't ever managed to do that successfully. When Melromarc had declared me a wanted criminal, they had deployed a bunch of troops, not to mention the other three heroes, to the border to keep me from getting across it.

"But we'd have to get through a few checkpoints. We might be able to buy our way through, but then we won't have enough money for the journey."

"You mean we can bribe our way out?"

"If you buy travel passes, then yes. I've only heard of it through the grapevine, but I hear it's like Edo-period Japan. It's easy to cross into the capital, but they make it hard to leave."

Judging from the way that Kizuna and Glass dressed, I was starting to think that this world had a definite Japanese aesthetic. But then again, L'Arc and Therese didn't dress the same way, so I couldn't say for sure.

But these travel passes—they sounded like tolls.

The merchant voucher that I had back in Melromarc was similar, but not the same.

"That's why it's so difficult to get out of the country."

"Sounds like a pretty controlled society."

"It's not as bad as it sounds. They mostly just restrict their citizen's movement out of the country. It's easy to head into it, though—to the capital. It's probably even easier now."

"Why's that?"

"They don't realize that I've escaped from the labyrinth, which means they aren't watching out for me. I can probably get close to the dragon hourglass."

"And what happens if you can do that?"

"Are they different in your world? If I get to the hourglass, I can teleport back to a safe place."

I'd played MMORPGs that utilized similar systems. Portal skills existed to teleport players around, but generally speaking, only the strongest players had access to them. They were normally used to escape dangerous situations or to return to town after completing a quest. That must have been what Kizuna was talking about, because the skill only returned her to a country or town.

There were devices in towns that you could use to teleport to other similar devices in other towns. They weren't the same as having a teleport skill of your own, but they were useful in their own way. A lot of games didn't even have teleport skills, and all the long-distance travel was done through systems like these.

To make matters simple, I'll refer to them as town portals from now on.

"The other idea is to wait for a wave to occur. I can see the hourglass on my status screen counting down again, so we could use that to hitchhike out of here."

"Hm . . ."

So we had a number of options.

The first was to try to get out of this country—which was the country that threw Kizuna into the prison. But to do so, we'd have to get through a number of checkpoints, which would cost money. And there was no guarantee that we'd be safe once we got to the other side.

Another option was to try to approach the dragon hourglass in this country. That wouldn't cost us any money, but there was significant risk involved in getting close enough to teleport.

The final option was to wait for the wave to arrive and summon us away. I wasn't very fond of that option.

"How long does it say we have until the wave arrives?"

"Um . . . About two weeks."

"That's a long time."

There was a limit on how long we could stay in this world. We were in a hurry, and I didn't want to waste time waiting around. Besides, we had to find Raphtalia and the others. Where were they?

I tried to use my slave and monster control skills one more time, but once again they didn't work. Lately, it felt like nothing was working. Raphtalia and Filo must have been in this world, but I couldn't seem to find them . . .

"First things first, we should work on getting your levels up."

"Good idea. We'll need equipment too—and money."

We would need money to get the equipment.

Kizuna had lent us some clothes, but to be honest they weren't that great. She must have chosen things that we were able to wear at our low level.

"We need to start investigating, so we should probably head to a nearby town first."

"Alright. And it sounds like we should stick together for now."

"Glad to have you two around, Naofumi and Rishia."

"Yeah, yeah. Rishia, without Raphtalia around, you're going to have to handle my offense. Oh, and if we have to fight any people, you'll be the only one that can hurt them. Don't let me down."

"Yes . . . sir! I'll do my best!"

I sighed. She was so annoying. Kizuna was clearly trying not to laugh.

Why did she have to act so weak? All that power she showed off in the battle with Kyo was going to waste.

We made it out of the forest and found ourselves in a relatively large town.

The town looked . . . How to describe it . . . It looked like Kyoto from the Heian period. At first I'd thought it was like the Edo period, but some things about it didn't quite fit in with that time period.

That's how the town looked, anyway—the people were another thing altogether. They didn't look like anyone I'd met in any world up until now. They had long ears, pretty white skin, and blonde hair. They sort of didn't fit in with their surroundings.

They looked like elves.

"In this world, they're called the grass people. They're like the demi-humans in the world you came from."

"They look like elves to me."

You know, they actually looked really good in the Heian-period clothes. I was surprised.

But I could tell why. They just looked like long-eared foreigners flopping around in baggy robes. They didn't wear their hair up in a topknot or anything like that.

Elves were a hunter-like race, but I always pictured them as wearing wizard-like clothing. I guess everyone had a different way of looking at things.

I found myself thinking that these Japanese-style clothes would look good on Raphtalia.

Aside from the elves, I also saw some semi-transparent people, like Glass, walking through the streets.

"Who are those people? They remind me of Glass."

"You mean you don't know? Those are the spirit people. People from other countries just call them spirits."

"Spirits?"

"You might think they are actually souls, but that's not quite right. But I can see why you'd think so. Their weapons are called things like Soul Splitter, after all. It's easier to explain if you look at your status menu."

I opened my status menu and looked at it.

My HP had been replaced by something else and was labeled "life force." And my SP was relabeled "soul power."

I was confused. What was going on?

"Spirits have life force and magic power . . . and if they wield a vassal weapon, then they also have soul power. But all those different powers are combined into energy for the spirit people."

"What? So when they use magic, they also lose their life force?"

"It seems that way. All their other stats exist as energy, too. They don't have levels. Energy is everything for them."

"They don't have levels?"

"That's right. But they can be very powerful when their energy levels are high. They have an exceptionally high defense, much higher than a human could have. They can survive attacks that humans never could—they're famous for it."

That explained why Glass was so monstrously powerful.

"The problem is that there's no way for them to recover their energy, unless another spirit person gives them some."

"So there aren't any items or spells they can use to recover?"

"That's right. Unlike humans and grass people, they can't rely on magic to recover in battle."

"I never knew that!" Rishia exclaimed, nodding her head.

She had fought with Glass, after all. Of course she would find it interesting.

I know I did.

I'd hit her with the full strength of Iron Maiden, and it hadn't hurt her. I'd burned her with the Shield of Wrath to no avail.

Huh?

"So if they could find some way to restore the energy they've lost, they could be really powerful, right?"

"Yeah, if something like that existed."

I remembered watching L'Arc dump a bottle of soul-healing water over Glass. It seemed like she had instantly powered up. Did that mean that there wasn't any soul-healing water in his world?

Hm . . . I'd have to investigate further. But before that, I needed to start gaining some levels.

"Okay, I got it. So can we hang out around here for a while?"

"It seems safe to me."

"We walked with Kizuna through the town until we came to a fairly large building. It was bustling with activity. The building looked like an adventurer's guild.

There were a lot of bulletin boards on the walls that were covered with job postings and wanted posters, promising cash rewards.

Kizuna scanned the postings and came jogging back over to us.

"It doesn't look like they've realized we've escaped."

"Good. But I've been wondering . . ." I said, indicating the back of the room where a crystal of some sort sat enshrined in a machine. It actually looked like a shaved-ice maker.

People filed past the machine and set pendant-like accessories on it, and then they tapped some buttons. It was almost like they were using a computer.

After a short amount of time a little puff of smoke would come out of the machine, and it would produce an item.

"That thing? We don't need to worry about it."

"Why not?"

"It's a machine that simulates the drop item functionality that the heroes' weapons, and the vassal weapons, already have. Crystal people like Therese use them the most. They're a race of people that receive powers from special stones they call jewels. They built the machine, actually."

Well, well. I was learning a lot today.

I remembered when we were out leveling with L'Arc in the Cal Mira islands. They had talked about drop items as if they were a typical, pedestrian thing, even though I'd thought they were only possible with the legendary weapons.

So it was looking like drop items weren't a rare thing at all in this world.

"Well they aren't as good as the legendary weapons, as far as probability is concerned, but you can choose certain drops and it will make them for you once enough has been saved up. With luck they can even get magic out of things, right on the spot."

"Is that so . . ."

The people of this new world seemed to have access to more skill subtleties than what I was used to. So they could absorb defeated monsters into those pendants and then use that machine to produce whatever drops the monsters had.

Before we went back to the world we came from, it might be a good idea to get our hands on one of those pendants. Maybe we could even learn how to make them. We'd be rich.

"That's amazing. To think of all the items you can get just from defeating monsters . . ."

"Itsuki could do it."

I wondered why most people in the previous world couldn't use drops. If there was some way to replicate the effect of the pendant, it was worth a try.

Chapter Four: Selling Drop Items

"Hey, are there pawn shops in this world?"

"Sure, there are shops. But . . . what is a pawn shop?"

I showed Kizuna the white box corpse that I'd stashed away in my bag. She cocked her head and looked confused. "Sure, you can use that thing as a box, but it won't sell for much. The drop item you get from it is worth more."

I was starting to understand. If replicated drop items were as common as they seemed to be, then shops would rather buy real drop items. I'm sure there were also times when raw materials were worth more than their drop items.

We did our best to absorb all the information we could at the guild.

"Looks like there's a lot going on—apparently there was a prison break in the next country over."

"There's someone just like us out there."

"Seems so—but at least they aren't looking for us. Oh, look. There's a sketch of the wanted people."

"That is seriously a rough sketch. I can't make heads or tails of it."

It looked like the sort of sketch that police officers made from listening to a witness's description. The face might as well have been a yokai or something out of a kabuki play.

"I've heard things about their prisons. They are supposed to be very rough. They have a way of negating your level gains and everything. I wonder how these people escaped?"

"You don't think it could be Glass or Raphtalia, do you?"

If it was, then we were about to walk into some serious trouble.

"Oh, I don't think so. What are the chances? I'm sure they're just fine."

"Right. Of course it wouldn't be that easy to find them. It wouldn't be like how you showed up just in time to save us from those kappa."

"Hehe."

"Haha."

Kizuna and I laughed dryly.

"Feh . . ."

Uh-oh. We were laughing but Rishia started whimpering as usual.

"Anyway, Glass is pretty famous in this world, isn't she? If she broke out of prison, I'm sure we'd hear about it."

"Yes, well. . . It's hard to know how much you can trust this type of information. They lie about the enemy state all the time. Saying things like people are on steroids when in reality their soldiers were literally giants . . ."

"Sounds like we shouldn't pay much attention to it then."

If it were true, that meant we'd have to find a way into the neighboring country.

We didn't have time to go chasing after every unsubstantiated possibility.

"There are rumors that the neighboring country is developing new weapons. I hear things about savage monster experiments. It's creepy."

"You don't think people are just having fun spreading rumors, do you?"

"Could be. Not everyone has entertaining lives like you and I do, Naofumi."

"The world might be like a game, but people can get used to anything, can't they?"

"Sure. But I hear they are researching teleport technologies, trying to duplicate the teleport abilities of the legendary and vassal weapons. They've already made a Return Transcript replica, but that's not all . . ."

"They're trying to make it so that everyone can use teleportation skills? That's unthinkable where I come from."

I had never heard of anyone trying to do anything like that in the world I'd been summoned to. Maybe I just didn't know about it.

We chatted for a while, and soon enough the sun began to sink low in the sky.

"Naofumi, what do I need to do to learn to read the writing here?" Rishia muttered, flipping through a book she'd taken off of the shelf.

That's right. Rishia not only couldn't talk to people of this world but also couldn't read anything that they wrote.

"I can't read it, either. I can only handle conversation because my shield translates for me."

Kizuna agreed. "Same for me. The only reason I understand what Rishia says is because my weapons translate it."

"Oh . . . I didn't realize . . . I thought that you understood our language."

"Kizuna, can you read and write the language here?"

"Just the simple stuff. Glass was very insistent on it."

"Wow . . . I'm impressed." I reached for the book that Rishia was flipping through. It was very old, but I thought I had seen some of the characters before. Sometimes, it even looked like there were kanji mixed in. Maybe I could read it if I had enough time to practice.

The language in Melromarc was very different from what I was used to, like English and Japanese, so translating between them was difficult.

I didn't have the energy to invest in study, though. My shoulders started to ache.

"It's getting late. What should we do?"

"There are some inns where we could rest. We should be okay since our escape hasn't been reported. No one has recognized me yet. I don't think anyone would, except for maybe some high-ranking officials."

"And you don't think they will report our escape soon?"

"I did hear some rumors about something popping out of the labyrinth, but everyone is saying that whatever it was disappeared immediately. We should stay cautious, but I think we're okay for now."

I wasn't sure I felt safe, but I'd still rather stay in an inn than out in the fields.

"Do you have money?"

"I sold some drop items I didn't need, so I've got enough to cover the three of us."

"Should I sell some stuff, too?"

"Like the box?"

"No, like drop items from the world I came from." I figured that they should be worth a lot, considering how rare they were in this world.

But then again, it might attract unwanted attention if I started showing off tools and items that no one had ever seen. They might not even be able to read the item names—like what had happened with my armor.

"That's not a bad idea. Normal things from your world might fetch a good price here."

"It would depend on the dealer. We don't want to attract too much attention."

Dealers decided what things were worth by considering their effects or their rarity. That worked fine if they knew what they were dealing with, but how would they react when they saw something brand new?

The best test would be to see if Kizuna recognized the items first.

"Well, I think we're all tired today. Let's save the money talk for tomorrow."

"There's a larger town a little further down the road. Maybe we should head there first."

"I'm tiiiired . . ." Rishia sighed.

I knew how she felt. Adventuring in unknown lands really sapped your energy. Our levels were low, too, so we had to stay on guard all the time.

If we were going to make money and get better equipment, we should probably wait until after I'd powered up my shield and gained a few levels. I'd need a fair amount of money to make it work, anyway.

At least we'd gained a few levels since we woke up in the cell. Rishia and I were going to have to level up together. But I was still worried about her poor stats . . .

According to Kizuna, we were in enemy territory, which meant we would have a hard time recruiting additional party members. Still, I'd seen plenty of people that looked like adventurers out in the streets, so it wasn't necessarily impossible.

Kizuna led us to a nearby inn, and when we got to our room I started to think about what drop items I had that might sell for a good price. It was a difficult task, especially because I didn't know anything about the local culture, and I didn't want to cause trouble.

There was so much I didn't know, but Kizuna seemed to know what was going on, so I'd have to defer to her judgment.

"I'll show you a bunch of items that I have, and you pick the ones you think we can get a good price for."

"Okay."

I pulled out a few items that I'd stored in my shield, and Kizuna started to look them over. I didn't know how she was evaluating their worth, but it looked like a lot of the item names were still legible in this world. I was grateful for that.

"You've got so much stuff . . ."

"I guess so."

"What's in this bottle?"

"Magic water. It replenishes your magic power when you drink it. Don't you have that kind of thing here?"

"Not that I've seen. Normally people use earth crystals to replenish their magic power," Kizuna explained. She pulled a red crystal out of her weapon and showed it to me. "Holding this crystal replenishes lost magic power."

"Really? What a weird crystal."

"You think? The idea of drinking something to recover magic power would sound pretty weird to anyone from this world."

I decided to try it. I reached out and took the crystal from her. When I touched it, it snapped, cracked open, and disappeared in a puff of steam.

Dragon vein unlocked! Received 3000 EXP!

The words flashed in my field of vision as if I'd just won a battle.

That was a lot of experience points! Certainly nothing to scoff at!

"I just got a bunch of EXP from this thing . . ."

"What?" Kizuna gasped. Then she took the bottle of magic water from me and drank it. "Wow . . . This replenished my magic power, and then it gave me all the experience points I needed to power up my weapon."

"You power up your weapon with experience points?"

"Yeah. Aside from their levels, my weapons all accrue experience points as I use them. Then they get stronger through a leveling system. My wooden fishing rod is basically like a mid-level weapon."

"I see."

So Kizuna had her own way of powering up weapons. I wonder if we could utilize each other's systems, like I'd been able to do with the other heroes. I was thinking it over when my shield beeped to alert me that the healing medicine it had been compounding was complete. I took the medicine out of my shield and set it among the other items we were considering for sale.

"What's this?"

"It's a restorative item. Healing medicine. You rub it on your wounds to make them heal."

"I wonder if it's like our curing medicine?" Kizuna said, pulling out a similar-looking item.

"We drink this to heal our wounds. But that's right—I saw you rubbing medicine on your cuts after the fight with the kappa."

"There sure are a lot of differences. This really is a whole different world."

"The scary part is what happens when the items have different effects."

She had another good point. We had both experienced different effects when we used items from each other's worlds. The idea of getting weapon experience from drinking magic water sounded crazy to me. I'm sure she felt the same way about the crystal and I.

That reminded me of something important. I pulled out a bottle of soul-healing water and passed it to Kizuna.

"What's this?"

"It's called soul-healing water. It restores your SP."

"SP . . . You mean soul power? I've never heard of an item like that. From what I've heard, you can only recover lost soul power through weapon effects, or absorbing it, or by recovering over time."

Well . . . It looked like this world didn't have any way to rapidly restore lost SP in an emergency. I'd have to pay close attention to that. If I used a skill like Iron Maiden, which took all my SP, then I'd have no way to use other skills until I recovered my SP.

"When I fought with Glass and her friends, L'Arc dumped a bottle of this over Glass, and she became really powerful."

Kizuna looked like she couldn't believe what she was hearing.

And I could understand why. The implications were tremendous.

Glass's people, the spirits, depended on energy for everything, even their levels. If they had a lot of energy, then everything about them, their strengths and abilities, would grow very powerful.

But according to Kizuna, it was difficult to recover energy once you used it, and most of the time people were forced to wait for it to recover on its own. What would it mean if these the spirits suddenly discovered an item that would allow them to regain any lost energy instantaneously?

"You mean this stuff can recover a spirit's energy?!"

"That's what it looks like."

"Then this item is priceless! Any spirit out there would do whatever it takes to get their hands on it."

"So you think we should sell it?"

"No one will know what it is, so there's no telling what will happen. Are you okay with that?"

"Sure. Who do you think I am? I guess we decided what we're selling tomorrow."

I had gotten quite a bit of business experience under my belt when I was a traveling merchant back in Melromarc, so I had a few ideas when it came to making money.

"Then there's the magic water, power-up stuff. And I'd like to get my hands on a lot of those earth crystals."

"You think our power-up methods can be used at the same time? Should we try and share what we know?"

"Yeah."

The more I knew about how to power up my weapons, the stronger I would be. Anything that could help with that was worth a shot.

"Well I already told you about the weapon experience points, right? What else? There are slips of paper you can stick to your weapons to add different functions . . . I know of a bunch of different ways. I'll start with . . ."

I tried a few of the power-up methods that Kizuna told me about, but my shield didn't show any sign of reacting. Kizuna was having the same luck with her weapons. But she also said that Glass had told her about a power-up method and that she'd been able to make it work.

"Glass says that you can take the magic power from

defeated enemies, or any power that has leaked out of enemies and is hanging in the air, and absorb it. Then you can use it to power up your weapons. I was able to do that. So I want you to know that I do believe what you're telling me."

"Yeah, I feel the same way."

It's not that I didn't believe her.

I couldn't have used the methods I'd learned from the other three heroes if I hadn't believed in them first. So I don't think it was a problem with my belief in the ideas.

"I know that it won't work if you don't believe in it. So I'm trying. If it doesn't work, maybe it has something to do with coming from a different world."

"That could be it. The systems might just be so different that they aren't compatible."

"Too bad. If it had worked, we could have gotten really strong."

"Yeah."

Kizuna and I nodded in agreement.

The truth was that the power-up methods I'd learned were the reason I'd survived as many battles as I had. It was too soon to jump to final conclusions, but there was no point in sitting around fretting over it.

The next steps were obvious. The easiest way to get experience was to get my hands on earth crystals—and I would need money for that.

Chapter Five: Sales Demonstration

The next morning we crossed a bridge and followed the road to a large and vibrant shopping area. We set up shop in a corner and started calling out to customers. We even set out a straw mat to make ourselves look more like an official business.

Just to be safe, we bought some masks from a nearby store and wore them to hide our faces. There was always the chance that someone might recognize Kizuna, and we didn't want that.

I clapped my hands and shouted as loudly as I could, "Come on over! You'll never believe what we're offering today! Any adventuring spirit would be crazy to pass this up! We've brought this unbelievable medicine from a distant land far across the ocean! Soul-healing water!"

Pedestrians started to take notice, and soon we had a small crowd of skeptical but interested people gathered around. Rishia and Kizuna hung back a bit behind me and chimed in whenever I stopped yelling to keep the momentum up. I had to tell Rishia to stop talking so much, because no one could understand what she said and it just made the customers more suspicious.

"What does it do?"

Kizuna kept the rhythm up and didn't miss a beat. "Wouldn't

you like to know? There's so much I'd like to tell you, but I don't think you'll be able to experience its full effect. But you! Over there! Yes, you!" She yelled, pointing at a group of three spirit people that had worked their way into the crowd.

I followed her lead and called out to them, "You are the only ones who will understand how invaluable this medicine truly is! Won't you take a look? Won't you try it?"

"Oh, um . . ."

The three spirit people came closer.

"Don't worry. It's not poison, and you don't have to drink it! Applying just a small amount to your skin will make its effect clear! Please, try it!"

I poured a small amount into another dish and Kizuna passed me a brush, which I used to paint the soul-healing water on the spirits' chests. At first they all looked skeptical, but soon their eyes lit up and they started to smile.

"It can't be!"

"Is this for real?! I've never heard of such a thing!"

"This is the invention of the century!"

The other spectators looked at each other in confusion, not understanding what all the fuss was about. Meanwhile, the three spirit people were so excited about their experience that they were shouting at the top of their lungs.

"This stuff restores your energy! I can't believe it!"

The crowd grew louder.

"That's right! This medicine is made just for spirits! It restores energy—it's amazing!"

"Feh . . . You sound different than normal, Naofumi."

"You mean he acts different when he's trying to sell stuff?" Kizuna whispered.

I wished they would shut up. I had to act that way if I wanted to attract customers.

If we had tried to sell the soul-healing water at a pawn shop or an apothecary, the staff would have been suspicious of us, and we would have attracted unwanted attention. Besides, they might have asked us how to make it.

And even if they had bought it, they would have just sold it to someone else, which would be inefficient. It was better to cut out the middleman and sell it ourselves.

"Today we have five bottles of this exceptional soul-healing water for sale. Have you all had the chance to sample it?"

"That's right. Today we're selling one bottle for one tamagin!"

The first spirit person flipped open his wallet and pulled out a small little bar of silver. Did they say tamagin? Did this world really use Edo-period currency? Did they use kohan, too?

"Then give us more!"

The three spirit people looked serious all of a sudden, glared competitively at each other, and started to fight over our stock of soul-healing water.

"Please don't fight."

"We're limiting our sales to one bottle per customer! Please calm down!"

Of course they would want it—as far as they were concerned it was an amazing medicine that could get them out of any situation, no matter how rough.

Each of the three spirits purchased a bottle and left.

"We still have two bottles left. What do you say?" I asked the crowd.

The other customers still seemed to harbor some doubts. They must have thought it was a trick.

"I realize this is all quite sudden, so how about we use the remaining two bottles and allow all of the spirit people present to sample our medicine's incredible effects for themselves? Please line up!"

Once again, I poured the contents of the bottles into a dish and used a brush to paint the medicine onto the spirits who had lined up for a sample. I kept going through the gathered crowd until I had used up all of the remaining soul-healing water.

The line in front of our little stand had grown very long by this point, and the spirits that had sampled the medicine had all grown very excited.

Quite a few of them stopped me to ask how I made it.

I made it with my shield—jeez. It was possible to make it from scratch, but it was a real pain. But of course, I couldn't tell them that, so I just told them it was a professional secret of mine.

I was starting to get concerned about how much attention we were attracting, but then again, if I didn't sell the stuff then I wouldn't be able to get the materials I needed to power up my shield.

And I still had to buy an expensive travel voucher.

When I ran out of sample soul-healing water, I clapped my hands to get everyone's attention and announced, "Now that you've had a chance to sample our wares, what do you think? Surely you see that this is not a joke or a trick? Surely you have seen that we are selling genuine articles?"

Most of the spirits in the line nodded in response, and it was clear that the mood of suspicion had lifted. We'd earned their trust.

The timing was just right, so I continued, "However, this medicine is very difficult to produce, and therefore our stock is somewhat . . . limited. I do not think we have enough for all of you gathered here today. Therefore, I suggest that we meet here tomorrow, at this very same time and place, to auction off our remaining stock."

The crowd clapped. It was just the reaction I'd been hoping for. I suspected that some of the people that would come would be middlemen themselves, hoping to make a killing.

"Excellent! The auction will be for five bottles of soul-healing water, the same amount we brought with us today. I hope to see you all in attendance," I said, ending our business for the day. We left as soon as we could.

"Are you sure this is a good idea? Everyone will be watching us, and we might not even make very much money off it!"

"What's this about tamagin? I almost burst out laughing."

"Naofumi, do you know something about this place?" Rishia asked.

She was the only one in our group that didn't know anything about Japan.

"That's what they use for currency here, so you'll just have to get used to it. By the way, they use doumon, tamagin, and kinhan: 100 doumon is a tamagin, and 100 tamagin is a kinhan."

The currency worked the same way in the world I'd just come from. But these names were just too much. It took all the discipline I had to keep from laughing. It's like they were straight out of Edo-period Japan, only not quite.

"You're talking about the auction? No, it's perfect. The word will spread and all the nobility in town will come out to the auction."

"You planned that out?"

"People love gossip. The size of the line is proof enough that we aren't lying. Just wait. You'll see."

Heh heh . . . I hadn't done much business lately, so I'd

forgotten how much fun it could be. I really didn't mind making money through the mercantile life. In fact, I liked it a lot.

"Makes me think you must have some good con men as friends back where you come from."

"Feh . . ."

"Rishia, it's about time you stopped freaking out about every little thing we run into here. We need money to survive, get it? Kizuna didn't have that problem because she started out with money."

"Well that's true, but . . . but . . . I like business, too, you know. Just not as much as you do, Naofumi."

It was looking like we were going to spend all of our time until the next day chatting, so I decided to focus on fighting to level up while we had the time.

Rishia would need to level up first, so I stayed behind and she went with Kizuna to hunt some monsters in the fields around the town. When they came back, Kizuna looked concerned.

"It seems like there are a lot more monsters out there than usual. What could it be?"

"Is there an activation event going on?"

"What's that?"

"It's a limited-time phenomenon that occurs in the world we came from. The monsters give more experience when you kill them during it. Know what I mean?"

"Oh yeah, I've heard of something like that. I wonder if that's what's happening. The monsters seemed stronger than usual, too."

After that, I went out with Rishia to hunt the cardboard boxes. They were a little stronger than the one we'd fought in the labyrinth, and we got more experience for killing them, too. Hm . . . Well, there was no doubt that they were stronger than the balloons back in Melromarc. I had no idea why the monsters would be stronger in this world than they were in the world I'd been summoned to. But if everything was stronger here on average, that might explain why Glass and her friends were so powerful . . . right?

The next morning, we went back to the main street and set up our shop.

And of course we were careful to wear our masks.

By the time we were finished setting up, there was already a crowd of people waiting for the auction to start, and a lot of them weren't spirits. That's what I was hoping for. Anyone would want it. I was selling a medicine that replenished energy in a world where there were hardly any ways to do so.

There were researchers and middlemen merchants, adventurers that wanted it for use in battle . . . all sorts of people. Also, at the back of the crowd, there were some excited people that looked like they might have been government officials. They were probably in the service of the local nobility.

Kizuna swore that we didn't need any official permits to do business there. If we needed something like that, I would have sold my wares in secret, behind the market.

Of course there was still the possibility that the noblemen might use their authority to stop the auction, but they wouldn't do that. They wouldn't want an angry crowd on their hands, would they? If anything, it looked like they were planning on joining the auction themselves.

"What a fantastic turnout! Thank you all for coming, despite your busy schedules!"

I handed the bottles of soul-healing water to Kizuna and Rishia for them to line up on the table.

"Now then, the efficacy of this medicine has already been proven, so rather than review the facts that are already known by all, I would rather just start the auction!"

The crowd erupted in cheers. It was so easy—like dangling a carrot in front of a donkey.

I felt like I'd found a tree that grew money. People were easy to control when they really wanted something.

I'd learned that in an online game. In MMOs, you can go hunting and find rare items. Some games would allow you to automatically sell the items, but others would let you hold an auction to sell the items to people that weren't able to go on the hunts themselves. I'd made it a hobby of mine. I did it all the time.

So I felt really comfortable in the auction environment. It was easy to sell things to people when they were ravenous with desire. I could tell I was going to make a lot of money.

"Now then, let's start the bidding with the price I've already received for one of these bottles—one tamagin!"

"One tamagin, 50 doumon!"

"Two tamagin!"

"Three tamagin, 30 doumon!"

It didn't take long for the competition to heat up. Things were progressing just how I wanted them to. I just had to manipulate them to keep bidding.

Normally, it would be hard to get people to bid so aggressively over a single-use item, so I had to make sure I didn't push it too far. I had to watch out for the officials in the back, too.

Honestly, I just wanted to get a bunch of money and hightail it out of there.

"30 tamagin!"

The competition was growing fierce. The crowd had gotten louder.

Back in Melromarc, that would be the equivalent of spending 30 silver pieces on one bottle of medicine. "I hear 30 tamagin! 30 tamagin!" I clapped my hands.

The bids grew less dramatic after that. People mostly just raised their bids by a few doumon here and there.

Finally the auction ended, and the bottle sold for 30 tamagin and 83 doumon.

"Will that be all?"

The crowd fell silent.

"Very well then. Sold for 30 tamagin and 83 doumon!"

I took the money from the winner and gave him a bottle of soul-healing water. The man looked like a normal merchant. None of the noblemen participated.

I flipped through my wallet to take stock of the sales. Did I have enough to purchase a travel voucher yet? I looked over at Kizuna for advice. She shook her head.

So I didn't have enough. I might have even needed a lot more.

Well that wasn't going to work, was it?

Fine then! I'll just have to get crafty!

We shouldn't stay in the town for too long. With all the people around, things were bound to get chaotic.

I signaled Kizuna with my eyebrow, and she immediately understood. Rishia stood beside her, holding the bottles of soul-healing water, and Kizuna stuck her foot out and tripped her.

"Ah!"

She dropped a bottle of soul-healing water and it shattered. But unbeknownst to the public, I'd secretly switched out the contents for plain water.

"Oh no! What a waste!"

"Feh . . . I'm so sorry!"

"You're destroying our products!"

Before we left the inn that morning, we'd already agreed on the plan.

Rishia had been affected by Itsuki's warped sense of justice, so of course she was a little worried about the ethics involved, but it was how I wanted to do things, and she eventually agreed—not that she had a choice. I pretended to shout at Rishia, who continued to apologize, before I turned my attention back to the crowd.

"Apologies! Due to my clumsy employee here, we only have one bottle remaining! She's an illiterate fool! Hear me? I'll make sure you pay for all that!"

"Fehhh!"

The crowd started booing Rishia, and pretty soon they started throwing things at her. That was probably enough of that. If I let it go on for much longer, poor Rishia would probably lose her mind.

"I'm terribly sorry, but we are down to the last bottle. Everyone, please find it in your hearts to forgive her."

I took a deep breath, paused, and then announced as loudly as I could, "Now then, let us begin the auction for the final bottle of soul-healing water!"

"Three tamagin, 20 doumon!"

"Eight tamagin!"

"15 tamagin!"

"30 tamagin!"

Got 'em. Everyone had been holding back because they knew there would be later opportunities. But once they were faced with an unexpected setback, they lost sight of their limitations and really threw themselves into the bidding war. They couldn't help themselves. From where they were standing, they thought they only had this once chance to get their hands on a rare, unbelievable medicine.

They thought they'd never have another chance.

As long as you can get your customers thinking of things in those terms, you can get the prices to rise.

And rise they did.

"Three kinhan!"

"Three kinhan, 50 tamagin!"

Some of the town's noblemen had worked their way into the crowd and had started a bidding war with the merchants—it was the perfect situation to make the prices soar.

The rest of the crowd had fallen silent. They waited breathlessly to see how high the auction would go.

"Four kinhan!"

"Ugh . . ."

"Will that be all?" I asked, watching to see if anyone would continue the battle. "Sold! For four kinhan! Everyone, thank you! A round of applause for the winner, please." I clapped my hands to signal the end of the auction.

The winning nobleman came walking over and handed me the money.

So the first had sold for 30 tamagin, and the last had sold for four kinhan. Not bad at all.

The man was clearly wealthy, so I'm sure four kinhan wasn't too much for him to shell out. Still, the look in his eyes was curious. He could have been after the production method. He could even be an assassin.

I didn't care. I'd made a lot of money off of a single bottle, so I was pleased.

Back in the world I came from, the stuff helped people concentrate, and even then it was still pretty expensive. Of course it had a different effect on heroes.

Now I just had to keep an eye out and make sure no one tried to attack us.

"Thank you all very much for coming!"

The crowd cheered, and we hurried away.

Chapter Six: Otherworldly Equipment

"Feh . . . Everyone seemed so angry."

"Sorry. I could have had Kizuna do it, but you seemed like the better choice."

"Yeah . . ." Kizuna muttered, looking at Rishia.

Even with her mask on, Rishia looked like a klutz. She played the part perfectly. She didn't even have to pretend.

Though from a certain perspective, we only got all that money because of Rishia.

"But, Naofumi, that was pretty impressive. Where did you figure out how to drive the prices so high?"

"It's the best way to make the most profit off the least amount of medicine."

"Wouldn't it work the same way if we sold three bottles instead of two?"

"Business isn't that simple. If you can get people feeling desperate, it's easier to lead them to higher prices."

Had we sold five bottles, I'd estimate that the second bottle would sell for 35 tamagin, and the merchants would have figured out a market price by the third bottle.

There'd be a difference in the final price, but with a revolutionary medicine in front of their eyes, and the sudden loss of merchandise, they'd lose their cool and lose all sense of perspective.

Had there been any merchants that were convinced they'd found the goose that lays the golden egg, then things might have been different. But that wasn't the case.

So it made more sense to sell one bottle for a much higher price.

"If we had just sold the five bottles, then it would have come out to one kinhan and 80 tamagin. It might have helped spread the word more for future auctions, which could have helped get us higher prices down the road, but we don't have enough time for all that."

We had other things to focus on.

Kizuna said that this was an enemy country, so we needed money in order to escape it and get to safety. We had to get out of there before too many people started to think they could make money off of us.

"So do you think we can afford a travel voucher now?"

"Oh sure. We've got plenty."

"Great. Then let's buy the voucher and use the leftover money to get ores we can use to power up our weapons."

"I'm impressed. I have some friends that are merchants and like to make money, but none of them are as good at it as you are," Kizuna explained as she followed me down the road.

It was funny. After selling our stuff at our roadside stand, we were now about to become customers around town. I decided to head to the weapon shop first.

We walked inside the store and looked around at what they had for sale. There were katana and nagamaki. They also sold folding fans, scythes, and spears. All in all, the selection was completely different from the old guy's back in Melromarc.

Of course the weapon shop only sold weapons. All we could do was buy a new sword for Rishia. I bought one that seemed about right for her level.

"So where can I buy a shield?"

"Over at the armor shop."

I should have known.

The weapon shops in the last world had sold both armor and weapons, but that was generally pretty rare. I was kind of starting to miss the old guy.

We went to the armor shop next, but they didn't have many shields on sale—and the selection wasn't very good.

But I did find a shield that seemed to be made from the carapace of a horseshoe crab.

I'd seen similar things in games before. The rest of the shields on display were all pretty close to what the old guy had back in his shop.

Actually, I could transform my shield into most of them, if only my level was high enough to unlock them. There weren't very many to choose from, anyway.

The country had a very Japanese feel to it, so I shouldn't have expected them to have many shields for sale. I never heard of soldiers from the Sengoku period using shields, anyway. I wasn't sure why, but regardless of the reason, the fact remained that there weren't many shields available.

I guess it was the same back in the previous world. Aside from the old guy's shop in Melromarc, most of the other weapon shops didn't have a wide selection of shields for sale. I'd heard that most of them had been taken off the market because the national religion represented them as the weapon of the enemy.

"Want to get some new armor?"

"Yeah . . ."

"Well, we've got the budget for it, so let's get a decent set. If we can get one with chainmail on the inside, that would be best."

I pretended to spit at the suggestion, and Kizuna looked shocked at my behavior.

"Why do you have to be so rude?"

I thought my reaction was perfectly reasonable. There was nothing I hated more than chainmail. I'd never wear something like that.

"I don't like chainmail."

"Oh yeah? You get emotional about the strangest things."

"By the way, I know this is an armor shop, but why are they selling kimono and haori?"

It made for a refined atmosphere in the shop, but from the look of the tattered haori Kizuna was wearing, they didn't seem to offer much in the way of defense. Granted, they might have been made with magic or other special attributes, but I still didn't see why they needed to be sold in an armor shop.

"Why not look at their effects? Then you'll see."

I walked over to a kimono and haori and looked up their information. I was surprised . . . They seemed to have pretty impressive defense ratings. They were more effective than their appearance would have you believe. That must be why Kizuna was so attached to her haori.

"Glass gave this to me, so I . . ."

"Don't get sentimental on me."

The haori was really beat up, though I guess she had been wearing it for years. What wouldn't get beat up in that amount of time?

I certainly didn't want to walk around in a kimono or a haori.

They were all a bit expensive, too.

For the time being, I decided to make do with a decent set of armor.

But all the armor looked like it had come off of a samurai. It all was made of metal and lacquered wood. I guess I'd have to settle for the samurai look.

Rishia could probably use a breastplate, too. It would probably even look good on her.

Luckily the store was selling breastplates, so I bought one and had her try it on.

"Does it fit?"

"Um . . ."

"Looks like your kigurumi days are behind you."

Rishia had always worn a kigurumi, but now she looked more like a proper adventurer.

She had a kodachi at her waist, too, which made her look like a ninja . . . but could she move like a ninja? I had my doubts.

Would she ever be able to move like the old Hengen Muso lady?

I had my doubts about that, too . . .

"Alright, let's go."

The new armor clattered and squeaked as we left the shop. It didn't feel like it fit quite right. I should have expected as much, but the stuff the old guy in Melromarc made was really the best. The Barbarian Armor had a noisy chain that hung off of it, but it never bothered me the way that this new suit did.

Still, I couldn't complain about the defense boost it gave me.

We went back to the market next and looked for materials we could use to power up my shield.

If I didn't power up enough to get through the coming battles, then my chances of surviving for much longer were slim. I was still a pretty low level, so I would settle for a stopgap

shield that would last until I could access to stronger ones.

"So where do we get this travel voucher?"

"At that guild—the one we already went to."

"Ah, right."

Guilds always had these town hall kind of responsibilities. I guess these various worlds had that in common. Whatever, it could wait. I looked at a collection of earth crystals a shop had out for sale and started haggling to get a better price.

There were chunks of ore that helped recover magic power in this world—similar to what magic water did in the world I was summoned to. As I expected, they sold for about the same price. But when Rishia and I used them (probably because we were from a different world) they gave us a more experience points than the boss monsters we'd fought in the Cal Mira Islands. You can see why we would want them.

It looked like they gave different amounts of experience based on their size and purity. It basically meant that we could buy experience points with money, which was a very good deal indeed. What could be more convenient than that? Unfortunately, I didn't know how long I could expect them to work.

"Alright, let's go get this travel voucher and be on our way."

"Good idea. No reason to hang around here for any longer . . ." Kizuna said, casting a glance behind us.

I took the hint and followed her gaze. We were being

followed by a group of men. They probably realized that there was money to be made with our soul-healing water, and they wanted to capture us and force us to tell them how to make it.

"Why don't we get some ofuda for Rishia before we leave?"

"Ofuda?"

"They're a sort of magic tool. Really advanced users can take their own magic power and manifest it physically as strips of paper. People that can't use magic on their own can use the ofuda as single-use spells."

It actually sounded like a pretty good idea.

"I should probably get some, too."

"If I try and use an attack-imbued ofuda, by throwing it at a person, it never works. I have a feeling they won't work for you, either."

That sounded plausible.

My shield certainly wouldn't let me hurt anyone.

Even if I made a bomb and threw it at someone, it didn't do any damage, so I had a feeling the ofuda might work, or rather not work, in the same way.

Kizuna and I weren't really suited to battle other people.

Rishia was more versatile, but her problem was that she wasn't very good at anything. She might have been able to damage other people in battle, but she was such a bad fighter that it didn't really matter.

I couldn't say how useful ofuda would be for her until I

saw how they actually worked. At the very least, it would give her another avenue of attack, and that was certain to come in handy.

"But I . . . I can't use them . . ."

"You just have to throw them at the enemy or stick them on the enemy. That's it."

"Really? That's all?"

Kizuna led us to a shop that had a lot of different ofuda out for sale. There were wood ofuda, paper ofuda . . . even stone ofuda. They just looked like name tags to me.

They did look like they'd all been made with a lot of care, from the materials to the designs on the surface.

"Just take a simple fire ofuda with you. We can at least use it at night to get a campfire going." Kizuna purchased a bundle of fire ofuda and gave them to Rishia.

"Rishia, I don't know how magic works in your world, but focusing your magic power when you use these will amplify the effects."

"Oh . . . Alright."

I couldn't think of any reason to disagree.

Now to finish what we came here for. We had to find a place out of the public eye where we could use the earth crystals to gain some experience.

We pulled it off. I ended up at level 35, and Rishia leveled up just a bit more than I did. How come she leveled up faster than I did?

Oh well. At least I had leveled up enough to use the shields on sale at the armor shop and enough to unlock some of the shields I'd acquired back in the world I was summoned to.

We left the town as fast as we could and made our way to the capital.

Let me try to sum up some of the things I learned about Kizuna on the road.

Over the last few days, it had become clear that she was a very strong hero.

She could easily kill more than half of the monsters we encountered on the road. Her skills were very unique, though, and I still didn't understand them very well. I'll try to explain what I mean.

The first one she used was called Form One: Pitfall.

It opened a large hole in the ground in front of her, and any charging monsters were forced to either stop or fall into it. It was about waist deep, which wasn't really that deep when you think about it.

All it really did was make a hole. It didn't have any other appreciable effects to speak of, but it did interrupt the monsters' charge and opened up holes in their defenses. Once she saw a chance for an attack, she could take the monster out with one hit.

When attacking, she effortlessly switched between her

fishing rod, a bow, and her tuna knife. Her movements were clean and impressive to behold.

We came across a large scaled, crocodile-like monster called Massive Mandible. I held it in place and she swept in with her knife, skinning the whole beast with one quick move and killing it instantly. It was kind of amazing.

Another skill she liked to use was called Fishing.

She could hook the lure of her fishing rod onto the mouth of monsters and yank them up into the air. Then the monsters would crash back down to the ground and lie there, belly-up, leaving the perfect opening for a finishing attack.

Apparently, she had quite a lot of other skills. But we made it through a few days with only those two.

I did see her use one that involved a mysterious fishing lure.

I think it might have lowered the enemy's defenses . . . maybe. Rishia had followed up with an attack that did way more damage than usual, so I assumed it was because of the lure.

I could have asked her to explain, but I had pretty much figured it out just by watching, so I didn't bother.

Anyway, after spending a few days with her, I'd come to the conclusion that she was about as powerful as Glass and L'Arc. If only she could use her offensive skills against other people, she'd be a formidable opponent.

I still didn't know why, but we continued to gain more experience points from battle than I was used to, and Rishia had already reached level 42. The monsters were pretty strong, so I guess that explained why we were leveling up so fast.

Soon enough, we arrived at the capital.

"Security looks really tight."

"If we can just find a way inside, I think we'll be fine."

The town we'd left looked like it had come out of Japan's Muromachi period, but the capital looked exactly like a city from of the Edo period.

A large Japanese-style castle loomed tall over the city. But just like in the last town, none of the residents wore their hair in a topknot.

We stood at the entrance to the city and gazed off at an adventurer's guild in the distance, where we expected to find the dragon hourglass.

The enemy was everywhere. I wasn't sure who it was, but I knew that it included high-ranking officials and other smart people. They must have been prepared for the worst, because it looked like there were a lot of guards patrolling the area around the hourglass.

"I wonder what's going on . . ."

If they were making these preparations on the chance that one of the four holy heroes had escaped from prison, then they were already demonstrating more intelligence than the idiots back in Melromarc.

If Kizuna could fight people, then we might have been able to punch through their defenses by force. But with only Rishia capable of offense, that wasn't going to be easy. But it might not be impossible.

"Should we go out to the mountains and level up more? Then maybe we could come back and break through."

"You think this is a game?" Kizuna asked.

She was right.

How would higher levels help us break through a crowd of guards? It wasn't a very good idea.

"Besides, if we spend more time leveling, we'll just lose more time before the next wave comes."

"Good point."

I don't know what hourglass Kizuna was registered with, but if we were going to waste time leveling, we might as well just wait for the wave to teleport us out of the capital.

We'd spent five days on the road.

The next wave would come in nine days, and it would teleport us to another country when it arrived. But what good would that do us?

I could hardly remember what we were supposed to be doing at the time, but regardless, whatever happened, I couldn't afford to lose sight of the goal. We'd come to this world to punish Kyo for using the Spirit Tortoise to cause chaos in our world. But that possibility was looking further and further away. We had to stay focused.

We didn't have time to waste. We were supposed to find a way out of the country as soon as possible. Besides, people were after us. Who knew if we could manage to stay out of sight for a whole week?

Why was I a wanted man literally everywhere I went?

"Still, with all the guards out like this, I don't know if we'll just be able to sneak in undetected. This isn't a spy movie."

"Sure—but if it were that easy, it wouldn't be any fun."

"Feh . . . What are we going to do?"

"Kizuna, are you sure we can teleport out of here if we reach the dragon hourglass?"

"You're asking that now? Yes, if I can get to the hourglass, we'll be free. Trust me."

I wanted to protest that trust was exactly the problem, but I held my tongue.

"We'll look suspicious if we keep standing here, looking at the building. We should go somewhere else to talk."

"Yeah."

We left the area and made our way to a nearby riverbank to continue our conversation.

"What is that building used for? Class-up ceremonies?"

"You mean job-changing? It is used for that, too, but most of the time people go there to check their drop items. If you check your drops at the dragon hourglass, you almost always get more items than you would from one of those sketchy machines out in the country."

"So the heroes don't need it, do they?"

"Nope. Heroes can access their drop items whenever they want, so they don't come here very often."

"Maybe we should pretend to be normal adventurers to get close to the building."

"It won't work. You have to go through a thorough screening to get inside. You have to provide official identification. It's a very important site as far as the government is concerned."

Hm . . . I guess we couldn't make a forgery, either. We could probably pull it off if we had some connections on the inside, but I couldn't think of a way to make that happen, either.

"And there's no guarantee that a holder of a vassal weapon from this country won't attack us. We are in enemy territory, after all."

"Wait a second. This vassal weapon . . . is it a book?"

"A book? No. I think it's a mirror in this country."

"A mirror? How does it work?"

"I don't know. I don't know everything, you know."

That reminded me of something. I couldn't stop imagining the story of Snow White.

The mirror in that story would answer the queen's questions. It would go something like, "Who is the most beautiful in the land?" What if this person could ask their mirror questions, too, like, "Who escaped from the labyrinth? Where are they?"

I hoped it didn't work that way. That would have been bad news for us.

"But you know, there's really no telling how strong we'd need to be to break through the security and run in."

It's funny that we were worrying about all this when there was a time when I could have just broken right through whenever we wanted.

"I can't deal any damage to human opponents, but they would still have a hard time catching me. The only reason they got me into that prison in the first place was because I couldn't move . . ."

Kizuna didn't have any doubts about her actual power.

I'd seen her demonstrate her impressive power plenty of times already, and I was already assuming that she could restrain people, even if she couldn't hurt them directly.

"But I guess it's an important site, so it's probably safe to assume that the guards stationed there are all mature, skilled fighters."

"Yeah, but still . . ."

I'd be able to use the Shield of Wrath soon, and then I could use it to burn through the enemy lines. Maybe then we could break through and get to the hourglass.

"You and I might make it through, but what about Rishia? She could be a problem."

"How so?"

"If all the guards attack at once, you won't be able to protect her from everyone."

What? Something wasn't quite right here.

I won't be able to protect her? I'm the Shield Hero!

All I could do was protect people, and now she was saying I couldn't do that? Kizuna was getting a little too condescending for my tastes. Did she think I was just in charge of sales? Was I just the chef in the group?

"Kizuna, I hate to state the obvious; I really do. But I have a number of defensive skills that cover a wide area. I don't think I'll have any trouble protecting anyone that needs it."

"Oh yeah. Right."

"Exactly. Rishia's only one person. I can protect her easily."

"Feh . . ."

"What's wrong? Did I say something?"

"You sounded like you didn't think I could handle defense."

"I guess it is your specialty, isn't it? So do you want to try attacking from the front? We don't really need to pay too much attention to the battle. We just need to get through. And if it's really necessary, I have a way to deal damage to people. It comes with a heavy price, though."

"A curse series?"

"Something like that."

Considering how similar her weapons were to mine, I had assumed that she had access to something like the curse series.

Just like how I had the Shield of Wrath or the Sprit Tortoise Heart Shield that could do damage directly, I bet that she had access to a weapon or two that could go on the offensive against human opponents.

But just like the curse series, I assumed that offensive actions like that would come with a heavy price.

"I'd prefer to avoid it if possible. But it might be better than sitting around talking, considering how little time we have. If worse comes to worst, maybe you can use your teleport skill, Naofumi."

I had already checked to make sure that I was able to use Teleport Shield again.

I could use it, but none of the locations from the world that summoned me were available. The only places I could go were places in this new world that I had visited and registered.

"I don't know if I can still use it when we are close to the dragon hourglass, though."

There had been times and places in the past where I hadn't been able to use Teleport Shield. So there was the chance that we might make it to the room with the hourglass and then find ourselves unable to teleport out. It was probably better to be cautious about it.

"If that's the case, we'll just have to run to a place where you can use it."

"This plan is getting messier and messier."

"It's better than doing nothing, isn't it?"

"Yeah."

I thought of myself as the sort of person to attack from the front and power through the enemy . . . but I don't think I had ever actually done it. I had thought about it before—like the time when I was wanted by the crown and had to cross a border to escape. I'd planned on it, but the high priest showed up and revealed himself before I ever had to cross the border.

"Feh . . . We're going to charge the guards?"

"Don't be such a scaredy-cat. Of course that's what we're going to do."

"When this is all over, it would be nice to spend some time fishing and relaxing."

"Don't sound so wistful before the battle. It's bad luck."

"Ha! Good point, Naofumi. You know, maybe you and Glass . . . Yeah right."

"Give me a break. Let's get going."

We pretended to look disinterested, like it was just a normal day, and made our way to the city-hall-like building that housed the dragon hourglass.

But . . . something was going on. A throng of people crowded around the entrance.

Maybe we could use the chaos to our advantage.

Kizuna looked confused about whether or not we should sneak into the crowd. I locked eyes with her, and she nodded.

"What's all this about?" I asked a random person in the crowd.

"Don't you know? A genius from the next country over developed a way to duplicate the dragon hourglass teleportation powers of the four holy heroes and the people who hold the vassal weapons. He just teleported into this room to demonstrate it."

"Really? What kind of person is it?"

It sounded like whoever it was had set themselves up nicely. I stole a glimpse into the building through the front door. When they mentioned a genius inventor, I thought it might have been Kyo, but it wasn't

He looked like a character out of a manga and wore samurai-like armor over a school uniform. Did they even have schools in this world? It looked strange to me. He wore his hair pulled back into a ponytail.

He didn't wear his ponytail up high, like Motoyasu, just pulled it back and downward.

A flock of girls stood behind him.

He must have been the person that Kizuna and I had heard about back in the adventurer's guild: the one they said had duplicated the heroes' teleportation skill. I guess there was truth behind the rumors.

"We did it."

"That was amazing!"

"I knew it would work!"

The women standing behind him all shouted words of praise.

The guy was shaking hands with someone who looked like an official representative of the government.

We'd managed to show up just in time for the strongest security possible! I decided we should probably pull back and wait for the excitement to die down before making our attempt to charge through. So I turned to work my way out of the crowd when . . .

"Ahhhh!"

The government official inside the room shouted and pointed his finger at Kizuna.

"What are you doing here? Aren't you supposed to be in prison?"

"Damn!" Kizuna immediately took off running at the dragon hourglass.

She was right to do so. Once they knew we were out of the prison, they would increase security around the hourglass and we would never get a second chance. We had to go for it now, despite the risk.

Rishia was frantically looking around the crowd, unsure of what to do, like a stupid schoolgirl who didn't know if she should do what her friends said or not, because she didn't want them to make fun of her.

I grabbed her hand and yanked her over to me.

"Shooting Star Shield!"

The roughly two-meter barrier appeared around us, and it

pushed back the people in the crowd and the nearby guards.

"Get him!" someone shouted, and all the guards immediately readied themselves for battle. The adventurers near the hourglass, as well as the "genius" and his cohorts, all turned to face us.

When I deployed Shooting Star Shield to push back the soldiers, Kizuna took off running for the dragon hourglass.

But the soldiers charged with protecting the hourglass reacted very quickly. Furthermore, the interior of the room was like a city hall and full of desks, tables, and other obstacles.

Kizuna didn't seem to care. She jumped on top of the desks, leaping from one to the next on her way to the hourglass. The guards fired arrows at her, and one went straight through her haori—but she didn't stop.

I chased after her, using the barrier to push all the people out of the way. The barrier was a very powerful line of defense, but it also repelled anyone that wasn't in your party.

Swords and spears could get through it, but they weren't strong enough to break it.

That's when the "genius" and his friends all came after us.

I didn't like the look in his eyes. Something about them just pissed me off. They reminded me of Kyo.

"This cannot be permitted! Stop them!"

"On it!"

"Take that!"

The women behind him all rushed to attack us, slamming the Shooting Star Shield with attacks. How long would it last?

I didn't have time to wonder—the barrier shattered with a high-pitched crash.

"Feh!"

"It's fine. Stand back."

I'd sworn that I could protect her, but it was looking like that might be more difficult than I'd expected. If only Raphtalia had been there—she could have taken care of all these women.

I still didn't know what world I was in, but I couldn't deny that everyone here seemed to be stronger than where I'd come from. The monsters gave more experience when they died. That meant that the samurai and adventurers in this world would all be at higher levels for the same amount of work.

Kizuna had mentioned job-changes and class-up-type ceremonies, but that didn't mean that people in this world were limited to level 40 without going through one, did it? If these people had managed to get to relatively high levels, then maybe they'd have no problem shattering my Shooting Star Shield, considering that my level was pretty low at the moment.

I hadn't been able to power up very much, and I was paying for it.

"Take that!"

The genius shouted, and the women all fell back in response.

What was going on?

I actually hoped they would focus on me. Our mission was to get Kizuna close enough to the dragon hourglass for her to touch it. If I could distract the enemy, it would help.

Just when I was wondering what they were concentrating on, they formed a giant ball of fire in the air and hurled it directly at me.

It looked like the sort of attack I could send back at them if I got the timing right.

"Hya!"

I readied my shield, waited for the right moment, and used it to hit the ball of flame back at the genius.

"What?! Nooo!"

The ball of flame flew across the room and slammed into the genius, setting him aflame. He fell to the floor and rolled around, trying to put out the flames, which were burning ferociously.

"Gyaaaaa!"

Everyone started screaming. In all the chaos, I couldn't make out the genius's name.

"I'm not finished with you . . ." the charred genius said, climbing to his feet.

He was pretty tough.

He drew a sword from a scabbard at his waist and flew at me.

I raised my shield just in time to stop it.

"You fool. You blocked my attack without knowing how high my level is. I can slice right through this shield of . . ."

A loud clang echoed through the room, and I felt an odd shock run through the shield.

This guy . . . Just how high was his attack power? Sorry to break it to you mister, but it isn't high enough to get through my defenses.

"It's great that you're so confident, but it looks like I can stop your attacks without any trouble!" I shouted, pushing him back with all my strength. There was a momentary pause before the impact sent him flying backwards.

I looked over at Kizuna. The soldiers had nearly cornered her. They nearly had her surrounded, and were inching closer.

"Air Strike Shield! Second Shield! Dritte Shield!"

I sent the series of shields flying across the room and positioned them like steps so that Kizuna could jump on them to get over the soldiers.

"Thanks, Naofumi!" she winked back at me as she bounded up and over the shields.

She was right in front of the dragon hourglass.

"Stop right there!" the genius shouted, dashing across the room to stop her.

I didn't know what he was planning, but I knew I had to stop him.

"Form One: Pitfall!"

Kizuna didn't need me. She summoned a hole in the ground to stop the genius in his tracks. He tumbled into the waist-deep hole, lost his footing, and crumpled to the ground.

"Ugh! Damn it! That won't stop me!"

"You! Stay out of my way!"

He tried to jump out of the whole, but it was too late.

His women compatriots were running after Kizuna, blood in their eyes.

But before they could reach her, Kizuna reached out and touched the dragon hourglass. She looked back to find me.

"Let's go! Return Dragon Vein!"

A soft light, completely unlike the feeling I got when I used Portal Shield, filled the room and enveloped my field of vision.

"No! You won't get away with this!"

The genius shouted after us, his voice rattling with fury.

"Too bad. We don't have time to waste on people like you."

He glared at me with so much anger in his eyes that I wondered if it was the first time he'd ever lost a battle.

I guess I could understand how he felt, but we had our own goals we had to accomplish. We couldn't just hang out in his country forever. And I couldn't think of a reason to obey the laws of an enemy country that had thrown Kizuna and I in prison.

"I won't forget this! I'll make you pay!"

It sounded like we'd made a new enemy for ourselves. Oh well. I was going back to the world I came from once we finished what we had to do in this world. I'd probably never see the guy again.

Before the genius and his women could reach us, Kizuna's teleport skill activated, and the scenery around us changed in an instant. It was like . . . It was like we'd fallen back in to that hole of light we'd passed through on our way between worlds, but it was somehow . . . softer

Before I could comment on it, the scenery changed again, and we were standing before a desk staffed by people wearing western-styled clothing. It looked like we were in another city hall, but it was very different from the one we'd just left.

So . . . the escape was a success?

Everyone in the room turned to look at us.

"Ah . . ."

They all ignored me and stared at Kizuna.

"Kizuna-sama!"

"I'm back!"

"Welcome back!"

I looked around at our new surroundings.

An official-looking bureaucrat-type excitedly shook her hand, a huge smile plastered over his face. It certainly seemed like we'd reached a safe place.

"Do you think they'll follow us here?"

"Not if they are using Return Dragon Vein. It can only teleport you to a dragon hourglass you've already visited.

That meant they couldn't follow us. Perfect.

I kept looking around to make sure it wasn't some kind of trick, but it still seemed safe.

"Looks good to me," I said, and let out the breath I'd been holding.

Chapter Seven: The Legend of the Waves

The new country we found ourselves was much more western, not like the Japanese style of the previous country. It reminded me a bit of the world I'd come from before this one.

It suddenly struck me as strange that I'd come to feel nostalgic for stone castles that looked like they'd come from the European Middle Ages. Still, even if this country seemed like it was in the same time period, it also felt like a different country. If the Melromarc I was used to was like England in the Middle Ages, then this new country was like Germany in the Middle Ages, or something like that.

Everyone looked very happy to see Kizuna. They were kind to us because we had arrived with her. An important-looking person, maybe even the king, walked over to greet us.

"Kizuna-sama, I'm so pleased that you've made it back safely. Those in my service say that you were captured and imprisoned in the inescapable labyrinth. It seems they were not mistaken. Something will have to be done about this injustice."

We were led into the throne room along with Kizuna and had a lot of questions addressed to us as well. It was a bit annoying. But Kizuna assured us that they would help us search for Raphtalia.

"That's right. Thanks to the efforts of Naofumi, this holy hero from another world, we were able to escape from the labyrinth that is said to be inescapable."

The second that she mentioned I was a holy hero from another world, everyone started looking around suspiciously.

"Um . . ."

"Is there a problem? There is absolutely no question that he sacrificed much to help me. I suggest you treat him with respect," Kizuna barked, annoyed by the sudden air of suspicion in the room.

If I had announced something similar back in Melromarc, I don't think anyone would have believed me. What would happen here?

"You're absolutely correct! Forgive us!"

"Fine. But are you going to explain why you acted that way?" Kizuna asked. The official looked uncomfortable. She said nothing more but walked closer to him, looking pretty menacing. She was pretty good at this interrogation stuff. "So? Are you going to explain?"

"Y . . . Yes, of course. This is information known to our holders of the vassal weapons. So of course, it should be shared with you, Kizuna-sama, as you are a holy hero as well." The man who looked like a king cleared his throat and continued to speak. "The first thing you must understand is that the four holy heroes have a more fundamental role, a deeper responsibility, than simply protecting the people of the world in times of crisis."

"I've never heard anything about it."

"It is only touched on briefly in the legends."

Back in the world I'd come from, Fitoria had mentioned something similar.

She'd said that the waves would grow stronger if any of the heroes were missing before the waves came.

"A phenomenon known as 'the waves' visit this world. Kizuna-sama, I realize that you are familiar with these."

"Yeah, there's always a countdown until the next one running in my field of vision. That's for the waves, yes? But what exactly are the waves?"

"Ancient texts say that the waves are a phenomenon that occurs when different worlds momentarily fuse with one another."

Hm . . . I'd also suspected that might be the case, but now that I'd seen Glass's world with my own eyes, I knew it was true.

But that's not what I wanted to know.

"Next question. Why are Glass and L'Arc trying to kill Naofumi?"

Exactly. While we were on the road, I told Kizuna all about our fights with Glass.

"Because there is a legend that says that if the worlds are allowed to fuse any further, then the worlds themselves will be destroyed."

"What? Why would that happen?"

"I do not know. The legends do not say."

"Hm . . . Okay. So why try to kill Naofumi?"

"The four holy heroes are the keystone, or the fulcrum, of the worlds they represent. When the waves occur and the worlds begin to fuse, the heroes must survive the battle. If all the heroes of a world are lost, then their world will be destroyed while the lifespan of the other world will increase."

"Hmmm . . ." Kizuna murmured coldly.

I could hardly believe what I was hearing. A hero could extend the life of his own world by killing all the heroes of the opposing world during a wave event? I'd never heard such a thing—but it would explain why Glass and her friends were trying to kill me. That was how they could save their world—how they could extend the life of their world.

I suddenly remembered L'Arc saying something to a similar effect.

He said that we'd have to die for the sake of his world . . . Actually, come to think of it, Kyo had said something like that, too. When he was controlling the Spirit Tortoise, he'd said that our world was going to be destroyed, anyway, so he might as well make use of it. That must have been what he meant.

I wondered if that was what Keichi, the ancient hero, had been trying to say in the writings we found on the wall of the temple on the back of the Spirit Tortoise.

It was unbelievable. This information changed everything. Even if that was all we ended up learning, coming to this new world was worth it.

"Naofumi, this isn't good for us, is it?" Kizuna asked.

"No, it's not. But if you and I got in a fight, I don't know how either of us would defeat the other."

"That's not what I meant!" she shouted.

I immediately raised my shield to protect Rishia. Based on all the time we'd spent together, I didn't think she would attack us. But that didn't mean that we were on the same team.

Did Kizuna understand what I was thinking? She turned to the kingly character and shouted, "So we have to survive by sacrificing another world? Is there no other way? Did you even try?"

"W . . . Well . . ."

The man trailed off and turned his eyes away from Kizuna's piercing gaze.

"Oh jeez . . . So that's how it is. Did you think I would approve of this?"

"No . . ."

"Do you really believe everything written down in the legends? Are you really that stupid? Could you at least do some real research on the waves first?"

Wow, she was coming off as really self-righteous. It felt like a cold breeze blew through the room.

"Destroying another world should be a last resort, don't you think? It's not the sort of thing you should throw yourself into on a hunch! Besides, you know I can't attack other people, don't you?"

"Yes, but . . . you see, the four holy heroes exist to defend the world. Killing the heroes of other worlds is a task that falls to those who wield the vassal weapons."

Hm . . . That would explain why the portal between the worlds normally wouldn't let holy heroes pass through. I was only able to be here because of special circumstances.

If that was the case, then fighting on the front lines in all these battles had been very reckless. Had any of us heroes been killed, everything would have come crashing down. Sure, books and manga were more interesting when the protagonist fights in all the major battles, but reality wasn't so sentimental.

I recalled that Glass and her friends had mentioned that they used vassal weapons. That was the last piece of the puzzle: now everything made sense.

"It doesn't really matter either way. Neither Naofumi nor I have many options when it comes to attacking other people, anyway."

"It's true. And neither of us can really fight on our own very well."

It wasn't that I couldn't fight against other people at all. It was just that I had strong defenses, so I would guard the battle line and protect everyone else while they defeated the enemies. Kizuna must have figured that out, too.

Considering the circumstances, it meant that Kizuna was actually in a tougher situation than I was.

There are online games that include player versus player elements, but the hunter-type characters normally dedicated themselves to fighting monsters. They were very skilled at defeating monsters but not very useful when it came to fighting people. There were a lot of those kind of players in the game I used to play, but they never showed up for guild battles.

And that's exactly the sort of hero that Kizuna was.

Assuming that the seven star heroes used the vassal weapons in the world I came from, I couldn't think of a way that Kizuna would be able to survive an encounter with them. Even if she were able to fight other people, how would she feel about killing the otherworldly assassins that came after her?

If this were all a game, then both Kizuna and I were in a rough spot.

She had access to other weapons, similar to the Shield of Wrath for me. But that wasn't the sort of thing you wanted to rely on.

"Anyway, I think it's a little early to decide to destroy an entire world for the sake of your own. You don't know all the facts. I'll tell Glass and the others, so if you know where they are, you should tell me."

"Yes, well . . . Glass-sama found a revolutionary way to become much stronger than she was. When the last wave occurred, she took the boy and went to another world . . ."

Boy? Who was that?

I'm guessing L'Arc? If I was right, then I'd have to make a point of calling him that since he always called me Kiddo.

"Matching that up with what Naofumi told me, that would mean that they met up with Naofumi and his friends in the other world and then all came back here . . . right? Regardless, we'll have to find Glass before we can do anything else."

"Understood. But, Kizuna-sama, I would prefer if you were able to stay in a safe place while this search is conducted. There is the chance that this other world's hero may pose a threat to you."

"Naofumi wouldn't hurt me."

"Maybe I can get back to Japan if I kill you."

"Feh! What are you saying?!" Rishia shrieked.

She was so annoying. If I didn't show some steel from time to time, no one would take us seriously. Kizuna had been a very nice tour guide up until now, but who knew what secrets she might have?

"You wouldn't dare. I swear, you're so bad with people . . ."

"Think whatever you want."

"Regardless, I'll take care of convincing Glass and others. You take the time to rest up. We can't let the vassal weapon holders of this world just do what they want, even if Glass cooperated with them. It's barbarism."

"Sure. I don't have the time to sit around arguing with you people, anyway."

"Right? What's better than having a lot of allies?"

I had my own things to take care of, and yet . . . I couldn't ignore the serious problem posed by the information we just learned. Kizuna must have felt the same way. That was why she didn't want to buy into this whole story of heroes from other worlds being forced to kill each other.

"Fine. I get it. So what do you want to do?"

Honestly, my highest priority at the moment was finding Raphtalia and the others. We weren't going to get far without them.

"Let's focus on finding my other party members first. Then we'll need to go have a word with the country that's harboring the person who wields the book of the vassal weapons."

"That's all? Aren't you a little more angry than that?"

"No need to make it complicated. Anyway, we'll enlist the citizens to help search the countryside."

"You think they might be on the run, like we were?"

Had they ended up in a country where they couldn't use Return Transcript, then it would be really difficult to escape from that country's borders. I knew that from experience.

But if there were inescapable labyrinths like the one that

we'd been lost in, there was also the chance that Raphtalia and Glass were stuck in one, too. And if that were the case, we'd have to save them.

"Remember when I said I knew someone that was good at looking for people? I'm going to get them on it, okay? Call for Ethnobalt!" Kizuna said, telling the kingly man to call for someone.

Did that mean it was all settled now?

"Great. Thanks," I said.

"I believe Ethnobalt will be here by tomorrow."

"Hear that, Naofumi? So what do you want to do until then?"

"If you think this person can help us find Raphtalia and Glass, then I guess we'll just have to wait," I said, nodding at Kizuna. "We should be prepared to leave at a moment's notice."

"You have to take a break every once and a while, you know? But I'm all for being prepared, though."

Well, at least we had someone to guide us around this world—that alone made it better than the one I came from. Still, there was so much I didn't understand that it was starting to drive me crazy. Not that I'm the type to be intimidated by new cities or countries . . .

Chapter Eight: On the Way to the Hunting Hero's House

Kizuna said this Ethnobalt person was going to help us with the search, so we had to wait until the next day before we could leave.

"What should we do?"

"Good question. I can use Return Transcript here, which makes getting back easy. Come with me."

"What is it? Where are we going?" Rishia asked, cowering.

"Don't take us anywhere . . . weird. I'll use Portal Shield to escape if this is a trick."

"Oh, stop worrying. I can't believe you still don't trust me after all this time."

I guess she had a point. Maybe I was being overly cautious.

Had Raphtalia been there with us, she would have had a stern word or two for me.

Raphtalia . . . Where could she be? I was getting really worried.

"Anyway, stick with me."

"Fine. Lead the way," I said, following Kizuna.

We left the town around the castle and followed the winding road through the countryside. The scenery reminded me of Melromarc. I found myself reminiscing as we cut down monsters that attacked us. They didn't pose a threat, and we made fast progress.

So we left the town and made our way down the road for a little while, but soon enough we came upon another large town. From the look of it, it seemed to be made mostly of businesses and houses.

Looking back, I could still see the town around the castle in the distance. I guess this new town was a sort of satellite city. There were probably a lot of people that commuted to the castle from this town. It looked like there was a fishing harbor.

We walked through the town for a little while before Kizuna stopped, indicating that we had arrived. We stood before a large mansion built of stone.

"I had this house built. I wanted it to be large enough so that everyone could live here."

"Wow . . ."

The door was locked, but Kizuna pulled a key from her pocket and opened the door.

It creaked open slowly, and Kizuna waved us inside.

The interior looked like what you'd expect from a house built of stone, but it looked very . . . cultured.

The first floor seemed to be a parlor for guests. There was a table in the center, and I could see a kitchen in the back.

"I'm home!"

There was no answer.

After entering the building, Kizuna carefully checked to see if anyone was there, and then she climbed the stairs to the second floor. I thought it might be best to wait for her downstairs, so I found a chair and sat down to wait. Rishia found a chair and plopped down, too—she must have been tired from the journey, because she immediately started nodding off.

After a short while, Kizuna came back down the stairs.

"We helped ourselves to some chairs. Hope that was alright."

"Of course."

"So? What were you up to?"

"I guess I should have known, but . . . after coming back to my house, after being gone for so long, it's strange that everything is just . . . the same."

"Is it?"

Her own house . . . I had certainly never made a home for myself in any of these worlds, so I didn't really understand how it must have felt. But for Kizuna, this building must have really felt like home.

"There isn't even any dust. I was stuck in the prison for so long that I'd started to think this house would be gone when I got out."

"Good thing it's still here. You think someone came buy and cleaned up for you?"

"Maybe Glass did it."

"She looks like she'd be particular about that sort of thing."

"Yeah . . ."

I noticed photographs on a shelf in the corner of the parlor. Most of them were of Kizuna and Glass. A lot of them had L'Arc and Therese in them, too. There were other people that I didn't recognize as well. Everyone looked cheerful and happy. The pictures were filled with a palpable sense of friendship.

I didn't have to wonder if Kizuna's bonds with them were still intact—a glance at the well-kept state of the house was enough to confirm that they were still close.

I felt a little strange looking at it. It was almost like . . . envy. I didn't have many friends that I could take such joyful pictures with. Sure, I trusted Raphtalia, Filo, and maybe Melty with my life, but I couldn't think of anyone else to add to that list.

Rishia was really only with us because she didn't have anywhere else to go. And Eclair, or the old Hengen Muso lady, had only teamed up with us recently. I wouldn't consider them very close. And Raphtalia's childhood friend Keel clearly didn't trust me yet.

Kizuna's pictures made me wonder if I would ever have enough trusting relationships to take pictures of my own. A part of me thought that day would never come—that I'd never know that many people that would be happy to spend time with me.

I'd always known it was true, but it was hard to admit to myself.

I can't trust the people in these worlds, anyway. I'd made up my mind about that a long time ago and had given up trying.

When peace returned to the world and it was time for me to go back to Japan, I couldn't picture myself posing with anyone for a commemorative photo. I just didn't have that many friends.

"Can I ask some questions?"

"Sure."

"You told me a little bit about your life here, but can you tell me more specifics of how you came to know Glass and the others and about the life you spend together here? You don't have to tell me anything you don't want to."

"No, it's fine. Glass and I met a very long time ago," Kizuna said slowly, as if reminiscing on happier times.

When Kizuna first found herself in this world, she thought that she had just been teleported into a game, so she had spent her time leisurely fishing and thinking about leveling up. The crown had supplied her with plenty of funds, but the government was not very powerful, as it was in the middle of a battle for succession.

Kizuna met Glass in a neighboring country. The disciples of a famous martial arts school were in the middle of a ceremony to decide who would inherent the responsibilities of the fan of the vassal weapons. Whoever was chosen would have to use the fan to defeat a dragon that hunted in nearby lands.

Glass had been denied consideration at first because of her birth. But disciple after disciple was turned down until Glass was finally selected to wield the vassal weapon.

"What do you mean she was denied because of her birth?"

Glass looked very powerful and serious. You'd have to be a fool to not recognize her potential. Did she come from a strange family of something? Is that why people ignored her?

I could sympathize with a predicament like that—after all, I'd been summoned to a country with a religious prejudice against the Shield Hero.

"That's Glass's issue, and I don't think I should tell you about it without her permission. So just pretend you didn't hear it."

"Oh . . . Okay."

"So anyway . . . the disciples that were passed over were pretty resentful about it. So they got together and decided to cut ties with Glass. They told her not to come back when she left for her trial."

"Sounds like there are a lot of jerks in this world, too."

How petty can you get? Cutting ties with someone just because they were chosen over you?

"Well, they probably thought that Glass would die in the trial, and then one of them would be chosen to succeed her.

They ended up fighting among themselves, anyway."

"Okay, well enough of that. So how did you end up meeting Glass?"

"She was fighting monsters out in the fields of that country, and I happened to walk by. We hit it off right away and decided to team up. That's about it."

It was nothing like the start of my first partnership.

I was stuck all alone with no way to deal damage to monsters. I had to buy Raphtalia as a slave . . .

We'd had a totally different experience right from the start.

I felt like I couldn't have even-footed relationships with people. Raphtalia and I would probably never have the sort of relationship that Kizuna and Glass did.

"We ended up meeting more people, and our party grew. It was a pretty wild ride, but we always had fun," Kizuna said, pointing out different people in the photographs.

She ended up pointing to so many people that I couldn't help but feel how different we were and how special this home must have been to her. It must have felt irreplaceable.

I was a little jealous. After all, I didn't have anything like that. But I was fighting to get back to my own world. Being jealous of what she'd built here didn't make any sense.

At least that's what I told myself.

We decided to spend the night in Kizuna's house.

Luckily for us, there were a number of empty rooms, so we were able to really relax and get some rest.

Soon enough, night was upon us.

I was relaxing on the terrace of her house, looking out on the lights of the town, when I saw Kizuna leave. I wondered where she was going.

I looked back inside, where Rishia was silently writing something.

I guess it was fine. I could always use Portal Shield to escape if I needed to.

Careful not to make a sound, I snuck out of the room to follow her.

We made our way through the unfamiliar town, and soon enough I saw a beach in the distance. Kizuna held a lamp in one hand and walked toward the ocean. When she got there, she fit her rod with a new fishing lure and cast it out into the sea.

She was fishing?

I guess she really did love to fish. She fished whenever she had spare time.

"Hm? Oh, it's you, Naofumi."

"Is this a good fishing spot?"

"Not really. You can only catch herring here."

"Herring, huh? Can you catch Japanese fish here, too?"

When I was framed and exiled by the crown, I'd done some fishing. I hadn't recognized any of the fish I caught.

"Sometimes. If you really keep an eye out for them."

"Heh."

She finished reeling in the lure and then recast it.

"Fishing here, in this spot, really makes me feel like I'm back home."

"I guess it would."

"You might feel the same way when you get back to the world you came from."

"Maybe. I haven't really put down any roots there, though."

What was closest to my home? Melromarc castle? I didn't like being there at all. It was uncomfortable. Then again, I could always use a portal to return to it, so I suppose it was convenient in some ways.

I didn't have a house like Kizuna did. The closest thing I had was probably Filo's carriage—I guess I had spent a lot of time in there.

I decided to stop comparing myself to Kizuna. It was starting to make me feel bad.

"Hey! I caught something!" Kizuna shouted, yanking her pole and pulling up a splashing herring.

Oh jeez. She was just making it worse. She could do everything.

"So that's how you would normally do it. Now let's try my special method . . ." she said, attaching a new lure to the rod. It had a shining green jewel affixed to it. "If this goes well, I should be able to catch something pretty interesting."

"I thought you could only catch herring?"

"Well, let's just see what happens when I use the power of the holy weapon . . ." she muttered, casting and reeling and casting and reeling until the rod bent down sharply under the weight of something unseen.

"It's a hit!" she shouted, her eyes blazing while she rapidly reeled in the fish. The surface of the water started churning.

"It's huge!"

As she continued to reel it in, I saw that it was an enormous . . . herring.

She finished reeling it in.

"What do you think? Is this a whole new world or what?"

"That thing is a monster."

"Can't argue with that."

I had a feeling I'd be seeing fish again on the breakfast table. The thing was huge, though—too big. It probably wouldn't taste very good. Maybe it would be best boiled . . . Or maybe as sashimi. Then again, I've never heard of herring sashimi . . .

"So you can catch these big ones by changing the lure?"

"Yeah."

"Is it a skill?"

"Huh? No—it's an accessory. Don't you add them to your weapons?"

"No."

"It's pretty great. You should try it."

"To power them up?"

The rationale behind Kizuna's power-up methods didn't seem to apply to my shield, so I didn't have much hope for this new idea of attaching accessories to it.

"It is a pretty broad system. I can't catch large herring without using this lure, and when I check on my status, it says that there are changes to my fishing ability."

Hold on a second. I'd seen something like that

A long time ago, the old guy at the weapon shop had given me an accessory to attach to my shield. When I used it, it formed a barrier similar to Shooting Star Shield, but then it broke. I wondered . . . Could I gain access to more protection—protective abilities that weren't already innate in the shield—by attaching accessories to my shield?

It was worth a shot.

"I can use this lure in battle, too. I have to say, I really like it."

"Then maybe I should try it, too. Maybe I could even make it myself."

Thinking back on the accessory the old guy had given me, I hadn't thought that it was something I'd be able to make on my own. But I was starting to think it was worth a shot.

It would be ideal to ask the old guy how he made it, but at least I had Kizuna here to bounce ideas off of. "Do you need to do something special to make them? Like imbue them with magic power or something?'

"Hm . . . For that kind of thing you'd probably be better off talking to an imbue master or a professional craftsman. I hear the imbue masters need some sort of base to work from."

I guess the skills of a professional craftsman might come in handy.

"Then again, I hear that the accessories have unusual effects when used with the holy weapons or the vassal weapons. It drives the imbue masters crazy."

Even if I got my hands on an accessory that worked well here, it might stop working altogether when I got back to the world I came from. That wouldn't be good. It would be like using expensive and rare materials to imbue an item with special effects, only to have the pieces fail and end up with nothing. Still, it was worth a shot.

"I think I'll try it. I'll make something and see if it works."

"You're going to make it? You can make accessories? Want to make me a new lure?"

"Why do I have to make stuff for you?"

"Oh, you know . . . because of all we've been through together?"

"I guess I could try it—just for practice, you know? But I think a lure might be more complicated than anything I've done yet. Like working on a complicated plastic model."

"There are wooden ones and metal ones, too."

Sure, and there were lots of different shapes. There were sparkling bits of jewelry you could use to deck everything out like a gaudy person who just inherited a bunch of money. I didn't like that sort of thing.

But fish were attracted to shiny objects, weren't they? Without even intending to, I was already thinking hard about how to approach the lure project.

What about my own accessory?

I could just try to imitate what the old guy had made for me.

It was a sort of cover for the jewel in my shield. It had clipped right on top of it.

Besides, I didn't have any other compounding projects lined up, so I had the time to try it. I decided to just give it a whirl and not worry too much about the outcome.

Besides, the view from Kizuna's fishing spot was too good to ignore.

Chapter Nine: Shikigami

It was the next afternoon.

I cooked up the herring that Kizuna caught the previous night, and we had it for breakfast before returning to the castle to meet this person that was supposedly going to help us search for Raphtalia.

"They'll be here soon."

"Are you sure?"

Rishia stood there muttering to herself as she read something off of a sheet of paper. I was getting tired of waiting.

But I didn't have to wait for long. Kizuna shouted to the people in the castle, "Ah, they're here! Let's go."

"Finally. You heard her, Rishia. Let's go."

"Alright."

Studiousness was good and all, but what was she reading? From what I could tell, she was just repeating simple phrases like "good morning, good morning," over and over.

Rishia and I followed Kizuna to the throne room and found someone there dressed like a black wizard with a circlet on his head.

He looked like a young boy in heavy robes, and he held an ornate staff in his hand. His hair was light, bordering on silver. He had clear, clean skin, and his sharp eyes left a strong impression. They were red or maybe black. It was hard to say.

He was waiting for us, and he seemed to be . . . floating.

I think I'd seen someone that looked like him in one of Kizuna's photographs. It was probably the same person.

"It has been a long time, Kizuna. I continued to search for you this whole time. I'm sorry I never found you."

"What's done is done. I never worried about it."

"This one was very lonely without you. Please take him."

"Thank you. You watched after him for me, didn't you, Ethnobalt?"

"Yes. Glass took care of him at first, but she became very busy and had to travel to dangerous lands. Therefore, we decided it was best for me to take over."

Kizuna stopped chatting with the boy, and he passed her something that looked like a wooden ofuda. She shook it lightly, and a column of smoke shot from it. When the smoke cleared, a penguin was standing before her.

It was about as tall as my waist.

I called it a penguin, but it wasn't exactly a penguin. It had a very expressive face, and it was so happy that it was hopping up and down.

It reminded me a bit of Filo when she had just grown out of her chick stage, before she started talking.

What was it?

"Pen!"

"It's been a long time. I'm glad to see you, too."

"Pen!"

The penguin leapt at Kizuna and started rubbing cheeks with her. Filo used to do the same thing.

"That reminds me. This little guy started fussing about six days ago. Had I made the connection, perhaps I could have found you sooner."

"We were behind enemy lines. It wouldn't have been safe for you to come. It would have taken you this long to find me, anyway."

"It's nice that you're both reminiscing here, but is anyone going to explain what's going on?"

No one liked to sit around listening to people talk about things they didn't understand and couldn't join in on.

"Oh right. Sorry. This is Ethnobalt. And this guy is my shikigami, Chris."

"You mentioned those before. How are they different from other monsters?"

"Shikigami are, well . . . You get them from other people or items, and they aren't monsters. He's basically my bodyguard. Since I can't, you know, fight with other people.

"I still don't really understand. Go on."

Was it like anything I was familiar with? I knew there were online games where you could recruit monsters to fight on your behalf. But that was simpler than what she was describing. In those games, you could just send any monster you'd captured out to assist you in battle.

My relationship with Filo was sort of like that.

There were other similar systems, like summons, or the sort of suspicious attacks you could use by working with other players.

Every game was different, so the borders and categories didn't always line up. It was probably best not to make too many assumptions.

"I'm very pleased to meet you, holder of a holy weapon from another world. I am the holder of the boat of the vassal weapons. My name is Ethnobalt. I trust we will get along."

"I'm Naofumi Iwatani, the Shield Hero. The girl behind me is Rishia."

That was it for introductions.

The boy had a look on his face like he understood anything and everything, and . . . Well, actually, if I let his face annoy me, then we'd never get anything useful out of the conversation.

"Which means that you're like Glass, and you have a vassal weapon? Where's this 'boat' you mentioned?"

"It's right here," Ethnobalt said, pulling his robes up to show me his feet.

He was standing on a round platform of some kind, and it floated a few inches off of the ground.

It looked like a UFO or something that bizarre.

"I'm pleased to make your acquaintance."

He looked like he might be a demi-human or some other type of person unique to this world.

"Is there something strange about this guy? Am I imagining it?"

This Ethnobalt guy looked different from all the other people I'd seen since arriving in the world.

"I thought you might notice. Ethnobalt is descended from a race of great monsters that have protected the world for generations."

"Really . . ."

Then I realized who he had reminded me of. Something about the way he carried himself . . . It was Fitoria. It's hard to be specific about how he reminded me of her, but he did.

He looked like he was probably highly skilled with magic, but maybe he was actually a melee fighter. He gave Kizuna a penguin, so maybe he was actually . . . a penguin? If that were the case, maybe all of these worlds were watched over by bird monsters . . .

"His true form is a cute rabbit."

"Kizuna, please don't refer to me as 'cute.'"

"A rabbit? He's not a penguin?"

"Why would he be?"

"I don't know. You're shikigami was a penguin, so I just . . ."

"Pen?"

What was up with this penguin? He reminded me of the legend I'd encountered on the Cal Mira islands: the one about

Pekkul. I wanted to put a red Santa hat on his head—then he would look just like it.

"Oh, I see. That makes sense. I don't know why, but when Glass and I formed our shikigami, this is what he looked like."

"Hm . . ."

Well, that was fine with me. I didn't want to see what it really looked like, anyway.

Ethnobalt rubbed his chin for a while, apparently deep in thought, and then, having made up his mind, he transformed with a puff of smoke.

I found myself looking at a rabbit standing up on its hind legs.

The look of him once again reminded me of the islands— of the karma rabbit familiars we fought there. Were it not for his staff and the intelligent look in his eyes, I would have mistaken him for a monster.

But the more I looked at him, the more I was certain that he was this world's version of Fitoria. I was pretty sure of it.

"Would you prefer I take this form when we speak?"

"How rare! I almost never see you as a rabbit," Kizuna said.

"For the sake of Mr. Naofumi here . . . I wouldn't want him to doubt my words unnecessarily. I'd like him to be comfortable."

"Oh? Naofumi, do you like animals?"

I remembered how Filo would always hug me, but then

again, I was probably just imprinted on her as a parent from a young age.

"Okay. So I hear that you're good at searching for people?"

"Perhaps, though I wasn't able to find Kizuna when she was imprisoned in the labyrinth."

"It's great that you're humble, but give me a better idea of what you can do, will you? We've been waiting for you this whole time."

I didn't want to hear that he couldn't actually help us—but then again, if he was like Fitoria, then he would be unbelievably powerful. From what he'd said so far, it was safe to assume that he had been able to tell if Kizuna was in this world or not. The never-ending labyrinth must have been a completely separate world.

Whatever. I didn't know him, so I wasn't thrilled about having to rely on him for help.

I thought that he might be like Fitoria, but he didn't seem to be.

"There are many complicated methods. I wonder which is best," Ethnobalt said, producing item after item from under his robes.

They looked like the sort of things a fortuneteller would use. There were small sticks, crystal balls, and . . . ofuda? Then came the deck of cards . . . They must have been tarot cards.

I was starting to trust this rabbit less and less. He looked less reputable by the minute.

He might have been the hero of the boat of the vassal weapons, but I didn't feel like I could trust him.

"Ethnobalt, I was thinking you could grant Naofumi a shikigami."

"That is a good idea. A shikigami may prove to be a boon to your search effort."

"Why is that? What can a shikigami do?"

"Aside from helping with the search, a hero's shikigami can do a lot of interesting things. They certainly make good bodyguards."

"Pen?"

I pointed to the penguin in Kizuna's arms, and it cocked its head in response.

That's right. I'm talking to you.

Was it really Kizuna's bodyguard? It didn't look like it would be much help in a battle.

"But you can't let them die in battle."

"Oh . . ." I sighed. If you had to be so careful with them, what good were they as bodyguards?

I was starting to understand. These shikigami were like the "familiars" in the world I'd come from. I think I'd seen something about them written in one of the magic books. It had said that certain items were necessary to summon your familiar and that if you lost the item you wouldn't be able to summon them.

I hadn't paid very much attention because I didn't have a familiar, but thinking about it now, it did seem like a familiar that could protect me in battle would be a handy thing to have.

I had Raphtalia and Filo with me, though, so I had never felt the need for one.

"I had hoped that with this little guy helping me I'd be able to find you quickly . . ."

"But because I was thrown into the labyrinth, you had to give up, right?" Kizuna sighed. "Glass and I made this shikigami together, so I think it will help us find her current whereabouts. But that might not necessarily bring us to your friends, Naofumi. It will if they are all together, but there's no guarantee that they are, is there?"

" . . . No."

I had no idea where Raphtalia was. The slave spell couldn't tell me anything unless we were in the same vicinity. I had to prepare myself for a difficult search.

"Then let us perform the shikigami ceremony. It's easiest if done by the dragon hourglass, so I suggest we make our way there," Ethnobalt said. With a puff of smoke, he transformed back into his human form and floated out of the room.

We all went to the guild-like building that housed the dragon hourglass.

Ethnobalt waved his staff and then tapped it loudly on the floor. When he did, a magical geometric pattern appeared on the floor around him. It was formed of a faint phantom-like light.

Because the magic was being performed by a giant rabbit, it made the ceremony feel even more otherworldly than the class-up ceremony back in Melromarc.

"First we will need a suitable medium, as well as some blood from the person who will serve as the shikigami's master."

"A medium? You mean like an ofuda or a gemstone or something?"

"Yes, you'll need something like that to make a familiar . . . When I made Chris here, I used all sorts of monster parts for the ceremony. Glass and I decided on the ingredients because we wanted to make a shikigami that could be a powerful guard."

Hm . . . It sounded like a delicate process. I could sometimes get tunnel vision when working on a complex project. I knew other people like that, too—the sort of people that would freeze up when starting a new game or when they were given a bunch of points to assign when creating a character. Some people never manage to actually start the game, because they spend all their time worrying about the best way to allocate resources to their characters. Honestly, I had those tendencies myself.

Out of all the items and materials I had, which would produce the best result? Materials from the Spirit Tortoise or its familiars? During the battle, I'd managed to pick up quite a few materials. Then again, I'd probably end up with a turtle if I used those.

Sure, Ost had been one of the Spirit Tortoise familiars, too, but no matter what sort of familiar I got, it would probably be more focused on defense than offense. As the Shield Hero, I had the defensive bases covered pretty well as it was, so I didn't want a defensive shikigami.

"After you make one, you can always adjust it later on, so you don't need to worry too much about it. For now, just use any medium you have to give yourself a shape to work with."

"It really doesn't matter what I pick?"

"Normally it would, but the rules are a little different for heroes like us. I guess there's a chance that it will work differently for you, since you're from another world."

So the heroes played by different rules? Good. I guess I didn't need to worry about it.

Somehow this kind of made it boring. Still, I was glad—it would have taken me all day to make up my mind otherwise.

"I think it might be best to use something that belonged to the girl you are searching for. That way the shikigami will be able to help guide you back to the item's owner."

That was a good idea. I could make it specific to Raphtalia—but did I have anything that had belonged to her? I normally made a point of keeping my items to myself and letting Raphtalia and Filo do the same.

I had given her different pieces of equipment in the past, but I don't think she had ever returned any of them.

"Don't forget that you can also use the dragon hourglass. You can use it to produce any drop items you have stored in the shield. Do you have anything that might work?" Ethnobalt waved his staff, and an icon indicating my shield flashed in the air. Then a long list of the items contained within it appeared. My eye fell on one thing in particular.

"This . . ."

Raphtalia was a raccoon-type demi-human.

I saw that an item I had received from Raphtalia was being stored in the shield, but it was a strange material that never unlocked a new shield.

That's right . . . I had some of Raphtalia's hair from when I had given her a haircut way back when I had first purchased her from the slave trader. It was perfect. I didn't know if I'd be able to take it out of the shield, but I tried just believing that I could and selected the remove option that appeared. The shield emitted a soft light, and then Raphtalia's hair was in my hand.

"Let's try this."

"Very well. Now then, I will need a little of your blood," Ethnobalt said, using magic to levitate Raphtalia's hair before us. Then he used a small knife to prick my fingertip and drip a little of my blood onto a plate.

Memories of my first days with Raphtalia came flooding

back into my mind. When I bought her from the slave trader, we had performed a similar ceremony.

"Now then, I will begin the shikigami formation ceremony," Ethnobalt said, sprinkling a magic powder over the mix of Raphtalia's hair and my blood.

The boat on which he stood began to glow faintly, as if it were contributing power in addition to Ethnobalt's own magic.

The air in the room around us began to glow with small points of light, as if we were surrounded by fireflies. It was beautiful—and strange.

Soon I'd have a shikigami . . . Would it really help us find Raphtalia? We were using her hair to make it. If the thing was going to help us find her, then I couldn't think of a better material to use in its creation.

"We petition for one who will protect—who will serve. A vassal formed from a part of himself. A servant is born . . ."

The lights swirling around us gathered around Raphtalia's hair and engulfed it completely.

It was an amazing sight. It was so impressive to see that I would've really lost it if the ceremony had ended in failure.

A shikigami . . . I looked over to see Kizuna's shikigami, and it was hugging her. I hoped that mine would be a bit more relaxed and a lot less clingy.

Did this mean that I was going to have another party member?

I wasn't sure how I wanted to use it. Would it have levels the way that other people did? Or did it grow through an alternate system?

However it worked, it was going to serve as my protector, so I would have to devote some serious thought and energy to its growth.

"It's . . ." Ethnobalt murmured, hardly able to speak.

"What? Did we fail?"

"No . . . It just formed much faster than I was expecting. Just who was the owner of this item?"

The light in the room grew even stronger. It was blinking. I couldn't see anything, so I instinctively raised my shield to protect myself. Then the shield in my hands started to crackle—it was responding to the light!

"Feh . . ."

"Calm down! Ethnobalt? Is everything okay?"

"Um . . . No. No! I can't control it! Everyone! Run!" he shouted, dropping his staff and quickly backing away.

I still had my shield raised to protect Rishia from whatever was happening. Looking over it, I saw something floating in the space before us.

Shikigami . . .

Shikigami Shield conditions met!

Shikigami Shield
abilities locked: shikigami servant: shikigami
power-up

A large puff of smoke appeared with a flash, filling the room with blinding white light.

"Cough! Cough!"

I waved my hand to try to clear the smoke away from my face, but it wasn't moving. I had no choice but to grit my teeth and breathe it in as I looked at the ground to find the source of the explosion.

"Rafu!"

Something came bounding straight at me out of the smoke.

"Wh . . . What the . . . ?"

I caught whatever it was in an instant. I looked down and saw a small creature that looked like a mix between a raccoon and a tanuki.

It was hard to describe it more specifically than that. It was like a cute raccoon character from an anime I'd seen a long time ago—only a little bit different.

It was like a tanuki—it was brown with a fluffy tail and walked on four little legs like a chubby little dog. Its ears, however, were decidedly not dog-like. Finally, it had a strange little face that didn't exactly look like a tanuki or a raccoon.

Its tail was at least as fat and large as the rest of its body, and it looked like . . . Well, it looked like the kind of mascot characters that little kids get excited about. Still, I'd never seen mascot modeled on a tanuki.

The mascot-like, raccoon-like tanuki creature stood there with its arms crossed. Then it raised one hand, showing me its puffy little paw, blinked its eyes softly, and barked, "Rafu!"

"Is it safe to assume that this thing is my shikigami?"

I changed my shield into the recently unlocked Shikigami Shield, and just like when I had first registered my slave, a new option had appeared in my menu.

That cleared it up. This thing was definitely a shikigami.

It didn't seem to have levels like the rest of us did. Its stats also weren't particularly high.

I selected the shikigami power-up effect, and a menu appeared that seemed to allow me to manipulate the shikigami's stats using various items. It looked like there were a lot of different possible effects.

It reminded me of the options I'd had when designing the bioplant. But aside from those options, it looked like the shikigami could be powered up with items I had on hand.

"Rafu!" it barked, wagging its puffy tail and looking at me with love in its eyes.

It brushed against me. It didn't feel so bad. Its fur was a little stiff, but it didn't bother me. It was warm.

"Feh . . ." Rishia whimpered, stealing sheepish glances at us. Was she seriously afraid of this little thing?

"Pen!"

"For a second there, I wasn't sure it was going to work. However, it seems like the ceremony was a success!" Ethnobalt said, sighing with relief and floating back over in our direction.

"This is a shikigami?"

"Raful!"

The shikigami jumped up my shield, stood on its hind legs, and raised both of its paws in the air. It almost looked like it was showing off.

"Yes, it is. Did your weapon say anything about having items to power up the shikigami?"

"Yeah. There's an option for a shikigami power-up."

"That's it. I thought you'd probably enjoy playing with that."

"I figured you'd be the sort of person that liked that stuff, too."

"How could you tell? I get a little obsessed sometimes."

"Hm. Guess we have that in common."

"Heh heh."

"Heh heh . . ."

"Feh . . . I feel like a third wheel . . ." Rishia whined, upset that Kizuna and I were sharing a laugh. Was there anything that didn't make her feel threatened? All we were doing was agreeing with each other, and even that seemed to scare Rishia.

"Well anyway, I believe that this shikigami will be able to

help you find your missing friend. Let's leave with Kizuna to look for your friend and for Glass."

"Sounds good, doesn't it?" I said to the shikigami.

"Rafu!" it barked back, excitedly nodding its head.

The little thing was going out of its way to get me to like it . . . and it was kind of working.

Its voice even reminded me a bit of a young Raphtalia. Just a bit.

"Naofumi, aren't you going to give this little critter a name?"

"A name? I guess you're right. I shouldn't just keep calling it shikigami."

"Rafu!" the little thing proclaimed, proudly puffing out its chest.

I guess that was the only sound it could make. What a weird thing to say . . .

It sort of made me feel like I was doing something rude, something disrespectful, to Raphtalia—not that I had any other choice.

I'd chosen Filo's name because she was a filolial, so I guess it made sense to name this thing after Raphtalia.

"Alright, how about Raph-chan?"

"Rafu!"

"You're naming it Raph-chan because of the way it talks? Isn't that a little lowbrow?"

"Why did you name a penguin 'Chris'?"

Chris sounded like a character straight out of a western fantasy. It certainly didn't seem like an appropriate name for a penguin.

"Because, when we made this guy, I counted back from the day I'd been summoned to this world and realized that it was Christmas."

"Ah . . . so that's where you got 'Chris'."

I still didn't think it was a good name.

But you're wrong about why I named it Raph-chan. It's not because it keeps saying 'rafu.' It's because I made it with Raphtalia's hair."

" . . . That's not so different."

I wasn't going to argue. Besides, it kind of felt like a little too on-the-nose that the thing kept saying 'rafu' to begin with.

"Rafu!"

"Okay, okay. Fine. You want a different name?"

"Rafu?"

Raph-chan (tentative name) looked confused and then shook its head. "Rafuuu."

I guess she liked the name. If she liked it, then who was I to argue?

"She seems to have a developed a sense of self, hasn't she? Normally it takes a little longer for their bodies and minds to develop this much."

"Maybe it's because the materials came from another world. Could that affect the results like this?"

Raphtalia wasn't from this world, so maybe it was a special case. Not to mention that she had matured differently than a normal demi-human, because she'd been raised by a hero—me. She had matured very quickly, so maybe this shikigami was the same.

"Okay then, Raph-chan. Can you tell us where Raphtalia is?" I asked.

Raph-chan closed her eyes and puffed up her tail, apparently doing . . . something.

Was she using magic or some sort of special shikigami ability?

Kizuna turned to Chris and addressed him, "Can you tell us were Glass is?"

"Raful!"

"Pen!"

Both of the shikigami's barked and pointed in the same direction.

"Pardon the intrusion. Perhaps you could indicate the location on this map?" Ethnobalt said, pulling out a map of the world and opening it before the shikigami. Both of them immediately pointed to the same spot.

If they were both pointing to the same spot, then it was probably safe to assume that Raphtalia and Glass were traveling together, right?

Kizuna and Ethnobalt sighed and looked upset.

"What? Is something wrong?"

"They're pointing to a country that's like the place we escaped from—enemy lands. It's actually the country where that supposed genius scientist came from."

"You sure do have a lot of enemies."

"I know. These are troubled times, after all. All those politics are basically what got me thrown into the labyrinth. What to do . . ." Kizuna murmured, looking concerned.

I guess you had to deal with war no matter what world you went to.

Even still, this world seemed to be less stable than the one I'd come from.

Melromarc and Siltvelt often went to war with one another, but even they managed to join forces when the world itself was under threat from the waves. The other countries I'd heard of were all participating in international talks about the waves, too.

This world, on the other hand, didn't seem so cooperative. Everyone seemed to be at war with everyone else.

Maybe the relative peace of the last world was only possible because the queen of Melromarc was so good at diplomacy.

"But Glass and her friends are really powerful in this world, right? I mean, they were chosen to wield the vassal weapons, weren't they?"

"That's true, but . . . the very fact that they haven't used a dragon hourglass to teleport back here makes me think that they must have run into trouble."

If Glass was having trouble, how were we supposed to help? From what I'd seen, she was so powerful it was nearly unbelievable.

A dark, somber feeling had taken over the room.

Kizuna and I had had a rough time fighting our way here, but that was only because of the limitations of our weapons. Without those special limitations, I was sure we were actually really powerful and wouldn't have had a problem. Glass and the others didn't share the same limitations that we had, so if they were having a hard time, then things must have been really rough.

"Is that where the guy with the book of the vassal weapon is from?"

"No, but they are allies. There's a chance that Glass and the others have been captured and turned over to him."

"Then we better get going."

"Agreed—it's better than standing around wringing our hands. Let's go."

"That settles that."

There was no telling how much help Kizuna could be if we ran into human enemies, but we didn't have a choice. We had to get going.

"Kizuna, aren't you going to bring some friends with you?"

She seemed pretty much ready to leave, but she hadn't mentioned anything about bringing anyone with us.

"Ethnobalt doesn't like battles. I guess there are some people I could reach out to, if I had to . . ." She looked over at Ethnobalt, who awkwardly cleared his throat.

"It would take a few days to get Kizuna's companions together. They are all spread out across the country, engaged in various activities."

"Something could happen to Glass while we wait for them to get here. We should go on without them."

I didn't disagree with her reasoning. Building up a strong party wouldn't do us any good at all if Glass and the others were captured while we waited.

And it certainly seemed likely that Raphtalia was with her. If they were turned over to Kyo before we could get there, she'd be in real trouble—and I had to protect her.

We were always right on the edge of disaster.

I sighed. "Aren't there at least some soldiers that we could bring along?"

"There are soldiers, but they are not permitted to leave the country. They need to be here to protect it."

Just great. Everyone was shorthanded.

I'd always felt like I didn't have enough people in my party, but it was looking like Kizuna had the same problem I did.

"Let's go. Can we use the dragon hourglass to teleport there?"

"No, but Ethnobalt should be able to teleport us there."

"You are correct, Kizuna. I am able to use the power of my boat to teleport you there—but how will you return?"

"We could use my Portal Shield skill."

"That's a good idea. Let's set a time and place to meet up after the mission. Ethnobalt, you meet us there, okay? If we don't make it . . ."

"Understood. Take a communication ofuda with you. With any luck, we should be able to stay in contact through them."

That was a convenient item to have on hand. I was almost jealous, but then I remembered that we had something similar in the world I came from. There were machines at the guilds (I don't know how they worked) but they could send messages instantaneously to each other.

Ethnobalt led us out of the building and stepped down from the floating platform he had been riding. The small circular platform then transformed into a boat.

"Everyone, please climb onboard so I can begin the teleportation process."

"This thing . . . It reminds me a lot of a weapon I saw once," I said. I was talking about Fitoria's carriage.

Skills like Teleport Shield would only work for people that were in your party. But Ethnobalt's boat and Fitoria's carriage could teleport anyone that happened to be riding in or on them.

How did they work? Did they form a portal? I had no

idea how people got around in this new world. I had a lot of questions running through my head, but they would have to wait.

We left to begin our search for Raphtalia and Glass.

Chapter Ten: The Katana of the Vassal Weapons

We climbed into Ethnobalt's boat. I thought that the boat was going to fly through the sky, but when it started moving, it was more like a teleportation skill. The scenery around us quickly vanished and was replaced with a path of pale light, over which the boat proceeded.

If the boat could take us anywhere—even locations that we hadn't registered beforehand—then it was a really powerful option to have!

"I'm impressed every time I ride on this thing. It would have taken forever to travel on foot."

"How does it work?"

"It works by using the connections between the dragon hourglasses as currents."

Hm . . . So the hourglasses were all connected by lines, and the boat had the ability to sail over those lines. Did that mean that the boat could go anywhere in the world, as long as the currents between the hourglasses went there as well?

The system was more complicated than I expected.

"You can sail over things high in the sky and use the boat to get the drop on unexpected enemies. We've done that a few times."

"So Raphtalia and Glass are somewhere nearby?"

"Somewhat. There are many defenses to watch out for, so I can only get you close."

"It's a big help"

Depending on how we used it, the boat could prove very useful. As for Ethnobalt himself, he apparently wasn't the strongest in battle.

"So we'll switch to flying in the sky from here on out?"

"That'd draw too much attention."

She was right. Sailing slowly through the sky was like asking the enemy to shoot us down. Maybe we could pull it off if we flew at a very high altitude . . . but then again, there were probably a lot of flying monsters in this world. We wouldn't want to run into them.

"I could offer some support fire or bombs, but that would only draw even more attention. It would be best if you only thought of the boat as a way to escape, not to battle."

"Okay. Then we will call for you after we meet up with Glass."

"Very well. And good luck," said Ethnobalt. At nearly the exact same second, the streaming pale light around us vanished, and we found ourselves standing on unfamiliar ground.

He said that we might run into trouble and that we couldn't count on him for backup, either.

"Okay, Raph-chan, take us to Raphtalia."

"Rafu!" she barked, pointing enthusiastically.

Kizuna's penguin, Chris, was pointing the same way.

We stood before a thick forest. It seemed to be mostly composed of pine trees, but there were tall copses of bamboo here and there, which lent this new country a Japanese feel, too.

We held open a map to get a sense of our bearings and began the search in earnest.

"What sort of country is this, anyway?"

"It borders the country that you and I just escaped. The two countries share a similar culture. But this one reminds me more of Japan under the Tokugawa shogunate."

At first I didn't really know what she meant, but it wasn't long before we came out of the woods and found a town, and then I understood what she was trying to say.

The houses were all made of wood, but there were a lot of signs out in the streets, the sort you'd seen in Showa-era Japan. The language looked like it was written right to left, and the architecture made the town look like it was in the midst of a modernization effort.

I even thought I saw street lamps with electric light bulbs in them. The mishmash of so many different time periods was unnerving—it didn't feel natural.

The adventurers walking in the street were dressed like the Shinsengumi. The rest of the villagers were also dressed in traditional Japanese clothes. I saw a lot of hakama.

"Is there some kind of checkpoint we have to get through?"

"I don't think it's that strict. I think the only checkpoints are on the border. It's a lot like the last country, but not quite so secure."

"You don't say . . ."

There certainly were a variety of countries in this new world.

In comparison, the countries in the world I'd come from seemed to be based on nobility and the rule of monarchs. That was at least easy to understand—not that I necessarily had it all figured out.

"Won't our clothes draw attention?"

"I don't think so. They aren't always on the lookout for foreigners here. They'll just think we are adventurers passing through. Look around. There are plenty of people dressed like us," Kizuna said, pointing.

She was right. There were plenty of other adventurers wearing armor similar to ours.

"That's great. We better find Raphtalia fast. The minute we find the others, we need to get out of here."

"I know what you mean . . . Chris, where's Glass?"

"Pen," the bird chirped, and pointed in the same direction that Raph-chan was indicating. We followed their lead and continued the search.

We followed their lead to a new town and ran into a very long line of people there.

"What's this?"

"I'll see," Kizuna said. She ran ahead to see what was going on. Then she came jogging back. "There's some sort of show going on. Everyone seems really excited."

"Hm . . ."

A show? I'd seen tents set up for a traveling show back in Melromarc, too. The proprietors would set up tents on the main drag in the marketplace. I never really cared for that sort of thing, though, so I'd never actually looked inside.

But there were so many people lined up it was hard not to be curious. There were more people lined up for this show than had attended my soul-healing water auction. The line seemed to snake through the whole town.

Could the show really be that impressive? Were the citizens just starved for entertainment because there was nothing else to do out here?

"Want to check it out?"

"I don't care—and we don't have the time."

"Good point. We don't have the time to waste waiting around in line."

"Rafu, rafu!"

"What is it Raph-chan? Do you want to see the show?"

She seemed very interested. She nodded vigorously.

Raph-chan had been formed out of Raphtalia's hair—if she wanted to see the show that badly, then I couldn't help but be curious.

"What is this 'show' you keep mentioning?" Rishia asked.

Kizuna stood on her tiptoes to try to read the sign by the building.

"It says, 'A young angel with wings on her back—literally fell from the sky! See her for only 40 doumon!' What do you think? A real angel?"

A girl with wings on her back? That sure sounded like Filo to me.

I was focused on finding Raphtalia, but I was going to have to find Filo, too.

"Hey Kizuna. Are there any races in this world that normally have wings on their backs? Does that sound like anything you've seen before?"

"Not particularly, no. What about in your world, Naofumi?"

"I've heard that there are harpy-type demi-humans, but I've never seen one. On the other hand, one of my party members is a girl with wings on her back. If you just got a glance at her, you might think she was an angel."

She did match the description on the sign.

She certainly didn't act like an angel—but you wouldn't know that just from looking at her. She could trick you if she managed to keep her mouth shut.

"Rafu!"

"Feh! Do you think it could be Filo?"

It could be.

And what if it was? I was about to walk right by the show. I wouldn't have stopped if Rishia hadn't asked Kizuna what was going on. Now what was I supposed to do? Line up on a hunch?

I walked to the front of the line and tried to overhear what people were saying inside of the building.

"Ya! Master! Mel-chan! Save Me!" I heard shouts of pain amidst the cracking of a whip.

She sounded like she was in a lot of pain. I'd never heard her voice sound that way.

"See what happens? Hurry up and cross the rope!"

"I . . . Ah!"

I could hear the shouts through the walls.

"What is that angel saying? I guess she's pretty upset. I don't like it . . ." I heard one of the customers mutter as they left the building.

That's right—no one in this world would be able to understand Filo. Even still, did they really think it was okay to capture her and treat her like an animal? Sure, she might look like an angel now, but she was really a giant bird monster.

"Fehhh!"

"Rishia, be quiet! If they realize that you're speaking the

same language, they'll probably try to grab you, too!"

"Feh . . ." She clapped her hands over her mouth and nodded silently.

"Is it really your friend?" Kizuna asked, her face serious. I nodded. "I know you want to help her, but that's going to be tough for you and I. Do you think Chris, Raph-chan, and Rishia can handle it?"

"If they try to sell her in an auction, we could try to raise the funds to buy her. Or if we can't get the money, we can get one of the town's noblemen to buy her to at least keep her safe . . ." I muttered. It was all I could come up with for the moment.

If a nobleman bought her, then we might be able to use the soul-healing water as a bargaining chip to get Filo back. But there was no telling how much he would ask about where we got it and how we made it, which could cause trouble. There's also the chance that they would just use Filo as a hostage to get whatever they wanted from us.

We couldn't spend too long staying in one place, but we couldn't do anything until we found out how Filo had been captured. If she had just been captured by normal adventurers, then we might be able to ingratiate ourselves with a nobleman and use his authority to get her back. On the other hand, if a nobleman had captured her to begin with, we'd be out of options. He could force us to do whatever he wanted in that case.

"What should we do? Should we hope for an auction?"

"We should avoid working with the nobility if at all possible. It would take a long time, and there's no telling what kind of situation we'd be walking into," Kizuna said. I could understand her caution. These people's allies had thrown her into the labyrinth, after all.

It was easy to imagine this country having prejudices at least as strong as Melromarc. I couldn't ignore the possibility that we might start conversations with a noblemen and then find ourselves thrown in a dungeon. We had just caused a ruckus in the next country over.

Luckily, judging from the reaction of the nobleman who'd bought the soul-healing water from us, we didn't have to worry too much about that side of things. Still, there was no reason to stick around any longer than necessary.

"Is there any way we can find out who is running this show? There must be someone in charge."

"Yeah, we can probably find out at the guild. With a line this long, it should be pretty simple to find out who is running it."

So we went to the guild and looked into the proprietor of the show—that was enough to cancel our plans of ingratiating ourselves with the nobility.

That's right. The nobility was already involved with the show's management. That didn't leave us with many options.

I motioned for Kizuna to come close, and I whispered in her ear, "Let's wait until nighttime, when everyone is asleep, and then try to sneak in."

Filo sounded like she was in a lot of pain, so there was no time to waste rescuing her. If we pulled it off, that would be that. If it didn't work, we'd just have to move on to the next plan.

"Okay."

"We need to secure an escape route. Better get moving."

"Alright!"

We had to get started on our preparations to free Filo. We might end up in a tough battle, so I decided I'd better figure out my shield plan. I'd need to start with one of the stronger shields that I already had and then use whatever materials I had to power it up.

There was the Nue Shield . . . It wasn't quite as powerful as the Chimera Viper Shield, so I would probably be able to use it. Out of the shields I could currently use, it was probably the best option.

Nue Shield (awakened) 0/35 C
abilities unlocked: equip bonus: defense 3
special effect lightning resistance: night terror; lightning shield (medium)

I decided to power up the Nue Shield and use it.

I thought the nue was a Japanese monster, and luckily the shield was still usable in this world. Also, when I powered it up, Lightning Shield (medium) became available. Before that, it was (very slight), which wasn't really good for anything.

I still didn't know what "Night Terror" was. It also appeared when I powered up the shield.

Regardless, rescuing Filo was now our highest priority.

Chapter Eleven: Rescuing the Angel

We waited for night to fall over the town before making our way back to the marketplace.

Kizuna and I crept lightly over the rooftops and approached the building where they were holding the show. I had to keep an eye on Rishia the whole time. I didn't want her stumbling and screwing up the whole plan. On the other hand, Raph-chan was quite a bit more dexterous than I'd expected. I didn't have to worry about her at all. She was just as light on her feet as Raphtalia.

"In this country, and in the next one over, there's a law that you have to carry a light if you go out after dark."

"It really feels like Edo-period Japan, doesn't it?" It was strange, because the town and the people in it looked like they were in the midst of a modernization movement. Everything was all mixed up. Not that I was particularly nostalgic for the Edo era. The townsfolk made it feel like an imitation version of Edo.

It was like foreigners had built it, wanting to make it really EDO-PERIOD JAPAN! For a Japanese person, though, it was clear that something was off.

"Running over the roofs like this makes me feel like we're

going to run into a ninja or something."

"I have a friend that's a ninja, actually. I think you might have seen them in one of my pictures."

I didn't recall having seen any ninja. This girl had way too many weird friends—and that includes Glass and L'Arc. As for Therese, I hadn't made up my mind yet.

"Really?"

"Yeah, I'll introduce you some day."

"I'll pass."

I couldn't stop picturing the shadows from Melromarc and their strange, annoying way of speaking. You'd think they would try not to stand out, but the shadows had a very distinct way of speaking. They were like lazy ninja.

"Alright, that's enough chat for now . . ." I said. We were getting close to the building. "You think she's in there?"

"There's no way to know for sure. Anyway, it looks like there are some rooms built over the showroom. If she's here, that's probably where she'll be."

That reminded me—if I was this close to Filo, shouldn't I be able to use the monster spell to find out where she is? I tried using it to get an idea of where to go next. It hadn't worked when we were in the labyrinth, and it hadn't worked when I tried it after we escaped. That had led me to mostly give up on it, but now . . . it was working.

I turned around to make sure I was getting an accurate

sense of where it was indicating, and sure enough, it looked like Filo was inside.

"Okay, great. I'll use a skill to make us hard to see," Kizuna said, pulling out her fishing rod and whispering.

"Invisible Hunter!"

There was a soft humming sound, and we were all suddenly covered in a thin film that made us invisible. I had nearly forgotten that Kizuna was the Hunting Hero. I'd assumed that she'd been able to sneak up on monsters and beasts, but I hadn't expected her to have such a useful skill.

Maybe it was because of the type of monsters I'd fought up until that point, but I had never learned a skill that could make me invisible.

Where would I even learn a skill like that? A Cloaking Shield? A Hiding Shield?

Raphtalia could probably do it.

"Raph-chan, can you use any stealthy magic?"

"Rafu?"

I guess not. She cocked her head to the side and looked confused. Still, she was made from Raphtalia, so I thought there might be a chance. I'd have to make a point of teaching her as many skills and techniques as possible.

"Should we get going?"

"Yeah. But how does this skill of yours work?"

"They won't be able to see us unless they use magic to

search us out. You have to be in our party to hear our voices and footsteps."

"That's great."

"It took a long time to learn the ranged version of it, but I learned the simpler single-person version of it when I was still pretty low level."

"I wouldn't complain too much."

"Should I cast a spell, too?" Rishia asked hesitantly.

She probably could cast it, technically. Too bad she was so bad at everything she tried.

"Maybe if you were Raphtalia, but it's probably better that we leave it to someone who knows what they are doing."

"But I . . ."

"I know how you feel, but let's just leave it up to Kizuna's for now."

Kizuna hopped off of the roof and snuck off toward the building where Filo was imprisoned.

We jumped down after her and followed her to the building's back door.

"It's locked. I should have known."

"I don't know how to pick locks . . ."

"Yeah, and this lock . . . It will set off an alarm if you break it."

"They take security pretty seriously, don't they?"

"A craftsman might be able to disable the alarm . . ."

She had mentioned that there were times when you needed a good craftsman on your side.

I reached out and touched the lock. It looked very old. It would trigger an alarm if we tried to pick it. I focused my magic power and touched it again, and I was able to get an idea of how the device worked. It was clear that something would happen if you were to just start fiddling with it.

But I had an idea.

It looked like it would just make a noise, not necessarily send a notification to anyone. If it was like a burglar alarm, then I might be able to find a way to disconnect it.

"If I can destroy the alarm it's rigged to, do you think you can break the lock?"

"Hm . . . Yeah, probably. But can you do that?"

I focused my magic power into my hands and sent it all flowing into what looked like the most important part of the alarm.

"Beeeee . . ."

Just before the alarm could sound, the lock started sparking. The alarm sounded very quiet and low, like a rumbling hum in my hand, unable to make any more noise. Because I was holding the lock in my hands, the noise was concealed by Kizuna's skill.

"See?"

"Wow! Okay . . ." Kizuna said. She whipped out her tuna knife and quickly sliced the lock in two. Everything happened in complete silence. If I covered the pieces with dirt, it would probably take care of any noise.

"You said that you made accessories, didn't you? You're quite the craftsman, aren't you?"

"Back in the world I came from, maybe so. I can handle some simple magic-imbuing and that kind of thing. It's not difficult."

It wasn't difficult, but it had taken a while to really get a handle on the feeling that goes along with drawing power out of gemstones and things like that. I'd failed quite a few times before I got the hang of it.

On the other hand, breaking things was much easier.

For this alarm, all I did was focus on the part that emitted the sound and then poured my magic power onto it. It was sort of like dumping water on a computer motherboard. Had it been very sophisticated, it might not have worked. Luckily, it was a simple little thing, and it broke easily.

"And you can cook, too! You're very talented."

That's enough of that. Let's get going."

"Raphtalia was very complimentary of you in that way. She always said that you were skilled with your hands, so she wanted to have you make her some accessories."

That wasn't a bad idea, actually—I could help Rishia out by giving her accessories with abilities imbued in them to make up for her poor battle skills.

Now that she mentioned it, I remembered having that conversation with Raphtalia. With all of the training, the searching for the other heroes, and the battles with the Spirit Tortoise . . . I'd completely forgotten.

We snuck inside and took in our surroundings. The interior looked like an old row house, and there was a stove near the back entrance. There was a place to remove your shoes and a staircase leading up to the second floor. At the back of the room there were a number of empty cages. They must have had a few different things to use for their show, but for the moment, it looked like they were focusing on Filo.

"That's not the way," I said, stopping Kizuna from continuing toward the front room.

"How do you know? She could be this way."

"Now that she's nearby, I can see what direction she's in."

An indicator in my field of vision pointed the way to Filo's location, so the fastest way to find her was simply to follow it. The original use of the spell was probably to help owners track down escaped slaves—or monsters.

Either way, at least I could see where she was now. That made the search much easier.

We kept our shoes on and crept up the stairs to the second floor, where there was a hallway with a few rooms on either side. There were a few merchants, or maybe noblemen

(I couldn't tell), standing in the hallway watching over the rooms. They had drunk themselves to sleep and looked like they were passed out cold.

There weren't very many rooms, so finding Filo should be a pretty simple matter.

I looked over at the drunk, sleeping guards. I guess there were drunks no matter what world you went to. It was pretty dark, but luckily I'd acquired an ability to see in dark places a long time ago.

"Feh . . . Naofumi. Please don't let go of my hand!" Rishia murmured. It must have been too dark for her to make out her surroundings.

Kizuna, on the other hand, moved forward through the dark without hesitation.

As the Hunting Hero, she probably had no trouble at all seeing in the dark.

"Which way is she?"

The arrow in my field of view was pointing to the right, so I waved toward the closest door and we quietly slipped inside. Inside we found a futon laid out on the floor. There was a well-off-looking man sleeping in it.

Behind him, I could just make out . . . a sack of money?

He must have been making a pretty profit off of Filo's show.

Seeing the money really pissed me off. I'd raised Filo from

an egg—she was like my daughter! Hearing her pained shouts earlier that day had been bad enough.

I would have to make sure this creep paid for his crimes . . . but first we needed to free Filo. I turned back to the search, but I couldn't see her. I looked around the room, but she wasn't there.

I thought that I'd find her sleeping in her human form, maybe locked in a cage or something. I must have been wrong. Was she in her filolial form? I wasn't sure the floor would be able to support her in that form. She was a very large filolial, and the floor would probably have broken under her weight.

The only other thing I saw was a small birdcage in the corner . . . and the arrow in my vision was pointing directly at it.

"Pii?!"

The little chick in the cage noticed us and started to chirp and fly around the cage.

Damn . . . Wasn't there any way to get this monster—or wild animal—to stay quiet?! The man would wake up if the bird kept making a racket.

"Naofumi! This guy is going to wake up!" Kizuna said, pulling out her tuna knife and pointing it at the birdcage. She wanted my confirmation before she killed the monster inside.

But . . .

"Kizuna, wait a second. Why is that little thing causing my monster spell to react as if Filo is here?"

"I don't know, but that's just a little chick. I think they call them humming fairies."

A humming fairy, eh?

But why was my spell reacting to it?

"Pii! Pii!"

The humming fairy chick threw itself against the bars of the cage, extending its wings at me. The way it held its wings out . . . It reminded me of how Filo used to try to hug me when she first turned into a human.

"Could it be? Are you . . . Filo?"

The humming fairy chick nodded. That settles that.

"Well, be quiet. If you make too much noise, this guy will wake up."

Filo nodded and stopped making noise. She jumped up onto a perch and sat quietly.

What was going on? Why was Filo a different kind of monster? Why was she in a little birdcage?

There was an ofuda stuck on her back, and she looked gloomy and depressed.

Maybe the ofuda turned her into a different monster so this guy could keep her in a little cage.

"Should I break the birdcage?"

"Just a second. We don't know if it's rigged with an alarm."

"Let's check it out."

I focused my magic power and reached out to touch the

cage. It felt like there was some kind of amplifier inside, and it was resonating with the ofuda on Filo's back.

"What does that ofuda do?

"It's a servant ofuda. People use them to control monsters and use them as servants. When the monsters aren't being used, the ofuda can be used to hold them prisoner, too. But this one is strange. Normally, the ofuda fuses with the monster's skin."

"Maybe because I already own her. The ofuda might not work the way it should, because I already have a monster spell cast on her."

These people were real creeps. Based on how upset she'd sounded earlier in the day, I assumed that they were treating her terribly. But they were people, so neither Kizuna nor I were going to be able to attack them. That left us with Chris, Rishia, and Raph-chan to rely on.

"Rishia, do you think you can take him out while he sleeps?"

"Feh . . . I can try, but I don't know if I'll be able to."

Damn it . . . We didn't have any way to make this guy pay! I didn't think it was a good idea to trust Rishia with the job. And Raph-chan wasn't strong enough to attack a person on her own.

"There are some things we could do to raise Rishia's attack power, but it's probably not worth the risk of being discovered. Let's focus on escaping while we still can."

"What about Chris? If he's strong enough to handle it, we should let him."

"Pen?"

"If we let Chris do it . . . he won't just hurt the guy. He'll probably kill him."

How strong was this shikigami of hers?!

"If we take the ofuda off of her back, will she be free?"

"It won't be so easy to get it off. Many ofuda have special magic applied to them . . ."

"This one doesn't seem to be working properly, though, so hopefully we can just rip it off."

"Pii . . ."

"If it has a lot of different settings and effects, then it could cause trouble."

It might kill her if she got too far away from her master—or it might tell him where we were. We were right in front of him.

I looked into the optional effects of the magic spell I had applied on Filo to see if there wasn't something I could do to make escape easier. The magic spell itself was a very powerful one. I decided to try to activate it.

"Filo, this may hurt a little bit. Bear with me."

I activated the monster spell and checked to see if it was working properly. A magic circle appeared in the air over Filo's stomach, and she began to writhe in pain.

And then the ofuda peeled up and twisted on her feathers. When she realized the ofuda was loose, she cocked her head to the side and started pulling at it with her beak.

I guess a little strip of paper and a powerfully applied monster spell weren't in the same league.

"Piii!"

"Kizuna, Filo is about to pull the ofuda off. The birdcage seems to be connected to it, so we'd better destroy it."

"Are you ready?"

"Yeah. I don't see any alarms on it. Even if there was one, we don't really have a choice here."

"Okay," she said. Then she drew her tuna knife and quickly sliced the cage to pieces.

The cage clattered loudly to the floor in chunks. At nearly the same moment, the monster spell circle on Filo's chest sparked, and the ofuda peeled off completely.

I immediately deactivated the monster spell. Filo transformed into a human and threw her arms around me.

"Master!" she shouted, raising her head to look up at me. "You're here! You're really here! This isn't a dream, is it?!"

"I'm really here. It's not a dream."

Filo was on the verge of tears. She was finally standing right before my eyes.

"Rafu?"

Raph-chan poked her head out and barked at Filo.

"Hm?"

"Rafu!"

"Master, what's this thing? It kind of smells like Raphtalia!"

Her sense of smell was as good as ever.

"Her name is Raph-chan. She's a creature called a shikigami. We made her out of Raphtalia's hair, so that's probably why she smells like her."

"Oh wow! Nice to meetcha, little, big sister!"

"Rafu!"

They smiled at each other. I started to smile, too, when . . .

"What the hell?!"

The sleeping man jumped to his feet—very awake. He clearly knew that he was about to lose Filo—the goose that laid his golden eggs.

"Who are you?! Show yourselves!" he said, pulling a katana out from under his pillow. "That bird is mine! I'll take her back now!"

"Damn . . ."

Kizuna's skill must have stopped working, because once the man noticed us, we quickly came back into full view.

"Boo!"

"How did you manage to get the servant ofuda off of her? No matter—I'll cut you down and take her back!"

I felt something snap, like a string pulled too tight. It must have been the limits of my patience. Was I letting this guy get away with too much?

"Okay . . . So you beat up my friend here, and now you're going to act all tough?"

I didn't feel like holding back anymore. Making this guy suffer was my highest priority.

"Rishia, Kizuna, I want to give this guy a taste of hell—any problem with that?"

"We're not going to run away?"

"Run away? Ha! Not until I torture this guy and destroy his soul."

"Ra! Fu!"

What's that now? Raph-chan understood how I felt? She was smiling devilishly.

But that's not the way that Raphtalia would have responded, so that made it clear that they had very different personalities. Raph-chan was an individual.

I took slow steps toward the creep that had captured and profited off of Filo. He had to pay. He had to pay for what he'd done.

"Stay away! Hya!"

The man swung his sword, but at nearly the exact same second, the Nue Shield's Night Terror effect activated.

A low rumbling emanated from the shield and echoed through the room. Is that all it did?

A split second later the man yelled, "Stay away . . ."

"Kyaaaaaaaaaaaaaaaaa!" A shrieking, high-pitched, nearly supersonic voice split through the room. It sounded like nails on a chalkboard, only much louder and longer.

Kizuna, Chris, Rishia, and Filo all immediately covered their ears.

"Feh . . ."

"What's that sound?"

"Ah . . . Ugh . . ." The man who owned the show tent started shaking.

"Ahhhhhh . . ." His face quickly twisted into one of extreme terror.

"No! Stop! Stay away!" he shouted, shaking his arms and running over into the cover of the room.

The shield must have had a powerful effect on the enemy—he looked like he was crippled with fear. It must have dug deep into his subconscious fears and brought them to life in his mind.

"Rafu!" Raph-chan puffed up her tail and a started to cast a spell. It looked like she could use the same kind of magic that Raphtalia could—illusion magic.

I squinted in the dark and could just make out the owner of the show, cowering and running from something. It looked like a ghost or something . . . Was the skill using his past traumas to torture him?

"How can you turn against me? How can it be?!"

It looked like he might have been having hallucinations—like maybe all the poor things he tortured for his business had risen up to exact revenge on him.

"Someone! Someone please!"

No good. I couldn't have him yelling for help.

I walked over to the cowering businessman. He was terrified and randomly swinging his sword, so I grabbed him by the shoulders to stop him.

"What do you want?!" he yelled and swung the sword at me. I stopped the blade.

There was a loud clang when it hit my shoulder.

Then Lightning Shield (medium) activated and electrocuted the man. He twitched violently in front of me.

"But how . . . You . . . You monster!"

"Calm down . . . The terror has only just begun."

"Naofumi . . . you sound so villainous," Kizuna said.

"You'll pay for what you did to my friend. Shield Prison!"

I wouldn't take damage either way, so I enclosed myself in the prison with him. Then I shoved the Nue Shield against his ears and blasted him with Night Terror. That's when I realized I could control the volume of the shrieks.

"Ahhhhhhhhhhhhhhhhhhhhh!"

The man's screams echoed through the prison. They were loud—and annoying.

"Fine then . . . Maybe you'd rather answer some questions. Where, and how, did you get your hands on Filo—I mean, on this angel?"

"Why would I tell you?!"

"Don't want to talk?"

I raised the Night Terror volume even higher.

"Gyaaaaaaaaaaahhhhhhhhhhh!"

I turned the volume back down and told him, "I suggest you start talking soon. Personally, I've got no problem with watching you suffer all day long."

"Whh . . . I . . ."

I smiled, and the man's eyes filled with terrified tears. He must have been leaking everywhere, because a liquid seemed to be running down his legs.

But that wasn't nearly enough to make up for all he'd done to Filo. She must have been terrified! I don't think any of the creatures whose misery he'd profited from would be close to satisfied yet.

"See?"

"My parents gave her to me! They said they found her unconscious!"

"Who are your parents?"

"They're nobility in the town!"

So they found Filo when she was unconscious, thought they could make money by showing her off, and captured her. What creeps!

"Who else is helping you run your show?"

"I'm nobody! I was just tasked with the running the show, as a representative of a local family!"

So there were clans that basically ran the town here? The place was organized like the Edo period, so maybe they were magistrates. It sounded like people were in positions of power strictly because of their families. I decided to ask Kizuna about it later.

I'd probably gotten all the information I could out of this disgusting businessman.

"Thanks for the information. As a reward, I'll provide you with supreme terror. Did you think it was already over?"

"Rafuuuuu . . ." Raph-chan cooed, seemingly enjoying the sight. That's it, Raph-chan. We can enjoy his misery together!

"Ah . . . Ahhhhhhhhhhh!"

You know, there's really nothing better than watching someone you hate suffer. It was such a relief to watch this piece of trash howl in fear. If only I could make Trash and Bitch suffer like this, back in Melromarc.

"Ahhhhhhhhhhhhhhhh!"

He was leaking liquid from all the holes in his body and vomiting, but I kept on dealing him more terror. I liked watching him writhe and struggle.

Finally, like a switch had been flipped, his eyes rolled back into his head, he foamed at the mouth, and then he fainted.

"Don't think that passing out will save you."

"Rafu, rafu!"

I pressed my shield against the man's ears and continued to use Night Terror.

Even though he was unconscious, it still seemed to be working. His limp body started to twitch. He might have been asleep, but I was injecting terror into his dreams.

I liked this skill. I could use it to torture people. I'd have to remember to use it the next time I came across a jerk like this.

It was a psychological attack, so there might be people that it wouldn't work on.

No matter—I continued using Night Terror to fill the man's dreams with fear while I waited for the Shield Prison around us to disappear.

"Ew . . ." Kizuna muttered, looking down at the unconscious man.

He had leaked all manner of things from every part of his body, and his face was still twisted in terror, like he was being tortured in his dreams. He looked like someone that had seen one of those videos that would kill you if you watched it. He had an unbelievably violent and pained expression on his face.

Humans were actually pretty tough. They could go through all of this and still not die.

"Feh . . ." Rishia was scared of the man's pained expression.

If I used Night Terror on Rishia, she'd probably lose her mind in a heartbeat.

Not that I would do that . . .

"Alright, we got our revenge. Now let's split."

"Right . . . Remind me never to piss you off. But you know, saying 'let's split' like that makes you sound like a criminal."

We had just committed a crime, hadn't we? This was illegally breaking and entering—even if we were rescuing a hostage.

"Thank you, master!"

"Yeah, yeah."

A loud beeping sound rang out through the night outside.

I opened the wooden shutters to look outside, and I didn't like what I saw. The building was surrounded by scowling men.

"You think they're out to expose the crimes of the show?"

"I doubt it. I think they must know we're here."

We'd used Kizuna's skill to stay hidden, and we hadn't run into any guards on the way in, but there was still a chance that we'd been noticed without knowing it.

"Come out and surrender!"

Yup . . . There was no doubt what they were after.

The townspeople had gathered around the building to find out what all the trouble was about.

"What should we do? How are we going to get away with all those people out there?"

"Rishia, I'm sure you know the answer to that. Think back on all the time you spent with Itsuki . . ."

"Feh? We would all proclaim Itsuki the Bow Hero and fight on his behalf."

That's what Itsuki did? What an idiot.

Well, I guess the Bow Hero was a pretty famous person back in Melromarc. He could probably use his notoriety to get out of a tough spot. He might not have had to escape all the time.

"So how do we escape?" Kizuna asked while Filo threw her arms around me.

Before answering, I invited Filo into our party and waited for her to accept.

"Here's the plan: Portal Shield!"

I chose a location outside of town that I'd registered before we snuck in to save Filo.

In a flash, our surroundings completely changed, and we were safely out of trouble.

I hadn't known if we were going to be successful in our attempt to free Filo, but I had always planned on using Portal Shield to escape.

"Wow!" Kizuna yelled, quickly looking around to get an idea of where we were. "That's totally different than Return Transcript!"

"You mean the rules are different?"

"I guess? This skill of yours is great for getting away from a pursuer."

"Let's hope it worked."

It was the middle of the night and very dark outside, so I would be surprised if anyone could figure out where we'd vanished to. We'd be in trouble if anyone recognized us—you could never be too careful.

"Anyway, we're done here, so let's split."

"Okay!"

"Alright!"

"Oh jeez, I guess we still have to run for it."

So after teleporting to the edge of town, we took off running into the night.

Chapter Twelve: Humming Fairy

We traveled through the night, putting plenty of distance between the town and us. By morning, we had reached the next town down the road.

"These criminals are wanted for crimes committed in the area. If seen, report them to the authorities immediately!" read a wanted poster pasted to a board in the new town. There were rough sketches of us, apparently drawn from eyewitness reports.

Good thing they'd only seen us in the dark. The sketches had very few details that could be used to identify us. Then I saw it . . . The poster included a sketch of Raph-chan. That would give us away in a heartbeat, so we'd have to hide her.

"Raph-chan. Sorry, but if anyone sees you then they'll know that we're the ones that freed Filo."

"Raful!" she barked. With a puff of smoke, she transformed into an ofuda that fit in my hand. The design on the slip of paper moved back and forth. I guess I could call for Raph-chan at any time.

Kizuna did the same thing with Chris.

As for Filo . . . Unfortunately she'd spent more time in the show, so the drawing of her was actually very accurate. No one would mistake her—she was a young girl with wings on her back, after all. Kizuna read the poster and said that it included information about how we had stolen Filo.

"Pii!"

Filo turned into her humming fairy form and hid inside of my armor.

"They say that news travels fast, but it's kind of amazing that the news beat us here."

"They made quick work of it, didn't they?"

We could probably escape without too much trouble, but how long would we be able to keep it up?

"What did they do?" I heard a passerby comment on the poster. I decided to listen in on the gossip.

"They kidnapped that angel girl from the next town over—the one you could pay to see."

"Are you sure a real angel didn't come and take her? I heard she vanished."

They were making it sound like Kaguya-Hime.

Considering how Japanese the country looked, I guess that sort of story fit with the scenery.

But maybe without even meaning it to be, the townsfolks' gossip was pretty close to the truth.

We'd better keep moving.

"What should we do about leveling her up?"

Filo was at level 1, just like I'd been.

Man . . . What if we were all returned to level 1 when we crossed between the worlds?

"She's like Rishia. If I'm with Kizuna then we won't level up, but Rishia and Filo should get experience, so there shouldn't be too much trouble. At least we got over the first hurdle."

My own levels had progressed well, and I had managed to power up my weapons a fair bit, too.

But . . .

"The real question is what happened to Filo. Why isn't she a filolial anymore?"

That's right. Filo had been turned into something called a humming fairy instead.

She could still transform into her human form, but that would get us noticed by the authorities.

"Filo, I'm sure you already know this, but don't transform into human form. They'll catch you again if you do."

"Pii!" she chirped from the space between my plates of armor. She didn't seem very worried.

"I was hoping we could use Filo to pull a carriage for us. How are we supposed to get around now?" If we had Filo in her filolial form to help, we could have covered a lot of distance very quickly. I'd been counting on it, but it's not what we got. Instead she was stuck as some other monster, something from this world.

"We could call for a human-powered rickshaw. We have

enough money for it. What do you think?"

" . . . Who's going to pull it?"

"Considering what we've got to work with, probably you, Naofumi. You probably have some skill that would make it easier, don't you?"

"Ha! Don't make me laugh!"

How awful would that be? Rishia, Kizuna, and Filo all lounging inside while I tugged at a rickshaw? But as for Filo, I could just have her pull it in her human form. We could go on a journey, pulled along by a little girl.

It sounded crazy, but Filo actually had pulled a carriage while she was in human form before. It wouldn't look good, though—it wouldn't look good at all. Plus, we'd really stand out in a crowd.

"Filo, do you want to pull a carriage?"

"Pii!" she shook her head no.

I had no idea what sort of creature a humming fairy was, but it seems they didn't like to pull carriages.

For the moment, we needed to focus on keeping up our momentum. We didn't need anything in the town, so we just walked right through it and kept on going. Once we were out of town, I took Filo out of my pocket.

She quickly turned into her human form and jumped in front of me.

"Whew!"

"We better not let anyone see you in human form, at least until we make it out of this country."

"It was so scary!"

"I bet it was. You sounded really scared."

"Thank you, master!" Her stomach grumbled loudly. "Master, I'm hungry!"

"Yeah, I bet you are," I said, handing her some dried fruit we'd bought at the market.

She greedily stuffed them into her cheeks.

"I want . . ."

"Don't talk with your mouth full."

"I want more!"

Her stomach was actually rumbling as she ate. It was a pretty impressive feat. I wondered if it had something to do with the fact that her monster form was still a chick. Maybe she was still growing.

When she was in human form, she used magic to form her shape. But maybe when she crossed over to this world, her monster form was returned to a baby. I would have to find an authority on the subject to ask them about it.

"Kizuna and I won't get experience from it, but we should probably take a road that will lead us to lots of monsters."

"We could go fishing, too!" Kizuna said, grabbing her fishing rod and flashing a smile.

What was the deal with her? Did she really like fishing that much?

"Fishing huh . . . If you can get food for Filo we could do some—as long as it doesn't take very long."

"I can catch more fish here than I can in Japan, but it can take longer to get a bite."

"No fishing then. Either that or break the rules and catch them with your hands or something."

"I would never! There is a code of honor among us fishermen! I cannot break it!"

Kizuna was even more into fishing than I thought. But there must have been "illegal" ways to catch fish in a world like this. Maybe she could use thunder magic to hit a river with a lightning bolt, and then all the fish would just float to the surface. Seemed like a good idea to me.

Why did she have to be so particular about it? Is that what qualified her to be a hero?

. . . Yeah right.

"Well, hunting is easy enough, so I could always do that. You've got some more friends on your side, too. Just don't forget what we came here for."

"How could I? I'm here to find Raphtalia," I said, touching Raph-chan's ofuda. I seriously could not relax without Raphtalia nearby. I was almost thankful to Raph-chan for being there, because she was the closest I could get to Raphtalia for the moment.

Having her there made me feel a little better.

"Hey, master?"

"What?"

"Who is this lady?"

Filo certainly waited long enough to ask about Kizuna . . . They'd already spent the whole night together.

"I'm Kizuna Kazayama. Naofumi and I have been traveling together. I'm one of the four holy heroes from this world."

"Oh wow! Nice to meet you, fishing lady!"

Filo had a tendency to refer to people by whatever they happened to be holding.

"Sorry, Filo, but Kizuna's weapon isn't actually that fishing rod."

"That's right," Kizuna said, changing her weapon into all sorts of different things before Filo's sparkling eyes.

"What? What? What? Wow!" Filo shouted while she followed the rapidly changing weapon with her eyes.

"So, Filo, what do you think I am?"

"Um . . ." For possibly the first time ever, Filo didn't seem to know what to say.

Kizuna looked like she was really enjoying herself.

"Though I have to say, I don't mind being called 'fishing lady.' I kind of think of myself that way."

"Then stop playing with Filo."

"I was just having a good time."

"Okay, I'll call you . . . Kizuna ne-chan."

What? Filo actually learned her name?

But "ne-chan"? That felt kind of weird, considering how much Kizuna looked like a barely legal loli-girl.

"Naofumi, you look like you're thinking about something nasty."

She noticed! I looked away.

"Why are you looking away?"

"Do you care?"

"Maybe a little."

"I just thought it was funny that she called you ne-chan, even though you look like an underage loli-girl."

"Hey now!" Kizuna snapped.

Filo ignored our conversation and interjected, "I shouldn't call you Kizuna ne-chan?"

"No, that's just fine. Nice to meet you, Filo-chan."

"Yay!"

"Shouldn't you be Kizuna-chan?"

"Naofumi."

I looked away again.

Kizuna and Filo shook hands, and then Kizuna changed the subject. "Okay, so how about we look for Glass while doing some monster hunting to help Filo-chan level up?"

"Good idea. I'm worried about her levels, but we can focus on them once we get somewhere safe."

We had to focus on finding Raphtalia for now.

I activated the slave magic again to see if it worked. Just like last time, it didn't.

We were going to have to depend on Raph-chan to find her.

What if she had been captured and abused like Filo had been? I don't even know what I would do if that were the case.

If Filo was Kaguya-Hime, then Raphtalia . . . Raph-chan . . . was Bunbuku Chagama.

I just hoped it wasn't Kachi-Kachi Yama.

"We're going to stop in the towns we pass through, right?"

"Do we need to? We've got the shikigami to lead us."

I guess that was true. But we should still try to gather whatever information we could. Who knew when we might need it?

"The demi-humans in this world are mostly elves and dwarves, right? People with beast ears and tails are sort of rare, right?"

"Yeah, I don't see them very often."

That didn't bode well for Raphtalia. Someone might have tried to capture her.

I hoped she was alright, but I was starting to worry that she'd been captured just like Filo had. Hopefully, she was still with Glass and the others. Glass could probably protect her—she was strong enough to defeat the other three heroes without breaking a sweat.

We kept pressing onwards, helping Rishia and Filo gain some levels along the way.

Chapter Thirteen: The Hunting Hero's Skills

"Ah—It's so gooooood!"

That night, I cut up some monsters we killed and grilled them over a fire for Filo.

Raph-chan was eating a lot, too—and smiling the whole time.

The sun had gone down, and we were camping out for the night.

"Do you like that, Filo-chan?"

"Yeah!"

"Naofumi sure is a good cook."

"I hate waiting for the blood to drain out, though."

Monsters were full of blood when you killed them, which didn't taste very good. They were very gamey meats, which I tried to hide with spices. It worked a little, but the meat still struck me as pretty stinky.

"Can't you use some skills to get around it? I have some skills that help with breaking down monster corpses."

"I guess . . ."

It was true. She had better skills when it came to butchering monsters. When she did it, we ended up with higher-quality meat.

. . . But it still tasted gamey.

I guess it didn't matter, as long as Filo and Rishia didn't mind—and they didn't seem to.

Filo was definitely in the middle of a growth spurt, because her stomach was constantly rumbling. It reminded me a lot of when I'd first started to raise her back in Melromarc. She was a real pig back then.

However, she was gaining levels unexpectedly fast. She had already reached level 30.

That must be how the opening game functioned in this world.

As if to keep up with her rising levels and food intake, Filo's monster form was changing, too.

I thought that her monster form might mature into something like a filolial, but instead she had grown into a falcon-like monster.

"What sort of monster is a humming fairy?"

"Oh, they're birds that really like music. They turn into all sorts of different forms as they grow up."

"That's right! Master, lookie!" Filo said, tottering away from us.

Then she started to flap her wings.

Filolials can't fly, though they can jump pretty well.

So even though Filo had wings on her back when in human form, they were basically just decorations. They didn't move very much. She could use them in battle or open them up and catch the wind, though. That way she could dodge attacks quickly. So they weren't useless, but she certainly couldn't use them to fly.

But . . .

Filo lifted off of the ground.

What? But filolials can't fly! But then again . . . I guess Filo was a humming fairy now, so maybe that meant that she could fly.

"What do you think? I can fly!"

"Wow, that's amazing."

Filo's monster half changed somehow when we crossed between worlds.

"That might let you use a whole new fighting style when you're in your human form."

"Yeah! Flying is fun!"

Well, there was nothing wrong with that. If Filo could fly now, that sounded like good news to me.

"What forms of attack do humming fairies generally use?"

"Well, they are birds, so they normally attack like other birds—with their claws. They are also great singers and can manipulate sounds"

"Filo, can you use any of your skills from when you were a filolial?"

"Um . . . I'm not strong enough to use them now, but I think I might be able to when I get stronger!"

She could probably still use Haikuikku and Spiral Strike.

With a puff of smoke, she transformed back into a bird and perched on my shoulder. She had the same coloring as she did when she was in her filolial queen form, but she was now a sleek falcon-like monster—nothing like the plump penguin-owl hybrid shape of the filolial queen.

She was actually pretty cool and just large enough to fit on my shoulder. She was kind of cute, too.

"Is she fully matured now?"

"No."

"I'm not?"

"She's at the middle stage of growth, called a humming falcon. She still has a few more stages to go through as she matures."

"Sounds pretty complicated. No more specifics?"

"I wouldn't call myself an expert, but I think the forms change as her levels go up. I also once heard a story about a legendary humming fairy . . ."

I didn't like the sound of that. It made me wonder if I'd run into another version of Fitoria or something.

"Master!"

"Hey, she can talk in her monster form?"

"She must have learned? I hear they can learn to talk, the same way that parrots can."

Ah, like Polly-want-a-cracker kind of stuff?

Everyone knows that birds can be pretty smelly. She was no exception.

"Rafu?"

Raph-chan, on the other hand, smelled great. She always kept herself clean, so she smelled way better than Filo.

"From what I've heard, they can mature into different forms depending on the circumstances. I wonder what Filo-chan will end up as?"

"I can turn small, too!" Filo chirped. With a flash of light, she turned back into a little chick.

That reminded me—when Filo was in her filolial form, she could still change back and forth between her filolial queen form and her normal filolial form. She might not be able to hold each form for a long time, but it would be convenient if she had a lot of different forms available. Filo could be a real handful.

"If she can fly with us on her back, it might be a good way to get around."

"Back in the world I came from, there are flying dragons that get used that way. Do you have them here?"

"Yeah. Humming fairies can do that."

That would be great! She had always been a bird that was basically a replacement for horses. If she could fly, that would be even better.

"Here we have European dragons and Asian dragons. If

she can turn into different types of humming fairies, then she must be really talented!"

"Tee-hee!"

"Yeah, yeah. Whatever. You're amazing."

We went back and forth like that for a little while, and then Rishia joined the conversation. "Filo, would you mind speaking with me for a little while? I'd like to learn as much about this world's language as possible."

Rishia waved Filo over and they started looking at some written letters closely. Had she really already figured out how to read the language? I was reliant on my shield to translate for me, so I hadn't learned anything that would be of help to her.

"Okay! I . . . um . . . I guess I've picked up a little bit while I've been here!" Filo hopped over to Rishia and started explaining things. "Okay, so 'hello' is, um . . . 'hello'! And 'food' is . . ."

The only problem was that Filo was terrible at explaining things. Rishia scowled in confusion and looked like she was trying really hard to listen.

With any luck they might figure it out. Who knows?

I looked up at the night sky and worried about Raphtalia.

I wasn't very worried about Glass and her friends. They could take care of themselves. But Raphtalia . . .

I'd managed to meet up with all of my companions since we were split up crossing between worlds . . . everyone but her.

I hoped she was alright. I hoped she wasn't sitting somewhere alone, crying.

I pictured her that way, and then she grew angry in my imagination, indignantly shouting, "I'm not a child anymore!"

Filo turned into a little chick when we crossed over. What if Raphtalia was a child again? That would make the coming battles difficult.

Even worse—what if she had been transformed into a different kind of demi-human? She'd lose her characteristic tanuki ears and tail. That would make her face look different, too. What if I didn't recognize her? Maybe the slave spell would still work . . .

We continued our journey.

Then, a little while later . . .

"Thank you very much!"

Rishia had used a little of our money to go to a shop that looked like a bookstore. She bought a book and came back to meet us, carrying it under her arm.

That was all that had happened, but it made me notice something.

"Rishia, you . . ."

"Hm? What? Is something wrong?"

"You understand the language here?"

"Oh, yes! I studied very hard, and then Filo helped me perfect my pronunciation!" Rishia proclaimed, looking very boastful.

She had learned a whole new language just by reading over some books for a few days? What was with this girl? Her stats were just as bad as they'd ever been, but I couldn't deny that there was a genius sleeping inside her.

Back in the last world, she'd known other languages besides what they spoke in Melromarc. She could read other alphabets, too.

But she figured out how to read and speak this world's language in only a week?

Rishia . . . you've got to get out more. She was obviously better suited to studying than to wielding a sword.

"It took me forever to learn the language here," Kizuna said, wiping cold sweat from her forehead.

"Is it so difficult? Sure, there are some differences, but . . ." she looked puzzled by our confusion. Was she so smart that she couldn't even understand why we would have trouble?

But wait . . . Her stats were so much lower than other people's. That had to be a hint to the mystery. There must have been invisible stats, like intuition and intelligence, that all of her points had been allocated, to.

"You . . . You're really wasting all your talent on something you're not suited for."

The poor thing. I kind of pitied her.

It wasn't that she couldn't be useful in battle, but she was definitely better suited to a back-line support position, somewhere that a hero could protect her while she contributed to the fight.

God, Itsuki was so stupid! She should have sat him down and taught him a foreign language. That would have shown him. Then he wouldn't have been so rude to her—and to me.

Not that you could teach him or anything. He wouldn't listen.

"Feh . . . Why are you looking at me like that? You look like you pity me . . ."

"Hm?"

Actually, Filo was smart. She learned to speak our human language, and it only took her three days! I hadn't given it much thought until now, but it was actually pretty amazing.

Both of them seemed to have picked up most of the language in this world. There were two geniuses here that could learn languages really quickly, even without legendary weapons to translate for them!

"Rafu?"

"You don't have to talk, Raph-chan."

I had my hands full with Filo. I didn't need two talking pets.

"Boooo! Master is thinking mean things!"

Whatever.

Anyway, I figured it was safe to assume that Rishia's stats had been allocated to categories that weren't listed in the stats menu. I'd known she had an excellent memory ever since I spoke with her back on the Cal Mira islands.

Back when Itsuki saved her from a nasty situation, she was immediately able to remember that Filo and I had happened to walk by them on that same day.

Viewed from that perspective, she was really impressive.

"Hey, Rishia."

"What?"

"What did you study back in your world?"

Her family had been swindled out of all their money, so she must have done all her studying on her own.

"Until the waves came, I studied at a school in Faubrey."

"Oh really?"

Hm? That reminded me. I think the queen had said that Bitch studied at a school in Faubrey, too. Rishia and Bitch were probably within a few years of each other, too.

"How were your grades?"

"Aside from gym, they were pretty good. I worried so much I was never able to pick a major, though . . ."

I don't think I had ever seen Rishia respond to a question with so much confidence, so I assumed that her grades must have actually been fantastic. She looked like the kind of girl that would whine about how they hadn't studied at all, only to get perfect scores on all the tests.

She wasn't that great with magic, or with a sword, but if she was as smart as she seemed to be, then she would probably make a great scholar. Had she been born at the right place and time, she could have gotten a really good job. Poor Rishia.

Still, she was so indecisive that she hadn't managed to choose a major. That didn't bode well for her.

"Hey, Rishia," Kizuna said. "Will you teach me, too? I don't know if I'll be able to keep up, but I'll try!"

"Of course, I'll try."

Kizuna quickly turned around.

What was wrong?

"Ah, so she's so smart that she'll 'try' to teach me? Did you hear that?"

"Fehhhhhhhh!" Rishia whimpered, caught in Kizuna's trap.

"She must really be something?"

"Yeah, but it's not who she wants to be. She wants to be a champion of justice, fierce on the battlefield."

"That's totally not where she should be spending her energy!"

"I feel the same way. But she made a promise—a promise to get stronger."

"Naofumi-san . . ."

Kizuna and I went back and forth commenting on Rishia's qualities for a little while longer.

Chapter Fourteen: Return Dragon Vein

"This just in! Come have a look!" a man shouted in the streets, waving what appeared to be a newspaper.

The townsfolk shuffled passed him, snapped up papers, and stared at them wide-eyed.

I grabbed one, too, and showed it to Kizuna.

"Can you read this?"

"Let's see . . . It says that the holder of the katana of the vassal weapons was found but was able to escape. Now the whole country is searching for them."

"There's a katana vassal weapon here?"

A katana? Hm . . . Katana are pretty cool. I'd seen plenty of them in shonen manga over the years. They were probably one of the top three weapons used by protagonists.

Back in the world I came from, one of the holy weapons was a sword, but Ren used it, which kind of ruined the category's appeal for me.

Anyone from this world that used a katana would probably be really condescending and boastful. I'm not sure why I pictured them that way, but I did.

We'd better keep an eye out to avoid any unnecessary trouble.

"I'd always heard that no one had been chosen to wield the katana of the vassal weapons. It's stored under heavy security in an official government building in the capital. People can look at it, but apparently it's very difficult to even be considered for selection to wield it."

Considering how important the vassal weapons were, it only made sense that it would be carefully protected.

I didn't know how Glass or L'Arc ended up getting their vassal weapons, but I imagined it was a pretty difficult process. I kept picturing it like the sword in the stone—only capable of being drawn by certain special people.

. . . ?

Weren't the seven star heroes supposed to be just like the holders of the vassal weapons of this world? If there was an equivalent of the vassal weapons in our world, it was looking even more likely that it was the seven star heroes, especially because only chosen people were capable of wielding them.

Ost had said something about that.

It wasn't like anyone could just walk up and use the weapons, but still, if someone on bad terms with the government got their hands on a vassal weapon, they could probably do a lot of damage. That was why the government had to protect them.

"The katana is also a symbol of national strength here. It sounds like they are hot on the trail of whoever has it."

"Hm . . ."

Whoever it was, they must have been chosen to wield the weapon, so why would they run?

"Sounds strange to me."

"How so?"

"It almost sounds like all the specific information about the person with the vassal weapon has been intentionally omitted. It doesn't say if this person is alone or accompanied, if it's a man or a women . . . It doesn't say anything. Are there two men? Two women?"

What could explain the chase? Maybe the person who took the katana wasn't from this country at all, so they were trying to bring it across the border to another country. It was the sort of incident that could trigger a war.

I remembered the queen of Melromarc saying how much international tension was caused by the summoning and management of the holy heroes. Any country that could manage to control the heroes, or get them on their side in a conflict, would be much more powerful as a result.

If anyone with nefarious or political intentions were to be chosen by the vassal weapon, it was only natural that they would try to escape with it.

"Hm?" Rishia and Filo both cocked their heads.

Oh, I forgot to mention that I was holding Raph-chan, and she was constantly pointing in the direction we should go. She was so quiet and cute. We continued in the direction she indicated, and we came across a checkpoint.

"Stop right there! There are wanted criminals past this point. We apologize for the inconvenience, but please take a detour," barked a samurai-like man who blocked the road with a spear.

I was taken aback for a second, but realizing that it would be best to avoid any unnecessary conflict, we did as we were told and took a detour. But when we did, Raph-chan started pointing in a different direction. That settled it—we must have been circling around the area where Raphtalia and the others were.

I was immediately relieved, but I started to worry just as quickly, because it sounded like they were stuck in a place with criminals—like they were caught in the eye of a storm. Worse, there was the possibility that Glass and her friends were caught up in conflict with the wielder of the katana of the vassal weapons.

My heart thumping in my chest, I turned to Kizuna and asked, "What should we do?"

"Do we have a choice? We sneak in over the rooftops."

"Wait. There are other options."

"Like what?"

"Filo."

"What?"

Filo was a humming falcon now—that meant she could fly.

Could there be a better way to scope out the situation?

She was riding on my shoulder at the moment, which was her new favorite place to sit. She seemed to prefer staying in monster form these days, probably because of the trauma she'd suffered while in human form.

When we went to a new town, she stayed in monster form and tried to never leave my shoulder. Between her on my shoulder and Raph-chan in my arms, I looked more like a monster trainer than a Shield Hero.

"Go fly around for a bit and see if you can't find Raphtalia in there."

"But . . . But what if they catch me?" she said, clearly scared.

Considering she looked like a normal bird, she probably did have reason to be worried. A hunter might just shoot her out of the sky with an arrow.

"You'll be fine. You just look like any other bird in the sky. Besides, we left the country that captured you a while ago."

"Promise? Promise I'll be okay? If someone attacks me, you'll save me?"

"Of course I will. Have I ever lied to you?"

"Um . . . Yup!"

"Okay, I guess I did. But I'm not lying now. Will you do it for me?"

She didn't even have to go far. She could stay within sight

of us. I just wanted her to fly up and look from a higher vantage point. There shouldn't be any trouble.

Even if she were to be attacked, we'd know immediately.

"Okay!"

Before I sent her into the air, I decided to check on the slave spell one more time. I opened the menu, and I could hardly believe my eyes.

Raphtalia was no longer listed there.

What the hell was happening?

I broke out into a cold sweat, and a shiver ran up my spine. Something was wrong.

What if she . . . What if she was dead?

"Rafu?"

I hugged Raph-chan close and tried to calm my pounding heart.

No . . . I knew it wasn't true. I could feel it. She was alive, and she was somewhere close by.

"Rafuuu . . ." Raph-chan put her paws on her cheeks as if she were embarrassed.

I patted her on the head.

"Master, what are you doing?"

"Nothing, it's fine. Go on up and check things out. Raph-chan, you keep pointing us toward Raphtalia."

"Rafu!" she barked, and pointed again in the same direction she had been before.

That meant . . . Right—Raphtalia was still alive. There had to be a different explanation for why she'd vanished from the slave spell menu. The spell must have been removed somehow.

Right. That's the explanation I decided to stick with until I heard differently.

"Okay, Filo, head on up."

"Okay!" she said, flapping her wings and soaring up into the sky above us. I watched her grow smaller as she pulled away from the ground.

She seemed safe. There were no arrows flying at her yet.

Eventually, she came fluttering back down to us.

"Um . . . It looks like some people are being chased!"

"Who? Who's being chased?"

"They were wearing hoods, so I couldn't see. I was going to get closer, but they were being chased by scary monsters, so I flew back here."

"Scary monsters?"

What was going on? Were there monsters in this town? It was unlikely that they were wild. They were probably like Filo—serving at someone's bidding.

"Then I guess we better get in there, at least to check that our friends aren't the ones being chased."

Kizuna flung her fishing lure and hooked it onto a nearby rooftop and then used the reel to pull herself up. It was a very quick process.

"Air Strike Shield! Second Shield! Dritte Shield!"

As for myself, I used my skills to form a makeshift set of stairs and climbed on them to reach the rooftop.

"Come on, Rishia."

"Feh . . ."

Once we were all up on the roof, we quickly and quietly moved away from the guards that blocked the way into town. As we made our way over the rooftops, Raph-chan and Chris slowly began pointing in a different direction. Finally, we came to an empty lot, where there was a fair distance we'd have to cross to get to the next roof over.

We decided to climb down first and then make our way back up the other side.

We jumped down to the ground and prepared to cross the lot, but there was a group of people in robes waiting for us.

"Damn . . ."

We were supposed to be finding Raphtalia! We didn't have time to deal with these people. I didn't want to end up meeting whoever was chasing these guys. At least we had covered our faces with masks before entering the town.

Maybe we should run away with Portal Shield until we could figure out a better plan.

I readied my shield and prepared for a fight, but then . . .

"Raful!" Raph-chan chirped, pointing energetically to one of the people before us.

Chris was doing the same thing, thrusting his wing at the group of robed people.

"Naofumi, you don't think . . ."

What?"

"Could it be?"

I slowly removed my mask to let them see my face. Kizuna and Rishia did the same things.

Then, as if the robed people had completely lost the will to fight, they lowered their weapons and stepped forward.

"Kiddo! Is that Kizuna with you?!" the tall man at the front of the group shouted as he removed his hood.

It was L'Arc.

Then he pulled off his robe to reveal clothes that looked like the Shinsengumi. He must have been trying to blend in with the rest of the people in this country.

Apparently the simple fabric clothes around here still had decent defense stats. The light-blue patterns on the haori actually suited him pretty well. He could get away with any fashion he wanted.

To think it was L'Arc and the others that were being chased! I mean, I knew it was a possibility, but I had tried not to think about it.

And we just ran into them in the street! What a coincidence!

A person behind L'Arc came running over to Kizuna and shouted, "Kizuna! Where have you been this whole time?! And what are you doing with Naofumi?!"

It was Glass. She pulled off her hood and robes to reveal tears in her eyes. Then she hugged Kizuna close.

It was unbelievable. Glass had always been so stern and cold. I'd never even imagined her making such an emotional display. Of course, everyone had someone or something they cared about, but it still felt weird to see such a cool person look so happy.

"I'm very glad to see you again, but our pursuers will be here soon. Be on the lookout!" Therese said, removing her robe. She was wearing a hakama covered in a pattern suggestive of gemstones.

Had it been made with aizome? Maybe not . . .

Whenever she moved, the pattern itself seemed to move as well. Was I just imagining it?

There was still one person wearing their hood. Was it Raphtalia?

The person came running toward me—and Raph-chan was pointing.

"Ra . . . Raphtalia?"

"Yes."

She pulled off her robe to show me her face. It was her—Raphtalia.

She had rounded, fuzzy ears, long soft hair, deep eyes that you could lose yourself in, and a puffy tail that swayed beautifully.

I hadn't seen her in so long—she was more beautiful than I remembered.

She must have been happy to see me, too, because she came running over with a big smile on her face. She was dressed like a miko, in red and white robes.

I felt something unexpected when I looked at her—something like an electric shock.

I looked at her again. The miko clothes were very simple. There was a white cloth around her shoulders, embroidered with red thread that almost seemed to form a bow. But the red didn't interfere with the white cloth at all—it was so delicate that it somehow emphasized how white the white really was.

Below that she wore a deep red hakama. The outfit suited her very well.

It also seemed to have been specially made to accommodate her bushy tail.

She wore white socks and straw Japanese-style sandals.

Yeah . . . She looked really, really good in that outfit.

When we defeated Kyo and went back to our own world, I hoped she would still wear it.

I could hardly believe the way I was reacting. I didn't like miko any more than your average otaku, but I could hardly take my eyes off of her.

"You're finally here, Mr. Naofumi!"

"Sorry it took so long."

"No . . . I know how hard it must have been . . . Were you alright? Was everything okay?"

"Mostly. A lot happened."

We were thrown into an inescapable labyrinth. We got out to find ourselves behind enemy lines. Then we made our way to the capital, charged the security guards . . .

Yeah . . . a lot had happened.

"That outfit looks great on you."

"A compliment? From you? It feels a little strange."

Did I really not compliment her?

"You should keep dressing like that when we get back to where we came from."

"Do you like it that much?"

"I think it looks good on you."

She blushed. She must have been embarrassed.

I guess she was still a kid.

"Doesn't it? I thought so, too!" L'Arc shouted. I wondered if he was the one that picked out her outfit. He clearly knew what he was doing—his perverted peeping had served him well.

We were so caught up in our reunion that it took the howl of an approaching beast to remind me where we were.

We'd relaxed for too long.

"Kizuna, use the ofuda."

"Hold on," she said, slapping an ofuda to her forehead and concentrating.

But . . .

"It won't work. Something is blocking the signal. We'll have to get out of here to call for him. And it doesn't look like L'Arc and the others will be able to use Return Transcript, either."

"Should we use Portal Shield?"

"Can we?"

"There might be too many people."

I had never checked to see how many people could use Portal Shield at once. But this wasn't the time to start worrying about it.

I sent Raphtalia a party invitation first.

"Portal . . ." Before I could finish saying it, something felt strange. And it wasn't just me. Everyone else was feeling it, too.

An icon blinked in my field of view.

Teleportation not available.

What? This was the first time I'd been unable to use Portal Shield since I woke up in this world. There was only one other time that I'd felt this strange—when we were fighting the Spirit Tortoise.

"Well, well . . . Did you really think you were going to get away from me? Hm . . . Looks like there's a few more of you than there was . . ."

I looked to the source of the voice to find who had been chasing Raphtalia and the horde of monsters he was controlling.

"You! It must be destiny that we'd meet here! I'll make you pay for last time!"

Whoever it was spoke condescendingly to us.

I'd seen him before.

That's right, it was the supposed genius scientist that we'd run into when we used the dragon hourglass to teleport out of the capital.

"Oh yeah, you were there, weren't you? I can't remember your name though . . ."

I'd rather have avoided meeting him again, but I was honestly starting to look forward to the fight.

He seemed to have more women following him than last time. Something about him really irked me. Maybe it was just that he reminded me of Motoyasu.

"I'll get you back for last time!"

"Criminals! Come with us peacefully!"

"Yeah! How dare you embarrass us?" he smiled. Surrounded by his gaggle of women, he looked very pleased with himself.

These people were starting to really piss me off. Was I the only one that thought that these women might not really like him? What was he trying to compensate for by keeping them around all the time?

Actually, I probably looked the same way to him. Better to drop the subject altogether.

"You mean you're in our country but you don't know my name?!"

"You fools!"

"Then listen up! I'll tell you whom you stand before. I am the hope of the people, the greatest alchemist in all the land . . ."

Okay, actually he wasn't the same as Motoyasu. Women liked him for his affected sense of charm. I started to think that this guy was actually more like Itsuki. What made me feel that way?

The never-ending preface to announcing his name took so long that I actually missed his name when he finally said it.

"—THAT'S who I am! Now you will know true fear! There's no reasoning with the likes of you!"

"Sure, whatever. Hey—what did you say your name was?" I couldn't remember what he'd said.

Maybe it was because of all the things I'd been through with Itsuki, but even if I could remember these types of faces, I couldn't bring myself to care enough to learn their names.

"You insolent fool! I'll carve my name into your chest! You won't forget it then!"

If he was so unimpressed with me, why did he want me to remember his name so badly? He made no sense.

A large white tiger prowled behind him and roared. The beast looked wild. A rope of drool dangled from its gaping mouth.

But something felt off about this whole thing. I'd spent so much time in this new world that my intuition had gotten sharper than it had been.

"It certainly looks like you are in cahoots with the thieves. It should come as no surprise that I find you repulsive."

"Thieves? What are you talking about?"

"Mr. Naofumi . . ." Raphtalia said, looking at me with repentant eyes. Then she opened her robe and showed me the weapon she had hidden inside. She was holding an unsheathed katana.

Let's see here—time to review the facts. Whoever had the katana of the vassal weapons was on the run . . . and Raphtalia had disappeared from the slave spell menu.

And the authorities were after whoever had the katana . . .

These jerks were probably the people chasing after it . . . but . . .

I knew what was going on, but I wasn't ready to admit it to myself yet.

"Why did you run? Wouldn't the citizens respect you? Greet you with open arms?"

Raphtalia was being pursued by the government. She was being treated like a thief—even though she was with people as powerful as Glass and L'Arc.

"You see . . ."

Chapter Fifteen: The Katana's Choice

I'll try to sum up Raphtalia's story.

Raphtalia, Glass, L'Arc, and Therese found themselves in enemy lands. They were thrown into a prison that kept them from utilizing the power of their levels. It was even worse than the place where Kizuna and I had been locked up.

The prison constantly kept magic spells that limited the abilities of its prisoners and then gave an equal amount of power to the prison guards. At least their prison was theoretically escapable, though, unlike the labyrinth we were stuck in.

Anyway, cooperating with Glass and L'Arc, Raphtalia was able to escape by using her illusion magic. Even if her power was restrained, the wielder of the katana of the vassal weapons wasn't going to lose so easily.

We'd relied so much on Raph-chan to find her that we completely ignored the information available to the public at the guilds. If Raphtalia and Glass escaped from prison and the whole country was after them, it would have been all over the news.

Why didn't they travel in secret, like we'd been doing?

"How did you get the katana? Didn't that just put a target on your back?"

"If our actions came to light, it would give the enemy an excuse to attack our country. We wanted to avoid that, so we tried to manipulate the news, which backfired on us," explained Glass.

That would explain why we hadn't been inundated with news about the escape.

They had to avoid it for political reasons. It wouldn't look good to put up wanted posters of the heroes that were supposed to be protecting the world. The katana was a symbol of national strength here, so they would obviously want to secretly dispose of whoever had it and go back to boasting about controlling an unassigned vassal weapon.

Those weapons really made things complicated. Anyone that got their hands on one would become an instant symbol of power.

The holy heroes that were summoned didn't have that problem, because the powers were limited to the person that had them. There was no competition involved.

The queen of Melromarc said that certain tools and items were necessary to summon the heroes, but procuring and managing those items must have been a lot easier than dealing with the vassal weapons.

Back in the world I'd come from, it was easy to check if the people who held the vassal weapons were alive or dead, which must have simplified some of the international diplomacy.

"Okay, so that's why you were so hard to find. What happened after that?"

"Well, after we escaped from the prison . . ."

They decided that they had to get out of the country, so they concealed their identities and travelled to the capital, hoping to use the dragon hourglass to escape. They were very powerful, so they planned to force their way to the hourglass if necessary. It was basically the same plan that Kizuna and I had decided on.

Glass and Raphtalia did some leveling up on the way to the capital.

"This girl here was really tiny, you know? She looked like she was ten years old," L'Arc explained.

"I thought her maturation might have reset. I guess I was right."

At least she hadn't turned into something else entirely, like Filo!

Maybe it would have been nice, if she could transform like Raph-chan, but I doubt Raphtalia would have been excited by that.

"Too bad she grew up so fast, eh, Kiddo? You probably wanted to see her as a child!"

"I've seen her like that before . . . Still, if I had the chance again, it would have been nice."

And in a miko outfit? That would have looked so good on her! She would have been so cute.

I better watch out. I was getting way too excited about these miko clothes.

Whatever. I would just have to cherish the memories I already had of Raphtalia's childhood. I made a mental note to ask L'Arc for details later.

"Mr. Naofumi!" Raphtalia shouted, her face red with anger.

"It wasn't easy, you know. Growing up again. I had to go through all those growing pains all over again."

"It's not just growing pains, is it?"

"What do you mean?"

"When you were little, you used to eat as much as Filo."

"I was growing!"

That was true. That was how demi-humans matured.

"Okay, so why do you have the katana?"

"When we got to the capital, they were in the middle of displaying the katana in the town square. A lot of people had arrived to compete for the nomination."

"Even if we were in enemy lands, we realized that another wielder of a vassal weapon may appear, so we split up and mixed in with the crowd to observe the event," Glass murmured softly. She looked upset. I was guessing the story didn't end well.

They were in enemy lands, but they still wanted to see what kind of person was using the vassal weapon there. Considering how crazy the man with the book of the vassal weapon was, I could understand why. On the other hand, if the holder in this land was reasonable, it might have been useful.

"Yeah, and then you all took off running! The country was seriously about to entrust the katana to me, but you had to show up!" interjected the genius scientist guy.

Ugh. I was about to lose it with this guy.

Didn't he care about avoiding war between the nations? If all he cared about was his own country, what were his thoughts about the waves?

"Then this guy came with a group of high-ranking officials and stood before the crowd. With everyone watching, he attempted to remove the sword . . ."

I tried to picture the scene in my mind. The obnoxious man before us looked at the katana where it sat, plunged deep into the heart of a boulder. The people in the crowd were on the edge of their seats, thinking they were about to witness the birth of a new hero. The guards were doing all they could to keep the crowd under control.

They guy walked forward slowly, one step at a time. He reached for the hilt . . .

But just before he could touch it, the blade flashed with blinding light and . . . flew from the stone and shot at the crowd like an arrow, only to land in Raphtalia's outstretched hand!

"And that was how the katana came to choose me to wield it."

"I should have predicted as much. After all, she was able

to cross between worlds with myself and L'Arc. We are only able to do so because we have the fan and scythe of the vassal weapons," explained Glass.

Raphtalia was very powerful.

She wasn't a hero, but she'd gotten through plenty of hard times with me. I could think of a lot of rough spots that I couldn't have survived without her.

"And?"

"This guy here didn't like the fact that I was chosen, so he had me declared a thief! Then he brought out these vicious beasts to chase us down! We ran for a long while, but they never let up."

"That katana was supposed to be mine! Therefore I will require its return!" the genius yelled at us again.

I looked over at Raphtalia, silently.

Honestly, I couldn't see why a vassal weapon from Glass's world had chosen Raphtalia to wield it. Aren't the people with the vassal weapons supposed to cross over to other worlds and kill the four holy heroes in the previous world? Wouldn't that mean that Raphtalia was now my enemy?

And why did it choose someone from another world?

It didn't make sense.

But then again, I'd been summoned from another world to be the Shield Hero. I guess that didn't make sense, either.

"I asked Therese and Glass to tell the katana that it had

chosen incorrectly. I asked them may times, but the katana will not leave me," Raphtalia said.

"Can't you let it go? If I could let this shield go, I'd have dropped it a long time ago."

What was this about talking to the weapons? If you talked to them, would they leave you alone? I wished I could be rid of the shield. Being stuck with no means of offense was no picnic.

Sure, I'd managed to put the shield to pretty good use, but I figure you should be able to protect people and also be able to do other things, too!

Fine.

"Shield, are you listening? Get out of here."

"Don't say that! You could lose everything!"

"I must kill you to reclaim my rightful place as the true owner of the katana!" the man screamed. The tiger behind him howled along with him.

"Oh please! Will you shut up for just a second?!" I yelled back at him.

I was getting really tired of listening to him complain. He was like a little kid that didn't get his way. He reminded me of the other three heroes—idiots, all of them.

"Alright, I think I understand. Basically, this guy doesn't like who the katana chose, so he's mobilized the whole country to hunt you down."

"Yes, that's about it. We've been able to fend for ourselves for a long while, but they just keep coming. We escaped from the capital a short while ago, and now we've run into Kizuna and Naofumi."

"Kizuna, Kiddo—you see the predicament we're in. Think you can help us out?" L'Arc asked.

As if I were some kind of hero?! Not that we would be of much use—neither of us could fight well against other people.

Besides, once we defeated these people, the country would keep sending more and more people out against us. If it didn't, then the government would look ineffectual and lose face. It couldn't let that happen, so it'd come after us with everything it had.

"Why don't you just show them what you've got? You're all pretty strong, aren't you?"

"They won't back off. These guys are pretty high-level, too."

"Heh. You may have vassal weapons, but no one from your country could ever hope to best us in battle. How foolish are you?"

"You're the fool! Blathering on and on just because you didn't get what you wanted!"

"What was that?!"

The vassal weapons were just like the holy weapons weren't they? Didn't they exist to protect the world? If the weapons were necessary to protect the world, how could this guy live with himself? He'd kill a hero just because he didn't like them!

That alone should explain why the katana didn't choose him.

"..."

Looking closer, I could that see Raphtalia, Glass, L'Arc, and Therese were all showing signs of exhaustion. Their journey must have been more difficult than ours had been.

I sighed and looked at Kizuna. She nodded.

"Fine. We can team up for a little while. I want to make Trash #2 pay for picking a fight with Raphtalia."

"Trash #2?!"

"Yeah, that's your name now. I know a piece of trash just like you back in the world I came from."

"You haven't changed a bit, Mr. Naofumi," Raphtalia remarked.

"Your nicknaming sensibilities are remarkable," Trash #2 said.

"Shut up. The point is that I've had it with pieces of trash like you!"

I stepped ahead of Raphtalia to protect her.

The enemy . . . Trash #2 . . . regarded my glare with condescension. He raised his hand.

. . . And two more tigers appeared behind him.

What was going on with these monsters? Were they the reason that I couldn't use Portal Shield?

"Rafu!" Raph-chan chirped, jumping up onto my shoulder.

"Thanks for the help, but you'd better hang back. These guys mean business," I said.

Raph-chan just wasn't strong enough to join the battle. She did what I said and ran over to sit by Raphtalia's feet.

"What is this little thing?"

"It's a familiar—they call them shikigami here. They made her with a ceremony for us. She led us to you."

"Rafu!"

"Oh . . . Is that so? Why does it . . . um . . . Why does it sound like it's saying my name?"

" . . ."

"You won't tell me?"

Oh jeez . . . But it wasn't my fault! I had to use something that would help us find Raphtalia.

"You see . . . Remember back when you were little and I cut your hair? I still had some hair stored in the shield, so we used it as a medium to make her."

"Oh, that's right . . . You used the shield to clean up all the hair . . . How dare you!"

"It's not my fault! They said that we had to use something of yours to make it work!"

"Rafu!"

Raph-chan jumped up and down and chirped at us both. It was like she wanted us to stop the fighting.

"Oh well. I understand."

"Rafu . . ." Raph-chan jumped up on Raphtalia's shoulders and pressed her forehead against Raphtalia's.

"Hm? What's . . ."

"What is it?"

"Oh. Something just popped up saying that the shikigami has been registered to me.

Hm . . . Oh, that's right. It must have been like how Glass and Kizuna made that penguin together.

"Um, Naofumi? We're kind of preparing for battle here. Can you focus please?"

The tigers were continuing to take slow steps toward us.

"What are these things?"

"The White Tiger is one of the holy beasts in our world. This seems to be a replica of it. It's like if someone made a replica of the Spirit Tortoise back in your world, Kiddo."

"What?!"

This thing was one the protective beasts from Glass's world?

What was it doing here? Weren't they supposed to be suppressed for now—isn't that what the blue hourglass was indicating?

"The White Tiger was defeated in the past, but they made a replica version of it to use in battle. They are considered a powerful weapon of war in this country. Kizuna—you better watch out."

"A protective beast? You mean the ones in the legends? Glass and I have heard something about this country using them. We've already fought them, haven't we?"

"Yes, and they were bigger. They aren't too powerful, but with this many of them, we may have trouble."

Even Kizuna knew about them, which meant that I was the only one in the dark!

"If you know all about them, will you tell me already?!"

"You didn't seem to be interested."

I guess she was right about that. I was really focused on trying to find Raphtalia. And if we had the time to sit and chat, I'd rather have used it on leveling up.

"Feh . . . We're fighting now, right?"

"Oh yeah. Things might get rough. These things are supposed to be pretty strong."

It would be great if she would awaken to her true power, like what had happened in the battle with Kyo. But I couldn't count on that happening, and she'd be in danger in the meantime. I better make sure she understands the situation.

"Rishia, I'm sure you understand this, but the people we are about to fight are trying to kill Raphtalia and Glass. Don't hold back."

"Oh . . . Okay!" She drew her weapon and readied it.

She didn't exactly fill me with confidence.

I wasn't going to place any bets on her. I'd just have to do what I could to make sure she didn't get herself killed.

"Imma do my best!" Filo said, turning into human form with a puff of smoke. She prepared to cast a supportive spell. It looked like her fighting style had changed substantially when we crossed between worlds. Not that I was complaining.

"Don't forget about us," Glass said.

"Yes," Therese echoed. They both readied themselves for battle.

We better choose our target.

"It looks like those White Tiger copies are preventing me from using Portal Shield. If we can get rid of them, I can teleport us out of here. Let's do it."

"Okay!"

"Hya!"

There were a lot of people in the fight, so we had to try to stay organized.

"Alright then. You may have the vassal weapon, but I'll show you what true power looks like!" Trash #2 shouted, drawing a katana from his waist.

He was surrounded by women and tigers.

"Naofumi, you know that I can't attack people, right? Can I leave the women up to you?"

"Got it. Kizuna, you focus on the tigers."

"No problem. They're my specialty."

The tigers roared, and the battle began.

Chapter Sixteen: No Incantations

I had to get a handle on what we were working with.

Without taking any unnecessary risks, the strongest shield I had access to was the Nue Shield. It didn't have the best counter-attacks. But I had used all the power-up methods I knew on it, so it had a very high defense rating. I hadn't been forced to delay powering it up because of any lack of materials.

Listing my team members in order of strength, I'd start with Glass, then L'Arc, Kizuna, Raphtalia, Therese, Filo, and end with Rishia. I had no idea if I should consider Chris or Raph-chan as fighters or not.

Chris was standing at the front to protect Kizuna and was in a staring contest with the tigers. Raph-chan was standing next to Raphtalia, watching the fight with her fur all puffed up like she was ready to join in.

If these White Tiger copies were really like the Spirit Tortoise, if they were really copied from one of this world's protective beasts . . . how strong should we expect them to be? Underestimating them would be a mistake, so I decided to think of them as opponents that even Glass would have trouble with.

As for their master, Trash #2 . . . He had all those women with him, and if the battle dragged on for too long, reinforcements would probably show up. If we ran away, they would keep chasing us, and the number of our pursuers would only increase with time.

We had a chance at victory . . . but only if we started soon.

"Ha!"

"Grrrrr!"

One of the tigers flashed its claws and ran for Kizuna and Glass.

Glass snapped open a fan and blocked its attack.

"You're form is all wrong!" Glass shouted, swinging the other fan to counter-attack. But the tiger was fast, and it leapt backwards to avoid being hit.

Its speed was impressive. These things were tiger-*like* monsters, right? Back in my world, I'd always heard the tigers were the strongest animals on land. That meant they were probably pretty strong in this world, too. And if they were copied from one of the world's four holy beasts, then depending on the game, they might be one of the final bosses.

But—I had to remind myself—this wasn't a game. Still, I expected them to be very powerful.

"Fehhh!"

"Rishia ne-chan! First Wind Cutter!"

A tiger leapt for Rishia, but I grabbed it by its back leg to stop it in time for Filo's wind spell to slice it in the neck.

It didn't do much damage. At least we stopped its attack.

Damn . . . Filo had always been one of my strongest attackers. If she wasn't doing much damage, then this battle was going to be tough.

"Don't move, Kiddo! Flying Circle!" L'Arc used a skill to send a disc of light flying at the tiger that I was still holding.

The disc slammed into the tiger and a spray of blood erupted from the wound, but it wasn't enough to seriously hurt the monster. It's white fur slowly turned red.

"Grrrrr!" the White Tiger roared with anger.

"Naofumi! Shining Stones! Crimson Flame!" Therese shouted, sending a ball of red flame hurtling at the tiger and me. Therese's balls of flame had a special property—they never burnt me.

"Grrrrr!"

The beast burst into flames and writhed in pain.

"Don't forget about me!"

"I'm not! Air Strike Shield!"

A shield appeared in mid-air to stop Trash #2's katana.

"What?!"

"I'm guessing you don't know what this shield is capable of, so you'd better be careful. I thought you'd figured that out the last time we met!"

He probably didn't realize that I wasn't capable of attacking on my own, which was all the more reason to make him wonder what I could do.

"Arrggh!"

"What?!"

I dug my feet into the ground and summoned all my might to throw the tiger at Trash #2. It flew through the air and slammed into him.

"Aghhh!"

It didn't do any damage to speak of, but it was enough to break an opening in his defenses—which was enough time for me to cast a spell.

I wanted to use the one that Ost had taught me—Liberation.

I had yet to cast it by myself, and I didn't yet understand how to set the range of its effect. But I had to do whatever I could to help the others in the battle, so I chose the next best thing.

"Zweite Aura!"

First, I'd start with Glass, which would help her deal out damage as quickly as possible. I'd cast support spells on everyone in order of their strength, which should maximize the utility of the spells.

"Thank you!" Glass shouted. She matched her breathing with Kizuna's, opened her fans, and used a spell so gracefully she looked like she was dancing.

"Circle Dance Zero Formation—Reverse Snow Moon Flower!"

The air filled with peels of flame, like dancing flower petals, which shot at the enemy. But they weren't enough to kill the tiger, which grunted and snorted at the petals that stuck to its face.

The monster was covered in small lacerations, but they weren't enough to turn the tide of battle.

"Shining Stones! Protection Powder!" Therese cast a spell that lowered the tiger's defense.

L'Arc found an opening and dashed at the monster, swinging his scythe with all his might. It dug deep into the monster's flesh, tearing through the skin and muscle and exposing the bone. The startled tiger leapt away.

I turned to Trash #2 and said, "Wish you hadn't been so condescending?"

He scowled, "The thieves think quite highly of themselves. I'll show you what I'm truly capable of!"

Trash #2 opened his hand and thrust his palm forward. Numerous balls of flame erupted from it and shot at us.

What? How did he do that? I never saw him cast a spell.

He probably knew that if he sent a big ball of flame at us, we'd block it and send it right back at him. That was why he opted to shoot a bunch of smaller ones.

"He didn't even have to use an incantation?!" Therese gasped, unable to believe her eyes.

I understood her surprise. Casting a spell normally involved chanting some incantations. I'd once read a story about someone that could manipulate their magic power without having to chant anything.

"How's that?"

"It's okay," I said, calmly blocking the balls of flame with my shield.

Based on what I'd seen so far, it was more powerful than a first-level spell but less powerful than a Zweite-level spell.

I guess they might have been difficult to defend against, which might have made them useful against someone with lower defenses than myself.

But the little balls of fire made me wonder what level the guy was at. Maybe he wasn't very strong at all. Maybe he could do some damage if he got a hit in when I wasn't expecting it, but from what I'd seen, I didn't think he'd be able to defeat us.

"You mustn't underestimate him. He has abilities worthy of one who holds a vassal weapon," Glass said, worry evident on her face.

I guess their levels probably were pretty high then.

"Hyaaaaaaa!"

"I'll make you pay!"

"Shooting Star Shield!"

Trash #2's women came running at us with their swords, but I deployed my Shooting Star Shield barrier to block them. It would be easier to block them all with the force field than it would be to try to stop each of their attacks separately.

Their attacks clattered against the barrier. The barrier had broken last time, but I'd powered up the shield substantially since then, and it looked like it was going to hold.

If the barrier would hold, then . . .

I rushed forward, using the barrier to push the enemy back.

"I'm going in!" Raphtalia shouted. The barrier threw the women off balance, and she rushed forward to take advantage of the opening.

"It won't work!" Trash #2 barked, sending a barrage of flames flying at Raphtalia to disrupt her attack.

She spun on her heels, swinging the katana around her to repel the balls of flame, and then jumped back behind me. She did it all in one fluid motion, and I have to say, she looked pretty cool doing it.

"Take this!" a woman shouted. She dropped the spear that the barrier had twisted in her hands, pulled a kodachi from her pocked, and leapt at me.

"Naofumi!" Rishia yelped, throwing the ofuda she'd received from Kizuna.

Probably because of the mysterious magic inside of it, the ofuda flew in a remarkable path across the battlefield and attached itself to the attacking woman's hand, which then burst into flames.

"Argh!" she shouted, running back behind Trash #2.

Rishia was doing pretty well for herself! Maybe she had a knack for throwing ofuda.

Actually, that reminds me of our battle with Kyo. She'd thrown a sword at Kyo and hit him with it. Maybe she was suited for throwing weapons.

"We're not finished with you yet!" Trash #2 shouted, shooting a number of magic spells at us quickly.

The first one was fire, then water, then wind, then light, and on and on. He kept throwing spell after spell at me, switching the element each time.

I didn't get out of it unscathed, but it also didn't hurt too much.

It was like I kept getting scratched or slapped.

"HA! Take that! And that! And that!"

The balls of magic were flying so fast that the air around us filled with dust, and it grew increasingly difficult to see.

"Zweite Aura!"

While the air was filled with dust and smoke, I took the opportunity to case boost spells on everyone, including myself. Once our stats were boosted, the already ineffectual spells raining down on us proved even less bothersome.

It was like walking in the rain without an umbrella.

"Grrrraw!" growled another tiger that leapt at us from the smoke.

The tigers were the enemy's main offensive players. I wanted to think that Trash #2 was concealing his true power to surprise us, but it really looked like he was already throwing everything he had at us.

"Kizuna! There's another tiger over here!"

"Yeah, there's a bunch of them! Give me a minute! Can't you hold them off?"

I'd have to make do with what I had for the moment—there were too many other enemies that Kizuna had to deal with.

The rain of spells continued, annoying as ever.

Trash #2's cohorts weren't rushing in to attack. They must have been vulnerable to the rain of spells. Instead, they hung back and cast spells. Sometimes they shot arrows or threw knives.

"Filo."

"Whaaat?"

"What do you think?"

"Hm . . ." She pointed her finger at Trash #2. A blade of wind shot from her finger and sliced into his arm.

"Ah?! What?! How?!"

The blade had cut deep into his arm, and he was forced to stop casting spells, so he could tend to the wound.

"You seem to be proud of yourself for casting spells without an incantation . . . but aren't you forgetting the most important thing?" Maybe I shouldn't give the enemy advice, but I couldn't hold myself back from addressing him as the smoke cleared. "I am the Shield Hero and the source of all power. Hear my words and heed them. Heal them!"

"Zweite Heal!"

The single spell was enough to heal all of the damage that his barrage of spells had caused, and we instantly recovered from any wounds we'd sustained.

"What was that magic? I've never seen anything like it!"

It was pretty impressive that he could cast spells without incantation, but Filo copied him without much effort.

I'd read something similar in a magic book once. It had said that experienced wizards could cast spells without an incantation but that the power of spells cast that way would be substantially lower. That much should have been obvious—it was like swinging a weapon without putting any effort into it.

If you swung a sword without putting any energy into the swing, it might break the skin but it wouldn't do much more than that. The damage caused by an attack was proportional to the amount of power behind it. That was why his spells were so weak.

I guess they might have been useful as a quick follow-up attack to a throwing knife or something, but the main problem was that there wasn't any power behind them to begin with.

"Answer me!"

"You want to know?"

Incantations were an essential step in giving shape to your magic power. They were the step where you focus your power so that you can use it. True, it did speak to his experience that he could command magic without an incantation, but skipping the incantation would definitely limit the level of magic he could use. It meant that he was skipping steps when giving shape to his power.

Maybe that was possible with simple spells, but as the spells grew more powerful and complex, it grew more difficult to shape the magic power without an incantation.

Anyway, we were in a different world now, so the magic seemed to work a little differently here—and judging by his reaction he'd never seen the spells that we were using.

"Um . . . Master? I don't think I have enough magic power to do anything stronger than that!"

"Oh no? Do you think you could make it more powerful if you leveled up more?"

"Yeah! I can just charge it up and bam!"

I couldn't figure out what she was trying to say, but if genius Filo said she could do it, then I guess she could do it.

"But . . . if I could, um, chant the thing . . ."

"Filo, I know."

"Oh!"

I cut her off. I didn't want to give the enemy any more hints than I needed to.

She had a point. If someone was powerful enough to cast a spell without using an incantation, how strong would their spells be if they took the time to use one?

Timing was important in battle, but if he could make the time to chant an incantation without being interrupted, his spells would be much more powerful. Using spells without incantations would be good for catching the enemy off guard, but in general it was probably better to chant spells when you found the time in in the middle of battle.

That's what Therese was doing. She chanted incantations while keeping an eye on the rest of the battle.

Was Trash #2 just trying to show off? Why would a wizard be chosen to wield the katana of the vassal weapons? He didn't seem to have a solid grip on reality. He drew some other katana from a scabbard at his waist and came running at us.

"Taste my steel!"

He was much quicker on his feet than I expected. Maybe magic wasn't his specialty after all.

The last time we'd met I didn't get a good look at his skill level because I'd simply blocked his attack with my shield, but now I could see that his movements were studied and skilled.

After I put all the other heroes' power-up methods to use, normal adventurers' movements seemed slow and laborious to me. But this guy was very quick on his feet. I wasn't sure I could keep up. Of course that was probably only because I was at a lower level now.

He was good on his feet. Now I could see why he'd wanted the katana. But that didn't explain why he had the skill to use magic without incantation.

"Grrrrrrraw!" a tiger roared and leapt at me to join his attack.

Wait, no—it was after Raphtalia.

I couldn't let it get to her! Its flapping tail brushed by me, and I reached out and grabbed it, stopping the cat in its tracks.

"Grrrraw!"

The tiger was furious, and it turned to attack me alongside Trash #2.

Good. As long as it wasn't after Raphtalia.

"Mr. Naofumi!" she shouted, brandishing her katana and rushing at the tiger.

"Crescent Moon Sword!"

A flash of light like a crescent moon shot from her sword and tore the skin from the tiger's back.

" . . . !"

I stopped Trash #2's katana with my shield, and the Nue Shield's counter-attack triggered, activating Lightning Shield (medium).

"Wha . . . Ahhhhh!"

Electrocuted, Trash #2 dropped his katana and jumped away from me.

"What the . . . ? What are you?! How did you stop my attack?!"

"You're just now figuring this out?"

He must have thought I was a MOB.

MOB was a term we used in the online games I used to play to refer to weak or backup players.

He must have been shocked to discover that my defense was actually much higher than an MOB. Who's a weak backup now!?

"It's that freaky shield you've got! I know you're friends with the thieves, but tell me your name!"

He was talking nonsense again. I ignored him and looked for Kizuna. She was struggling in a battle with one of Trash #2's women.

"Kizuna, leave the humans up to Glass or me!"

"That's what I was thinking! Do you mind?"

"I don't like to receive orders from Naofumi, but he happens to be correct. L'Arc, Therese, come with me!" Glass announced.

"Got it!"

"Understood. It's necessary so that Kizuna can best command her skills."

"Great power in these stones, hear my plea and show yourself. My name is Therese Alexanderite, and I am your friend. Lend me the power to destroy them!"

"Fusion Technique: Burning Disc!"

"Fusion Form: Reverse Burning Snow Moon Flower!"

Glass's and L'Arc's skills combined, forming a burning flame that sent the woman who was attacking Kizuna flying.

"Gyahhhhhh!"

But it wasn't enough to kill her. She slowly tottered back to where Trash #2 was standing and started to cast healing magic on herself.

We just weren't strong enough to finish them off.

"These guys are tougher than I thought. Don't give up yet, Kiddo!"

"Who's giving up? I'm taking care of the weak ones, so I guess I might get a bit careless."

"What was that? I'll show you!" Trash #2 complained. I didn't care.

Even after seeing his skill with the sword, it was still clear to me that the White Tiger copies were the greater threat.

Glass and L'Arc held vassal weapons from this world, so they were really powerful. I'd seen their strength firsthand back in the Cal Mira islands. When we ran into them during the Spirit Tortoise incident, they'd had weakened somewhat. But they were definitely much stronger now that they were back in their own world.

"Tell me your name!" Trash #2 shouted angrily.

"Calm down a bit, will you? If you want to know that badly, I'll tell you. I'm the Shield . . . Hero. I've got this shield, but all I can do with it is defend people. My name is Naofumi Iwatani. I'm from another world." Hearing myself say it all felt strange . . . I was the Shield Hero from another world who came from another world . . . How many worlds were there now? Whatever—it was the truth.

"What? There's no such thing as a holy shield! Stop with this drivel!"

"Then don't ask me!"

I didn't care if he believed me. Actually, the less he knew about the Shield Hero, the better.

"Listen up! We're focusing on this guy for now!"

"Okay!" the flock of women shouted in unison.

Well, well. Let's see . . . Kizuna was dealing with the tigers.

He probably wanted to use the tigers to fight Glass and L'Arc, since they were the strongest. Then he would focus on killing me, since I was defending everyone. His ultimate goal was to kill Raphtalia and take back the katana she held. It was a decent plan, but he wasn't going to get past me.

"Shooting Star Shield!"

The barrier appeared around my party.

"Mr. Naofumi . . ."

"We'll be fine. Rishia, Filo—watch out."

"They won't catch meeeee!"

"Good."

"Feh . . ." Rishia whimpered, but she held an ofuda, ready to attack.

Everything looked good.

Actually, come to think of it, Trash #2 was really proud

of himself for casting spells without incantations, but couldn't anyone do that if they used ofuda?

"Heh! Now I'll show you what I can really do!" he said, pulling out an ofuda.

Was he trying to pretend that he'd been holding back?

He obviously wasn't as strong as Kyo—so why would he bother holding back?

I had Rishia, Filo, and the vassal weapons on my side. If he didn't pull out all the stops, he was going to end up dead.

His reinforcements would show up before too long. It was time to end this.

"Let's go!"

Trash #2 focused his magic power on the ofuda in his hand while he sent spells at us without chanting their incantations.

"Now! Air Strike Shield!"

Right before he could shoot a spell at us, I deployed Air Strike Shield directly in front of him. He always attacked so directly, throwing his spells in perfectly straight lines. I couldn't wait to see how he reacted to this.

"Wh—"

The spell slammed into the shield and exploded in his face.

"Ahhhh!" Caught up in the flames, he screamed and jumped away.

Ha! It worked even better than I'd anticipated. Glass or L'Arc wouldn't have had any trouble dodging it.

"You! You . . . fool!" Trash #2's friends all brandished their weapons at us.

"Second Shield!"

I formed another shield to protect us and then quickly looked to Filo.

Knowing what I meant, she nodded and began to chant an incantation.

"I'm Filo, the source of all power! Hear my words and heed them. Wrap them in a fierce tornado and blow them away!"

"Zweite Tornado!"

The name of a newly available skill appeared in my field of vision. I'd used it before. It was a combo skill that had some offensive capability.

"Tornado Shield!"

A shield of howling wind appeared before the charging women, and when they recklessly attacked it, they triggered a counter-attack.

"Ahhhhhh!" they shouted.

A huge tornado spiraled out from the shield and pulled the women into it, and they went spiraling up into the sky.

"Mr. Naofumi! I'm going in!"

Just when I was about to suggest that Raphtalia cast an illusion spell, she charged straight for Trash #2.

"No matter how many times we have tried to reach an agreement, you continue to thirst greedily for this weapon.

I cannot tolerate it any longer. This comes to an end now," she yelled. She drew the katana, held it out horizontally, and then shouted a skill.

"Powder Snow!"

"Wha—"

The blade sliced and the impact exploded with blood.

She spun the sword to throw off the blood that clung to the blade. Then she turned it to face his crowd of supporters.

Trash #2 knocked backward at the waist after receiving such a skilled attack. But then the skill's effect became clear.

"Ah?!"

A fine snowy powder erupted from the opening of the cut she'd made, filling the air and turning everything white.

What the . . . ? It was . . . snow?

The snow melted a moment later, and Trash #2 tottered back upright.

"That was . . . pretty good . . . You stole . . . stole the source of my magic power."

The skill must have turned the magic power of whomever it cut into snow.

Trash #2 gripped an earth crystal that must have had restorative properties. He was trying to heal himself.

I wouldn't let him. I walked over and grabbed the crystal from his hand.

"Don't you touch that! I . . ."

He swung his sword at me, but I blocked it, and once again, Lightning Shield (medium) activated and electrocuted him.

His wound was . . . Yes, his wound was still open.

It hadn't cut him too deeply. I guess the skill was more focused on robbing the enemy of magic power than on dealing damage directly.

"Master!"

The reinforcements had arrived and were starting to surround Filo and Rishia.

Glass and the others were slowly hacking through the White Tiger copies, but more and more of them kept appearing.

Amidst it all, one person was acting strangely—Kizuna.

She kept randomly swinging her fishing rod and hitting the tigers with the lure.

Glass and L'Arc weren't focusing on attacking the tigers; they were clearly focusing on defense. The tigers appeared to be ignoring Kizuna for some reason.

I wondered if monsters had a kind of instinctual fear of the Hunting Hero.

Kizuna's lure hit Trash #2 next, but nothing happened.

"Naofumi, don't attack anything my lure has touched until I say so, okay?"

"Ah, alright. But . . ."

What was she up to? I was guessing it was a skill that lowered their defense or something, but I wasn't sure.

"Grrrraaaw!"

A particularly large tiger appeared in the middle of the prowling pack of monsters.

Was it their leader? No . . . I'm sure that Trash #2 was controlling them, so that would make him the leader.

Regardless, there was no doubt that the strongest White Tiger copy yet had just joined the fight.

Chapter Seventeen: Blood Flower Strike

"Hey, that one looks pretty tough. Alright, let's do this Glass."

"Yes!"

"Right on! I haven't seen Kizuna's skills in a long time," L'Arc added.

"Kizuna, it's all in your hands now. Phantasm!" Glass shouted, slapping open her fans and using a skill that filled the air with dancing flower petals. Delicate cherry blossoms flit on the wind, making everything look pink and fantastical.

The tigers swayed on their feet, their eyes rolling around in their heads. The skill must have made them dizzy.

What was going on? What was the plan?

"Here I go!" L'Arc shouted, throwing his scythe. A tornado erupted from where it landed.

The howling winds appeared to make Glass's skill even more effective.

"Oh power in these stones, here my plea and show yourself. My name is Therese Alexanderite, and I am your friend. Give me the strength to stop them!'"

"Shining Stones! Paralysis Wing!"

Butterflies flapped out from her hands and joined the howling winds and flower petals.

The tigers lost their momentum, slowed, and then came to a complete stop.

"It's a little tricky to stop so many of them at once. This would have been over a long time ago if there had only been one," Kizuna said, turning her weapon into the tuna knife.

"But it's the end now—and we have won. Behold the true power of the Hunting Hero," Glass declared.

"Naofumi . . . Actually, Raphtalia, we'll need your help, too. When the attack happens, you go after the strong one that Naofumi is holding."

"Alright," Raphtalia said, turning to face Trash #2. I still had him cornered.

Then Kizuna held her tuna knife like Raphtalia held her sword, took a breath, and ran for the tigers. In a flash, she was already done with them.

"Instant Blade: Mist!"

"Hunting Skill: Blood Flower Strike!"

Raphtalia held the katana in both hands and flew at Trash #2.

"What?!"

"What is it?"

"The blade . . . It feels strange—like it cut unnaturally deep."

Trash #2 stopped trying to wiggle free from my grasp. I let him go.

He shook and shivered, and his face grew pale.

"Ugh . . ."

"Oh, it will hurt worse if you move. You should stay still," Kizuna added, tapping the frozen White Tiger copy with the tip of her tuna knife before returning to where Glass and her friends were standing.

I hadn't seen the attack at all, but suddenly all of the tigers collapsed, falling into bloody chunks.

The air was thick with the scent of blood.

The sprays of blood hung in the air, like red flower petals to match the pink ones.

Kizuna's skill was aptly named—it really did look like flowers of blood.

Trash #2's women and his backup troops stared at us speechlessly. They must have realized that if Trash #2 moved at all, he would fall apart into bloody chunks, just like what had happened to the tigers.

"I don't believe it! How could you defeat our most powerful weapons so easily? It's impossible! Impossible!"

One of the women pointed and shouted, "And by the weakest of the heroes, no less!"

Kizuna rolled her eyes.

I knew how she probably felt. I was used to people saying the same kind of things about me. I guess people only respected you if you could fight against other people.

"Do you even know anything about the Hunting Hero? I'm sure you realize that all the heroes have their specialties . . ."

That's right. Kizuna had said something about that. She couldn't attack people, but she made up for that with her special abilities against monsters.

"I may not be able to fight with other people, but that doesn't mean I can't fight. If you don't learn to separate rumors from fact, you'll end up dead."

The crowd of reinforcements started to murmur among themselves.

It was amazing. Glass and her friends had been struggling against those tigers for the whole fight, and Kizuna took them all out with a single attack. She was terrifying!

Looking back on the time we'd spent together, I couldn't think of a single time I'd seen her struggle in battle, except for when we were faced with human opponents. She had always defeated monsters without breaking a sweat.

I hadn't realized how terrifying my travel companion really was!

I wonder if she felt the same way about me—after all, I was a holy hero, too.

I couldn't do much by way of attack, but when it came to defense, I was far more impressive than anyone else I'd met.

I'd survived the Spirit Tortoise's main attack—wasn't that proof enough?

Just like me, Kizuna couldn't attack humans, but when it came to attacking monsters, she was the most powerful person around. I was actually grateful that her specialty wasn't the opposite . . . What if there was a holy hero out there that was specialized in fighting people? Wouldn't that be terrifying?

"Alright then . . . You've seen how easily we defeated your commander and your strongest weapons. Don't you think it would be best for you to let us go free?" Kizuna said, twisting her tuna knife so it flashed in the sun.

"Feh . . ."

"Rishia, Kizuna's on our side. Don't be scared."

"Mr. Naofumi, your new friend is really something . . ."

"I guess so."

"Rafu?"

Raph-chan had kept quiet during the battle. Or I guess she did try to protect Rishia.

That was fine. I had never expected her to be much use in battle.

On the other hand, I had seen Glass and Kizuna's shikigami, Chris, doing all it could to protect them during the battle. I still didn't have a firm grasp on what they could do, though—I'd been too occupied dealing with Trash #2.

"Raphtalia, your attack was really impressive, too. You must have gotten stronger since I saw you last."

"Do you think so? I've been so busy since I got here that I

haven't had the time to stop and reflect on it."

That attack of hers was really something. I was sure of it.

It was certainly strange that she'd been chosen by the katana, but it was starting to feel like destiny now. She'd really handled herself well in the battle.

She must have been through so much since we'd been split up, because she seemed more skilled than she had been. If we had to split up again, I wondered if she'd develop bulky muscles or something.

"You're thinking about something rude again, aren't you?"

"No. I was just thinking about how strong you've become and how dependable you've become."

"Oh . . . Well . . . What should we do now?" Raphtalia asked, staring at the katana in her hands.

It was a good question. Once we got back to the world we'd come from, was it safe to walk around with such a valuable weapon?

"Naofumi? Aren't you going to absorb some of these White Tiger parts?"

"Yeah, yeah, of course. But I've got a hostage here, so I can't move yet," I said, looking back and forth between Trash #2 and his women and the backup troops.

He must have been a pretty important person, because everyone seemed stunned by his capture. They clearly had no idea what to do. They knew that if they tried anything funny, he'd split in two at the waist—Trash #2 seemed to realize that he couldn't move at all.

"Take a good hard look at him. If you stay after us, you'll end up the same way," I said, squeezing in one last threat.

"Mr. Naofumi, you love doing that, don't you? Threatening people."

"If they don't really feel scared, these underlings of his will never learn."

"Sigh . . . I supposed you're right. It seems there are people like him no matter where we go . . ." Raphtalia murmured.

She was right. He reminded me of the other heroes back in our world—or of Trash #1.

"Alright, we have your vassal weapon. This whole debacle is because of his foolish recklessness. Don't forget that."

Didn't anyone in this world care about the holy heroes?

Didn't they respect Kizuna at all?

I guess I'd been through something similar back in the last world. There must have been people that didn't believe in, or trust, the heroes. You didn't want to get captured by people like that.

I walked over and absorbed the White Tiger parts into my shield, keeping an eye on the soldiers that hesitantly ran over to rescue Trash #2. We had what we needed, so we left. On our way out, I saw the gaggle of women casting healing spells on him. He would be fine . . . maybe.

"Don't let them get away! You must kill them all! Look at what they've done to me! The vassal weapon belongs to our country. We cannot allow them to escape—"

Raphtalia turned back to stop his tirade. "It's too soon. If you move in the next ten seconds, you'll still die. You'd better keep healing magic going for the next few days." Raphtalia bowed deeply and then raised her face. "We didn't pick this fight with you, and we do not wish for war. If you can consider the situation dispassionately, you will see that an alliance with Glass's county is in your best interests. When you reach that conclusion yourself, please discuss it with your government."

He didn't give up. "Wait!"

"You mustn't move!"

"Don't believe her! I've already cast healing spells on myself! You'll see!"

Slowly, the women and soldiers began walking after us. Trash #2 rose to his feet to join the fray, when . . .

" . . . How unfortunate. We truly wished to end this without any unnecessary bloodshed."

"I agree. I had hoped that your nations could form an alliance that could usher in an new era of optimism for the future of this world . . ." Raphtalia sighed.

Glass nodded in agreement. "Naofumi, you had better not watch. I've seen Glass and L'Arc slaughter people like this before," Kizuna said.

That just made me want to watch more.

Raphtalia seemed resigned to this outcome, reasoning that they had brought it upon themselves.

"Rishia, you'd better not look, either!"

"Rafu!"

"Feh . . . Why? What's happening?"

Filo and Raph-chan were trying to keep Rishia from watching.

I actually didn't need to watch to know what was going to happen. I'd seen it in anime before—that thing that happens when someone is instantly sliced up.

"What are you doing!? Hurry up and . . . ugh . . ."

First came a sickening, crushing sound. Then it was followed by the hiss of blood spraying into the air.

"Kyaaaaaaaa!" the women screamed.

"—Youuuuuuuuu!"

I couldn't make out what he was trying to say.

Too bad. I didn't feel a bit of sympathy for him. I didn't really care about his name, but I wonder what it was . . .

I could only think of one thing to say: "The world is rid of another piece of garbage, heh, heh, heh . . ."

"Mr. Naofumi!" Raphtalia shouted, chastising me.

I didn't see what was so wrong with what I said. This creep had been trying to kill her!

And he'd done everything he could to get in our way.

"Kiddo, I know you want to be cool, but I wouldn't laugh. You wouldn't want to see it by accident."

"I wouldn't mind . . . as long as it's not too gross."

I didn't really want to turn and look at the splattering gore behind me, but I still couldn't pass up the opportunity to gloat. There were plenty of people back in the world I came from that I'd like to die this way, but if they actually did, then it wouldn't be a good thing.

Anyway, that's how we won the battle and escaped.

We left the town over its rooftops.

"What kind of attack was that?"

It was so fast that I hadn't actually been able to see what happened. It looked like she had just cut the monsters with her knife. But it couldn't have been that simple—what was all that stuff she'd done with the fishing lure beforehand? That must have been setting up the killing move. It might have been a sequence of skills, like when I use Shield Prison and then Change Shield (attack) and follow those up with Iron Maiden.

"Hm? Oh, the skill connects all of the enemy's weak points and then cuts through them. It doesn't always kill them, though. Sometimes it just cuts very deep."

So it was actually a really strong attack, and the enemy only fell apart if the attack was strong enough to kill them.

"What were you doing with your fishing lure beforehand?"

"It's a skill called Lure Needle, and it multiplies damage. Anything hit with the lure will take double damage on the next attack."

That was why she told everyone not to attack until she was ready. If someone had attacked, then it would have taken the multiplier off of her follow-up special attack.

"The effect only lasts a little while, so I was in a hurry. If the enemy figures out what's happening too quickly, they can cancel the effect."

"It was pretty nasty."

So the lure lowered the enemy's defense for the next attack.

An attack like that could really mess up my strategy.

"It's not as simple as it looks. The lure only affects the area that it touches, so you have to make sure that you hit the enemy's weak point. It probably wouldn't do all that much against you."

I had experience with something similar in some games I'd played. There was a skill that worked the same way—strengthening the next attack in a sequence. I normally used it as a trump card during tough boss fights. But if the boss's defense rating was already really high, then it obviously didn't help as much.

The skill's effect only lasted for a little while, which made it pretty fickle to use right. I often felt like I was relying on luck.

Kizuna was clearly very skilled with it, though. She must have been an amazing fighter.

She couldn't do damage directly against human opponents, but she could probably use that lure skill to deal damage indirectly with the help of her teammates.

That was probably why Raphtalia's attack had been more effective than she had anticipated. Maybe that was the reason she sliced him in half.

Could they have really saved him if they kept casting healing magic on him? To tell the truth, I didn't really care that he had died. The world was better off without him.

"Hey, can you get in touch with him now? I don't know how many people I can take with me, but we could use my skill, too."

"One second," Kizuna said, holding an ofuda to her forehead and whispering to herself, "Yeah, I got him. He says he'll meet us at the agreed place. You want to go back first?"

"Probably. You've got Glass and everyone with you, so you should be fine. I'm not sure how many people I can take with me through the portal."

"You use the skill but don't know its limitations?"

"I've never felt the need to test it out."

Back in Melromarc, I didn't have the need to—my only friends were Raphtalia, Filo, and Rishia. I never tried to use the skill with Eclair and the old lady or Keel. I never tried to see how many people I could use it with. The cool-down time was pretty long, too, so I was careful not to waste it.

"Something tells me those women of his will be out for revenge . . ."

"I'm sure we can handle them—they don't have the tigers anymore. Don't you think, L'Arc?"

"Sure thing! With Kizuna on our side, we've got nothing to fear!"

Kizuna was like me in that she could handle herself fine, as long as she had teammates to work with. She'd be fine, as long as she was with Glass and the others.

On the other hand, all of our enemies were together again. If Kizuna turned on us, we'd never survive.

Kizuna, Glass, L'Arc, and Therese . . . I suddenly imagined them scowling and attacking me. I didn't think I could win.

How much did I really trust them?

"Alright then, we'll use my portal to teleport back to your country, ahead of you."

"Sounds fine to me. We should all be good. Let's split up."

"I'll see you soon. Alright then, we're going. Portal Shield!"

And so we left them behind and teleported back to the country they called home.

Epilogue: Together Again

We went back to the castle in the country that Kizuna called home and waited for the others to return. It didn't take long to receive word that they were back.

"Okay, but Glass, you know what I'm trying to say, right?"

"Oh. Um . . ."

Glass was sitting seiza-style and, apparently, being lectured by Kizuna. L'Arc and Therese were kneeling behind her. It looked like everyone was in trouble.

"What's going on?"

"Hm? Do you remember the stuff we heard about the waves a little while ago? I'm a little upset with Glass for just buying into it and going to your world to try and kill you," Kizuna said, crossing her arms.

"Kizuna, it's not that simple. I felt I had to do it for the sake of the world . . ."

"Of course you did. You heard a legend, assumed it was true, slipped through the dimensional rifts during a wave, and tried to kill the heroes you found. Is that right?"

"Yes . . ."

I could hardly believe my eyes. The stern, serious, samurai-like Glass turned her face to the floor in shame. I knew that her and Kizuna were close, but it sure looked like Kizuna was the boss.

"Kizuna. I know how you feel, but don't you want to hear our side of the story? Huh?" L'Arc asked.

"Yes, we were only trying to protect this world that you hold so dear . . ." interjected Therese.

Kizuna wasn't impressed. She narrowed her eyes and barked, "Fine then, answer me this. Can you think of a time when vassal weapons from another world came through the waves to kill the heroes here?"

"Well, um . . ."

"Can't answer me?" Kizuna snapped. Everyone turned their eyes away.

They could have just lied. But they knew each other well enough that they probably couldn't get away with it. Glass in particular looked like she'd be a terrible liar.

"No, no, I can't think of a time that happened. Not in this country or in another—though we are not privy to what happens in other lands."

Based on what I'd learned in this new world, I felt it was likely that whoever was in the world on the other side of the wave rifts was responsible for calming the waves.

"Wasn't it you, Glass, that said you hated the idea of peace built on the sacrifices of others? How could you say that and then rush off to murder people?"

"I . . ."

Kizuna was really interrogating her. I liked the sound of it. But they must have enjoyed their time together before Kizuna disappeared. Kizuna's house made that much clear.

"Okay, listen up. It's true that protecting the world and extending its life is important, but that doesn't mean you can kill other people to do it. I know that the legends are written that way, but don't you think we should look for another option before we rush into something like that?"

"Yes, but we did all the research we could. And yet . . ."

"You couldn't find another way, so you snuck off to murder the heroes? Is that it? If you can't find a way, maybe you should keep looking! Even if vassal weapons from another world did come after us, that doesn't give us an excuse to do the same thing!" Kizuna shouted. Glass looked intimidated.

I hadn't pictured their relationship like this at all . . .

They looked like children being scolded by their mother. My cheeks flushed.

"Mr. Naofumi, you're smiling."

"What are you laughing at, Kiddo? Are you enjoying this that much?"

Raphtalia told me off, and L'Arc joined in—but Kizuna glared at him and he backed off.

"What's wrong with that? You tried to kill me, and now you're getting a lecture. What's not to like?"

"Sigh . . . Glass is tough enough, but you're something else, Naofumi," Kizuna sighed, slapping her palm against her forehead. I didn't disagree.

L'Arc nodded along with the lecture but kept stealing glances at me.

I could see where he was coming from, but there was no need to worry. I didn't consider myself a champion of justice.

"At the very least, now that I'm back, I am firmly against this plan of yours to go to other worlds and kill their heroes!"

"Um . . ."

"Got it?!"

"Y . . . Yes!"

"That goes for L'Arc and Therese, too!"

"Right, yeah. Good—I didn't really want to fight with Kiddo. Destroying another world to save your own isn't really our style, anyway."

"Very well. And luckily we reached this conclusion before we were actually able to defeat Naofumi," Glass said.

L'Arc looked and Therese and then at me. They both looked happy.

If they were going to look at me like that, then there was only one thing to be said: "Then you shouldn't have tried to kill me in the first place."

"Shut up, Kiddo! Stop trying to act cool!"

"L'Arc!" Kizuna shouted, and L'Arc immediately closed his mouth.

Kizuna could really command a room.

We'd met by accident, but I was sort of jealous of her commanding presence. That's how the holy heroes should be. Either that or she was too good for the job.

"And, Glass, please think about this. You know that I can fight monsters but not people. What do you think would happen if someone with a vassal weapon from another world came for me?"

" . . ."

Glass didn't answer. I could see why.

Kizuna couldn't fight people. If someone with a vassal weapon came after her, she'd have to fall back and depend on her friends. But the heroes were summoned to the waves. Was she really being summoned to her death?

"Glass, I think there's a reason that the holy heroes are summoned to the waves."

"A reason?"

"Yes. We're summoned to the waves when we might be killed there. That makes me think that we might not need to fight in the waves at all. They summon us because they need us. If that's true, then maybe it's because the world gets more time until the next wave if the heroes stop it, or maybe they can stop the fusing of the worlds."

" . . ."

"I don't know if I'm right. But based on what you are

saying, if the heroes exist to protect the world, then there shouldn't be any reason for them to fight in the waves. And yet, isn't it the heroes' duty to do just that?"

Kizuna muttered that she hadn't been fighting in the waves, because she'd been stuck in the labyrinth. Then she gripped Glass's hand.

"They don't write about it in the legends. But I don't believe it. I don't believe that we are supposed to protect our world by destroying another. We can't do that."

" . . . Understood. I apologize."

Glass turned to me and lowered her head. I couldn't think of a reason to stay mad at them. They were clearly doing what they thought was right, and they were leagues better than the jerks that summoned me to Melromarc, only to lead me into a trap.

I knew that they were good people. After Kizuna disappeared so long ago, the state of her house was enough to prove it. They protected their friends. It was clear that they cared.

I was even a little jealous of their relationship.

If Raphtalia had been chosen by a weapon back in our world and I had gone missing—would she have done the same thing for me?

I looked over at her. Raph-chan was climbing up onto her head from her shoulder.

"What is it?"

"I can understand how Glass feels, so I won't say any more."

If it were possible, I wanted to have the sort of relationship that Kizuna had with her friends. It was nothing more than a wish, but I'd be happy if Raphtalia felt the same way about me as they did about Kizuna

"As long as you're not going to try and kill me anymore, I certainly won't pick a fight with you."

"Kiddo . . ."

"Naofumi . . ."

"Great. So we can all be friends, right?" Kizuna said, holding out her hand to me.

I slapped it away. "I'm not into that sort of thing." I wasn't the type to get all misty-eyed over sentimental friendship. I mean I liked that sort of thing in games and manga, but I hadn't had enough positive experiences in these worlds to justify taking the leap of faith that sort of relationship required.

"Anyway, we can certainly keep working together. I've got something I have to do, and I could certainly use the help."

"That's right. Didn't you want to get back the power that was stolen from your world's protective beast?"

"Exactly. That's why we came here—to make the guy with the book of the vassal weapons, Kyo, pay for all the chaos he brought to our world."

I hadn't forgotten. I had to avenge the Spirit Tortoise—avenge Ost's death.

Raphtalia nodded, and so did Rishia and Glass and then L'Arc and Therese. Everyone was very solemn.

"Kizuna, I can tell you this without doubt: Kyo is no longer fit to hold the book. The vassal weapons that we hold have begun to demand his defeat and subjugation," Glass explained.

"Well, if he's done all that you say, of course he needs to be taken care of. If your weapons are demanding it, then I won't stand in the way. Naofumi, I'll help you—so please, allow our cooperation to compensate for the harm that Glass and her friends tried to inflict upon you in the past."

"What does it matter if I forgive them? Our goals are the same. If we don't stop Kyo, this world will be in danger, too."

There was a good chance that Kyo was up to something with the power he had taken from the Spirit Tortoise. He probably had to do something before he could use it as he pleased. We had to find him before he could pull it off.

Damn . . . We weren't any closer to accomplishing our goal than we were when we first went through the portal.

"Got it, Kiddo? All that is well and fine, but look—everyone is here together for the first time in forever. Do you know how long Kizuna has been missing? Let's go all out and celebrate tonight!" L'Arc clapped his hands, and the attendants mulling about the castle all started running around.

It looked like they were getting ready for a party.

The whole castle sprang into action when he clapped

his hands. Just how much authority did L'Arc have here?

I suddenly remembered the king referencing a boy. Could it be?

"Hey, boy," I shouted.

L'Arc turned to me, wincing. "What? How do you know about that?!"

"I thought they were talking about you. You're a pretty important person, aren't you?"

"Not that I like it. I prefer my freedom!"

I had only heard a little from Kizuna, so I didn't know how she ended up meeting L'Arc. His father was the king and probably died, and the country was given over to a less-than-worthy prince.

L'Arc seemed like the sort of person that the populace would rally behind.

The country seemed to be doing pretty well, so maybe his reign was going well for the country.

He probably had good people working for him. He was charismatic enough to attract good people. I wonder if Kizuna's questing in the past had anything to do with it.

"So you see, boy, I'm going to keep calling you 'boy' as long as you call me 'Kiddo'."

"Fine, Nao . . . fu . . . mi."

"Hm."

He said my name, but looked really irritated by it.

Then he turned and whined, "No, it sounds all wrong! You're Kiddo, not 'Naofumi!'"

"That doesn't make any sense, boy!"

"I don't care, Kiddo! You guys take a load off for now. I'll call for you when everything is ready. Kizuna and Glass, you two take the time to get reacquainted," L'Arc barked, shuffling us out of the room.

Um . . . What next? I looked at Raphtalia.

"L'Arc likes to celebrate, doesn't he?" Ethnobalt said. He had been silent all the way back to the castle, but now he smiled and spoke up. "And yet, I think he is right. We should enjoy ourselves tonight. Kizuna, welcome back."

". . . Thank you. It's good to be back . . . with all of you," Kizuna said, looking at everyone. She looked like she was about to start crying.

How long had she been trapped in that labyrinth? I didn't know exactly, but it must have been a very long time. She'd returned to a place she thought she'd never see again. If I hadn't been so lucky, I could have ended up trapped, just like she had.

"A party? I wanna siiiiing!" Filo yelled.

"Raful!"

Filo and Raph-chan each happily jumped up onto my shoulders.

I let them. Then I turned to face Raphtalia and Rishia.

"They're right. We should enjoy ourselves tonight. To be honest, I'm exhausted."

"Feh . . . How wonderful to reunite with old friends!"

Yeah, they were right.

I hadn't been separated from Raphtalia for very long, but I had felt her absence starting to take its toll, so I could understand how Kizuna must have felt.

Glass looked so happy to see Kizuna again. She was beaming like a little kid. I couldn't help but smile, too.

"For now . . ."

"What is it?"

I looked at the unsheathed katana in Raphtalia's hands.

"Kizuna, I know everyone is really happy right now, but don't you think that Raphtalia should sheath the katana?"

"Oh yeah," Kizuna said, turning around and stepping back toward us. When she did, she left Glass standing there with her hand outstretched. Glass made a very disappointed face—it looked weird on her.

I was starting to think she might be a lesbian.

"Then let's go to a shop I know and get one made. They're really good."

Had we been in Melromarc, I would have had the old guy do it, but we were stuck in another world, so I decided to defer to Kizuna's judgment.

"Okay."

Kizuna led us out of the castle and into the town at its base.

"Well, if it isn't Kizuna! How long has it been?!"

Kizuna took us to a bustling blacksmith in the middle of town.

It was run by a very muscular, masculine woman with a red gemstone in her chest. She must have been one of the crystal people.

Therese's gemstone was in her forehead, so I guess different people had their gemstones in different places.

"I heard from Glass that you'd gone missing. I was worried about you! Now Glass can finally relax a bit. When you went missing, everyone had a rough time trying to console her."

"Romina, maybe we can save that for later," Glass quickly said, trying to shut down the conversation as fast as possible. I'd always thought Glass was cool and reserved, but she was starting to look more like a normal person.

"This is Romina. She's the best blacksmith I know."

"I'm Naofumi Iwatani."

"My name is Raphtalia. It's a pleasure to meet you."

"Filo!"

"Rafu!"

"I'm Rishia. Nice to make your acquaintance."

"Always nice to meet new customers. Hope to see more of you!"

The blacksmith reminded me of the old guy at the weapon shop back in Melromarc.

"If we bring you materials and money, can you make us new stuff?"

"Pretty much—though I reserve the right to throw out obnoxious customers!"

"You think I'm obnoxious?"

"Hmm . . ." Romina scratched her chin and looked me over carefully. "Actually I think we'll get along pretty well."

"Good."

There was something attractive to me about the profession—about the idea of finding potential in materials and then using them to make custom weapons and tools.

"People that can understand Mr. Naofumi's personality figure him out with a single glance. I'm a little jealous," Raphtalia said.

"What are you talking about?" She should know by now that I liked custom tools.

"So? I'm sure you stopped by for something other than an introduction."

"Naturally. We have a lot of materials that we'd like you to look at. Also, we need a scabbard for her katana," Kizuna said, dropping a pile of drop items onto the counter.

"Ah, I see . . . Oh hey, this is pretty good stuff!" Romina said. Then she looked at Raphtalia's katana. "Well, well . . . Would you look at that."

"Yeah, it's the katana of the vassal weapons."

"I didn't expect to ever see it! Alright then, I'll make you a scabbard for it."

"Thanks."

"No problem, I'm thrilled just to see it. I've got new customers, new materials to work with . . . What more could a blacksmith want?"

"Thanks."

Romina started measuring the katana and drawing up some quick sketches.

"Naofumi, why don't you have Romina make you some shields or armor?"

"Good idea."

"Hey, that reminds me. Didn't you have some armor from your world? I bet Romina would love to see armor from another world."

"Hm? Yeah, I've still got it . . ."

She was probably talking about the Barbarian Armor +1? that had gotten all beat up in the fight with the Spirit Tortoise.

I took out pieces of it I'd stored in my bag and dropped them on the counter.

"Maybe she could look at your stuff too, Rishia. Maybe she can make you something good," I said, pulling out Rishia's Filo kigurumi and putting it on the counter next to my things. "It must have been rough for you—coping without your kigurumi."

"Feh . . ."

Raphtalia looked at Rishia and started to say, "It's not like she was so dependent on it . . ."

She stopped and blinked.

"Okay, maybe she was."

"Fehh?!"

It was hard to sympathize with her surprise. After all, Rishia was the one that said she wore it so that no one could see her cry.

"What are these? Do they do anything?" Romina said, holding up our old armor and regarding them with suspicion.

"Hey, Filo."

"Whaaaat?"

"What happened to your claws?"

"They're gone!"

I sighed . . . It wasn't her fault. She'd been captured and turned into a sideshow.

She could have escaped if they left her with her claws—that is, if they were still in working condition.

I still had the Karma Dog Claws in my shield, so I took them out and put them on the counter, too. When they hit the counter, I discovered that I couldn't read any of the information about them.

"These things might have stopped working when we crossed between the worlds. Think you can do anything about it?"

"I might be able to do something with the armor here, but I've never seen anything like what these kigurumi and claws are made of, so . . ." Romina muttered to herself as she turned the articles over in her hands. She found the gemstone set in the center of the barbarian armor chest plate and pointed to it. "Fascinating! This is a core stone from the Dragon Emperor."

"Core stone? Dragon Emperor? What do you mean?"

"It looks just like the core from the Dragon Emperor that Kizuna defeated a long time ago. There must be a Dragon Emperor in your world, too."

"I don't know. I know that I got that when I defeated a Dragon Zombie, so maybe they are the same thing."

Actually, when I first met Kizuna, she said that she had originally been summoned to defeat a powerful monster called the Dragon Emperor. She must have been successful.

"These have fantastic effects. You better take care of it."

"Well, the armor is trash, so it isn't any good to me now. That's why I brought it to you."

"An excellent point. What is this armor called? I can't read it."

"Barbarian Armor."

"It certainly looks the part."

I guess I had taken the parts from a bunch of bandits . . . I mean—hey!

"Stop that! That was made for me by a very talented man!"

The truth was that the armor was really good, but its name made it come off as worse than it really was.

"There's potential here, so I'll see what I can do."

"How much will it cost? If you can't do it then maybe we don't need you."

"Mr. Naofumi, we're the ones making the request here. Please be a little more polite . . ."

"Who cares about that sort of thing? She's friends with Kizuna, so we don't need to stand on ceremony, do we? If she can't do it, she'll tell me so!"

"I . . . I suppose so . . ." Raphtalia sighed.

Romina burst out laughing. "You're quite the business man, aren't you?"

"Naofumi's even better than Alto."

"Really? That man is a monster when it comes to business."

"I was starting to suspect the same, but do you really think so, Kizuna?" Glass asked, casting a suspicious glance at me.

"Yeah, he's better. Alto takes the long way to a secure a sale, but Naofumi can sell the same thing in no time and no effort. He's really got a knack for it."

"Decide if you're complimenting me or insulting me."

We needed money, and we didn't have any time, so what other choice did I have but to play a little dirty at the soul-healing water auction? She didn't complain about it at the time.

Whatever. The truth was that I was pretty interested in

meeting this monster of business they were talking about. If he looked anything like the slave trader, I'd take off running in the other direction.

Raphtalia sighed and looked disappointed in me—but I really didn't do anything wrong!

"Well, don't you worry yourself over the money too much. You're friends with Kizuna, so I'll do whatever I can to keep costs down. I get some money from the crown, too."

"Glad to hear it. Also, try not to destroy it too much."

I'd grown pretty attached to the armor. The old guy that made it for me was the first person to trust me.

"I know, I know. But enough about the armor—what's with this crazy thing?" she asked, holding up the Filo kigurumi.

"Whatdya mean crazy?!" Filo flapped her wings, outraged at the implication. She must have thought she was being insulted. It wasn't so surprising that she said that, though. No one in this world had ever seen a filolial queen, let alone a kigurumi that looked like one.

"What are you mad about?"

"Oh her? She transformed for some reason when we crossed over to this world. Back where we came from, she looks like the monster that kigurumi is based on."

"Ah . . . I see. She looks so cute and funny, but you're saying her real form is . . ." Romina smiled thinly and turned away.

I couldn't blame her. Filo's filolial queen form was a strange sight to behold. She was huge and imposing—far more than a normal filolial.

"Regardless, if this is equipment from another world, I'd like you to let me study it a little. With any luck, I can make you something good."

"Got it. Good luck."

I didn't have anything to lose, considering we couldn't use the equipment in the state it was in. If she could make something useful with it, it would probably raise our chances of survival from here on out.

A part of me still felt like I was helping the enemy grow stronger, but it was the best option I had.

"Need anything else?"

"I think that's it for now—though I'd like to see what sort of shields you can make, too."

I would just use Weapon Copy to get my own version of whatever shield she made, and then I could sell it to someone or give it to one of my party members.

"Sure, but with so many orders to work on, I can't do them all at once. We should probably cut of this order here. Then I can work on other stuff when this is all done"

"That's reasonable."

"Great! I have to say I'm pretty thrilled to work on this stuff. I've been so bored with the projects I've had lately. This will really shake things up for me."

Who knew that blacksmiths had so many things to worry about? When we got back to the world we came from, I'd have to go pay the old guy a visit at his weapon shop. Maybe he was bored, too. Besides, he'd definitely be interested in seeing the barbarian armor after Romina worked on it.

If she used gemstones from this world, he'd probably be thrilled just to see them.

Isn't that the sort of thing that craftsmen got excited about?

We left our equipment with Romina and then left her shop.

"What should we do now?" I asked. Before anyone could answer, the air filled with crackling explosions. Fireworks burst in the air over the castle.

The townsfolk in the streets all looked up at the colorful bursts and smiled.

"For now, let's just enjoy the celebration they're throwing for my return. Doesn't that sound nice?"

Glass squeezed Kizuna's hand, smiled, and bowed deeply to me.

"Thank you so very much for helping our missing Kizuna. We will do all that we can to assist you, but for now, please enjoy the celebration."

I wasn't going to argue. We had to enjoy ourselves sometimes, right?

It was hard to relax back in Melromarc, anyway, and it didn't seem like anyone here was trying to take advantage of us.

"Alright then, let's take the night off. Raphtalia, Filo, Raph-chan, and Rishia—let's go!"

"Okay!"

"It looks so fuuuun!"

"Rafu!"

"Feh . . . What should we do first?"

"Look at all the food carts!"

"Fehhh!"

"What's the matter?"

"Yay! Foooood!"

"RaFUUUUU!"

We walked toward the festival that was filling the streets of the town. Glass and Kizuna walked behind us, as if they were watching over us.

It would still take a while to accomplish what we'd set out to do—punish Kyo for his misdeeds. But for the moment, I tried to convince myself that there was nothing wrong with taking a night off.

Character Design:
Ethnobalt

船（円盤）

エスノバルト

Character Design:
Kizuna Kazayama

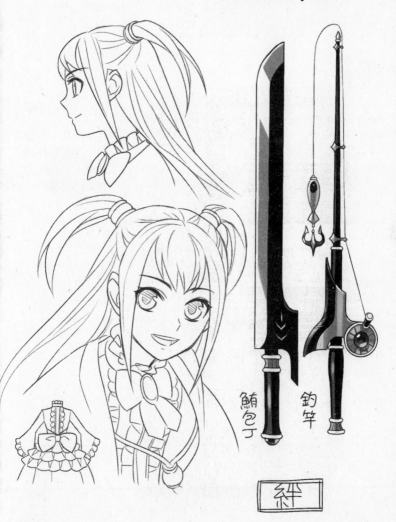

鮪包丁　釣竿

絆

The Rising of the Shield Hero Vol. 8
© Aneko Yusagi 2014
First published by KADOKAWA in 2014 in Japan.
English translation rights arranged by One Peace Books
under the license from KADOKAWA CORPORATION, Japan

ISBN: 978-1-944937-09-6

Written by Aneko Yusagi
Character Design Seira Minami
Cover Design by Yusuke Koyama
English Edition Published by One Peace Books 2017

Printed in Canada

2 3 4 5 6 7 8 9 10

One Peace Books
43-32 22nd Street STE 204 Long Island City New York 11101
www.onepeacebooks.com